Praise for previous books by

Catherine Palmer

Prairie Rose

"Highly recommended."
—*Library Journal*

"Begins with a bang and doesn't let up till the end. Expertly presents the tragedy and triumph of the human experience. Also successfuly illustrates many eternal truths about God's character."
—*A Closer Look*

Prairie Storm

"A fine addition to the entertaining series."
—*Library Journal*

"[This] bittersweet romance takes on themes of forgiveness and reconciliation with spiritual tenacity."
—*Romantic Times*

"Contains well-developed characters and an excellent plot. Easy to read and a great addition to the series."
—*CBA Marketplace*

Finders Keepers

"A romance that tackles deeper issues."
—*Library Journal*

A Victorian Christmas Cottage

"[An] engaging seasonal collection of novellas. Entertaining."
—*Library Journal*

HEART QUEST

HeartQuest brings you romantic fiction
with a foundation of biblical truth.
Adventure, mystery, intrigue, and suspense
mingle in these heartwarming stories of
men and women of faith striving to build
a love that will last a lifetime.

May HeartQuest books sweep you
into the arms of God, who longs for you
and pursues you always.

Catherine Palmer

PRAIRIE CHRISTMAS

Elizabeth White • Peggy Stoks

HEART
QUEST.

Romance fiction from
Tyndale House Publishers, Inc.
WHEATON, ILLINOIS

Visit Tyndale's exciting Web site at www.tyndale.com

Check out the latest about HeartQuest Books at www.heartquest-romances.com

HeartQuest is a registered trademark of Tyndale House Publishers, Inc.

Designed by Melinda Schumacher

The Christmas Bride edited by Kathryn S. Olson

Reforming Seneca Jones edited by Jan Pigott

Wishful Thinking edited by Ramona Cramer Tucker

Scripture quotations are taken from the *Holy Bible,* King James Version.

Library of Congress Cataloging-in-Publication Data

Palmer, Catherine, date.
  Prairie Christmas / Catherine Palmer, Elizabeth White, Peggy Stoks.
    p. cm.
    Contents: The Christmas bride / by Catherine Palmer—Reforming Seneca Jones / by Elizabeth White—Wishful thinking / by Peggy Stoks.
    ISBN 0-8423-3562-5
    1. Christmas stories, American. 2. Christian fiction, American. 3. Frontier and pioneer life—Fiction. I. White, Elizabeth, date. II. Stoks, Peggy. III. Title.
PS648.C45 P35 2000
813'.6080334—dc 21   00-037783

Printed in the United States of America

05 04 03 02 01 00
9 8 7 6 5 4 3

CONTENTS

THE CHRISTMAS BRIDE

Catherine Palmer

CHAPTER 1

Hope, Kansas
September 1866

I AM THE happiness of all the town!" Rolf Rustemeyer pushed back his chair and held up an envelope so the townsfolk gathered in Lucy's Bakeshop could see it. Even the postmaster, who was sampling one of the proprietor's famous cinnamon rolls, paused to stare at the big German farmer.

"You mean to say you have happy news for all the town," Rosie Hunter said, laying her hand on Rolf's arm to soften her correction.

"*Ja*," he said, beaming. "Happy news for the town. I have a letter from my home in the Old Country. Soon, I am marrying the Christmas bride."

Lucy Cornwall studied Rolf through the glass pane of the counter as she arranged the morning's display of sticky rolls. She thought the blond farmer had it right the first time. Rolf Rustemeyer *was* the happiness of the town of Hope. A frown never shadowed the man's face, a word of anger never crossed his lips, and he was always ready with cheerful encouragement or a helping hand for his neighbors. He strode into her bakeshop each morning before dawn and announced that it was going to be a very "goot" day. And usually, while Rolf Rustemeyer was around, it was.

"My father sends to me this letter," he continued, displaying the crisp white sheet of paper for everyone to admire. "In summer, I was writing to him. I tell my father I am too much alone. No wife, no childrens. I tell him to find me a wife."

3

"But what about Widow Hudson?" Seth Hunter asked. As Rosie's husband and mayor of Hope, he kept up with most of the town's goings-on. "I recall a picnic last summer when you were dancing with Violet Hudson and three or four of her children."

"Mrs. Hudson moved already to Topeka," Rolf said. "She sells her farm to me and goes away with her husband's parents."

At this news, Lucy turned to her wooden bins and scooped out a measure of oatmeal. She was pleased to hear that Rolf had acquired more property. The German had become the largest landowner in the county, and certainly the wealthiest. And she had to admit she was glad that his efforts to court the Widow Hudson were at an end. Violet was a sweet woman, but Rolf deserved someone younger . . . more gentle. . . .

"Has your father really found you a wife, Rolf?" Rosie asked.

"Ja." He scrutinized the letter again. "Ingrid Volkart is her name. She is living near Heidelberg with her mother and father and three sisters and six brothers."

"But, Rolf, do you know this woman?"

"Not yet. She comes by the boat and the train at Christmastime. Then we marry." He picked up his coffee mug and took a long swallow. "Goot, Miss Cornwall. Very goot!"

Lucy knew she was blushing as she kneaded the dough for the oatmeal buns she sold by the dozen. Why couldn't she say something to him in response? What kept her tongue frozen like a slab of winter beef? She could feel the eyes of everyone in the shop, so she turned quickly to look for her rolling pin.

"Ahh," Rolf said, setting down the mug. "And now, sun is coming up. Cows want to be milked. Chickens giving eggs. I better to go home."

"Rolf." Rosie caught his arm. "How soon will this Ingrid Volkart be here? Should we plan a wedding for you? What if you don't like her? And how will you—"

"I don't know answers," the farmer said. "God has the goot plan for Rolf Rustemeyer. When I make plans for myself in these matters, it does not go so fine. A while back, I try to marry with you, remember, Mrs. Hunter?"

Rosie smiled and took her husband's hand. She was due to deliver their first child within the month. "But God had a different plan," she said softly.

"*Ja*, and then I think maybe to marry Caitrin Murphy. But she marries with Jack Cornwall, there." He pointed at Lucy's brother, whose Irish wife was next door opening the mercantile for business.

"After that, I try the Widow Hudson." Rolf raked his fingers through his thick blond hair. "Is no goot for me to make plans, you see? Better to let God be the boss of it."

"But, Rolf, how can you marry a woman you don't even know?"

"Did Adam know Eve? They get along OK, I think." He frowned. "Maybe one or two small problems."

"Oh, Rolf, you've worked so hard to learn English, and you've built up such a fine farm. Why don't you marry a nice American girl?"

"Who, Mrs. Hunter? Who I shall marry?" He lifted his arms and spread them wide. "No one is here. No one!"

He started across the floor, his heavy leather boots thudding on the wooden planks. Grabbing his coat, he tossed it over one shoulder. Then he turned and looked directly at Lucy.

"Very goot cinnamon rolls today, Miss Cornwall," he said. "You are the best baker in all of Kansas."

Lucy couldn't bring herself to face him, so she nodded in acknowledgment of his compliment as he walked out the door. Yes, Rolf liked her cinnamon rolls and her coffee. He liked the sunny bakeshop with its cluster of round tables. He liked the blue gingham tablecloths and the shiny glass counter and the oven filled with fragrant breads. He even liked Lucy.

She pinched off a ball of oatmeal dough and rolled it into a bun as her morning customers began to don their hats and coats. Everyone in town liked Lucy. But they were wary of her, too, she knew. They all were aware of her troubled past—how she had been attacked by soldiers during the war and had given birth to a baby as the result of that violation. They knew that the child had been given up for adoption. And they knew that for months afterward, Lucy Cornwall had not been in her right mind.

Now, she wrapped a dish towel around her hand and opened the oven door to slide in the pan of buns. She wasn't so deeply troubled these days—not so others would notice, anyway—but the townspeople remembered how she had scrubbed her flesh raw in an effort to rid herself of the stains the soldiers had left on her. They recalled the way she had thrown herself in front of a stagecoach. They knew about the time she had waded into the freezing waters of Bluestem Creek, determined to end the torment of her bleak, black life.

But things had changed. Though her past had been difficult, Lucy had found a new sense of peace and joy. Strong, determined, and filled with hope, she could see that God was caring for her. With the encouragement of Rosie and Caitrin, Lucy had set up her bakery. Now she spent most of each day away from the Cornwall family's soddy, far from the bitter unhappiness of her mother, who had yet to accept the death of her husband, the loss of their Missouri farm during the War Between the States, and the attack on her daughter. Free to experiment in her new kitchen, Lucy had begun baking up such succulent treats that nearly the whole town turned out early each morning to eat breakfast and purchase fresh breads for the day's meals. She found pleasure in her accomplishments, and she looked forward to what each new day might bring. In the past few months, Lucy had joined the church choir, stitched herself three bright calico dresses, and learned how to weave colorful ribbons through her brown hair.

This Christmas, she had decided, was going to be the best ever.

She would trim her shop with swags of fresh pine boughs, set pretty red candles on every table, and bake dozens of cookies for the town's children to decorate. Excitement filled her as she thought of the money sack, heavy with coins, under her counter. Lucy planned to buy a length of red velvet and sew herself a beautiful, full-skirted gown. With the rest of the money, she would purchase a new hunting knife for her brother, a gilt-framed mirror for Caitrin, and the rose-bedecked hat that her mother had so admired in the mercantile. Lucy could hardly wait.

"Oatmeal?" Rosie asked, leaning against the counter to peer into the empty mixing bowl. "Oh, Lucy, you know how I adore your oatmeal buns. Seth, let's buy some. We can eat them with the chicken I'll be frying up for dinner. When will they come out of the oven, Lucy?"

"Not long." Lucy dipped a rag in her wash bucket. She liked to keep her counters clean. "Why don't you send Chipper down later? I'll put some buns in a basket for you."

"Would you do that? Lucy, you're so sweet." Rosie rubbed her hands over her swollen stomach. "Oh, I feel like I'm just ready to pop. And would you look at that? Seth's gone out the door without even thinking of me. He and your brother are all caught up in their plans for building the new school. Caitrin is longing to teach, but she can't do that and run the mercantile, too. Besides, I suspect she'll be in the family way before long. I've told Seth a hundred times that we need to find a spinster for the teaching job."

"That's true," Lucy said.

"What do you think of Rolf's announcement? A bride from Germany! I'll have to start teaching English lessons all over again. Well, Lucy, it's been a wonderful start to the morning, hasn't it? I'll send Chipper down the hill for the buns. I can't wait!"

Rosie waddled across to the coatrack. Lucy watched her lift a heavy woolen shawl and slip it around her shoulders. Sometimes Lucy recalled the months of her own pregnancy. She had loved the tiny life growing inside her. And at the same time, she had feared it might be a hideous growth, a kind of cancer that a great evil had planted inside her. But she had knitted eight pairs of booties, and she had stitched every yard of flannel she could purchase into tiny gowns and blankets. She had ached to hold her baby in her arms. And other times she had longed to rip it out of her body. It was the symbol of every pain and torment that had been visited on her.

Even now that her life had taken on such joy, there were times when Lucy found herself wondering what had happened to her baby. Lucy prayed daily for her child. Somewhere deep in her heart, she nurtured the dream that she might one day be reunited with her daughter.

"Look at that husband of mine," Rosie said. "He's halfway up the hill with Jack Cornwall. You'd never know they were once mortal enemies."

"God has worked miracles in Hope," Lucy said.

"Now isn't that the truth? When I think of all the things that have happened here, I just have to fall on my knees in gratitude. The way God gave Chipper back to Seth was truly a wonder. Then Jack Cornwall hid in the O'Tooles' barn and fell in love with Caitrin. And who would have thought a prairie fire would turn Jimmy O'Toole to Jesus? That's not even to mention the way your mother and Sheena O'Toole have come to—"

She stopped speaking and let out a yelp like a wounded pup. Lucy turned from checking on the oatmeal buns to find Rosie in a heap beside the front door.

"Oh, Lucy!" Rosie was clutching her skirts. "Something's happening to me. There's water everywhere! Where's Seth . . . where's . . . oh, no!"

Lucy hurried around the counter and sank to the floor beside the young woman. "Don't worry, Rosie. It's all right. Didn't

Sheena tell you about the water breaking? Sometimes it happens first, and that means the baby's on the way for certain."

Rosie was gasping for air. "But there's so much of it!"

"More than you'd suppose. Calm yourself, now. I'll fetch Seth."

"Wait, Lucy, don't leave me!" Rosie grabbed her hand and squeezed hard. "It hurts. My whole stomach hurts. It's so tight, like there's a big leather band around it. I'm afraid!"

"No, no. That's just the way it's supposed to feel. Stretch your legs out now. Lean back against the wall. There you go—"

"Oh, oh, ohhh!" Blue eyes wide, Rosie stared at Lucy. "What if the baby's born right here on the bakeshop floor? What if something terrible happens? What if—"

"Close your eyes, Rosie, and take a deep breath. Remember God is here with you right now. He's watching over you and your baby." Lucy stroked her hand across her friend's damp forehead. "That's right. Try to breathe. Now, remember, it usually takes a long time to birth the first baby. You'll be home in your own bed long before your little one shows his pretty face to the world."

"The pain's going away now." Rosie's eyes fluttered open. "I feel better. I feel like I can—"

"I forget my bread!" Rolf Rustemeyer announced, barging into the bake shop and swinging the front door into Lucy. "How am I eating my sandwich without the bread?"

He stopped, stared at the empty counter, then noticed the two figures at his feet. His tanned face went ashen.

"Mrs. Hunter! You are not well?"

"It's the baby," Lucy said softly, rubbing her shoulder where the door had hit her. "Mr. Rustemeyer, please go and fetch Mr. Hunter right away."

"But what is this wet on the floor and the skirt? She's bleeding?"

"Oh, I'm mortified!" Rosie cried. "Rolf, stop staring at me. Go away!"

"Never. I carry you to your house!" Before either woman could speak, he scooped Rosie into his huge arms and strode out the door. Lucy scampered beside him, frightened her friend would have another pain. What if Rosie cried out and Rolf dropped her?

"Put me down this instant, you great shaggy bear!" Rosie pounded on Rolf's chest with her bare fists, but he kept walking. "I want my husband. Lucy, where's Seth?"

"What's the matter with Rosie?" Caitrin Cornwall raced out of the mercantile, her bonnet ribbons flying. "I heard the shouting. Is it the baby?"

"It's the baby," Rosie wailed. "Make Rolf put me down!"

"Has she started her labor?" Lily Book, the pastor's wife, stepped through the church door. "I'm on my way!"

As the women of the town fell in behind the German farmer and his burden, Lucy stopped. Now Sheena O'Toole, her sixth baby due at any moment, came tottering across the bridge over the Bluestem. She was waving a handful of diapers and shouting advice as a string of children tried to hold her back by her skirts. Ben Hanks emerged from the smithy, while his wife and mother quickly joined the crowd hurrying up the road toward the Hunter family's white clapboard house.

Lucy let out a sigh and turned back to her bake shop. She needed to check the oven. Perhaps later she'd make up a basket of warm oatmeal buns and send them to Rosie. And one day, maybe soon, she would get the chance to see the tiny newborn. Perhaps Rosie would even trust Lucy to hold the baby.

"Wait for me!" Sheena called. "Colleen, do stop clutching my skirts. Sure you'll trip me up any moment."

Lucy paused for a moment in the door of her little shop. She felt grateful to see the townspeople come together for this event, just as they had rallied to stop a prairie fire, build a church, clean up after a tornado, and for countless other efforts. If the mercantile needed new glass windows, five of the townsmen arrived to install them. If the O'Toole children fell ill with croup, the women of

Hope took turns staying up all night and nursing them back to health. It was a good place, and Lucy thanked God daily for giving her a new life here.

As she started to step into the shop, Lucy noticed Sheena come to a halt and steady herself against the church wall. Bending over, the redheaded woman took several deep breaths as two of her youngsters skipped around her. She pushed their hands away and clutched her belly. Then she sank onto the ground.

"Sheena?" Lucy shouted. "Are you all right?"

"Glory be to God!" Sheena's face brightened as she spotted Lucy in the distance. "Sure I thought everyone had gone up to the Hunters' house. Move out of the way, Will, I can't see Miss Cornwall at all. Lucy, can you come here a moment, my dear? I'm afraid I've a bit of a problem."

Grabbing her skirts, Lucy hurried up the dusty road. She was concerned about her oatmeal buns burning up in the oven, but she knew she must help Sheena first. "Is something wrong, Mrs. O'Toole?"

"Aye, that there is. This baby of mine has made up his wee mind to have a bit of a race with Rosie's child."

"A race?"

"He's wanting to be born, so he is." Her round face was flushed and beaded with drops of perspiration. "You'll help me, won't you, Miss Cornwall?"

"I'll run for Mr. O'Toole—"

"No time for that. This is my sixth, and it won't wait for Papa. I can feel the head pushing down already."

"The head!" Lucy clutched her heart, trying to breathe. "But Mrs. O'Toole—"

"I had pains all night, off and on, but naught to fret about. The running must have hurried the labor." She grabbed her son's arm. "Will, take Colleen and run to the farm hot-foot and fetch your papa. That's a good lad. Miss Cornwall, help me into the church."

"You can't have a baby in the church!" Lucy cried.

"Shall I have it here on the road, then?"

Lucy clutched her skirts, paralyzed with uncertainty. Sheena was trying to stand, the children were scampering away, and Lucy longed to race back to her shop where everything was safe. Where she was in control. Where nothing could go wrong.

"Won't you help me, Lucy?" Sheena asked.

"I . . . I . . ." Lucy couldn't make herself move.

"Oh, you're useless, so you are!" Sheena snapped. "I should have known this would happen. Naught to help me but a weak-headed googeen. God have mercy!"

She pushed herself to her feet and leaned on the windowsill. Breathing hard, she began to shuffle toward the church door. Lucy bit her lip, praying for courage, fearful she might faint. She needed to go back to her shop. She had to take the oatmeal buns out of the oven. Then she ought to wash the counters. Scrub them until they sparkled.

Groaning in agony, Sheena fought her way to the door. Lucy swallowed. She couldn't do this. Couldn't help. Didn't know how. What if she made a mistake? What if the baby died? What if Sheena died? She should run. Run back down the hill to her shop.

"I can't . . ." Sheena tugged on the door handle. "It's locked, is it? Oh, have mercy on me!"

Lucy gritted her teeth and sent up a desperate prayer for strength: *Father God! Oh, God, please help us!* Crying out, shattering the bonds of fear, she lunged at the door. The handle turned. The door swung open. Sheena toppled to the church floor. Lucy fell to her knees beside the woman and threw back her skirts.

"Are you there, Lucy? Are you there?" Sheena cried. "I must push it out! I've no choice!"

"I'm here," Lucy whispered. "Push, Sheena."

With a loud wail, she arched her back. Lucy cupped her hands. A small, damp head slipped into her palms.

"Is it out?" Sheena cried. "Lord have mercy on my soul, I'm dying!"

"Push again!"

This time the baby's shoulders emerged, and then all at once the rest of the tiny body slid out into Lucy's hands. Gripping the slippery baby, she ran her finger around the inside of the rosebud mouth.

"Breathe, child!" Lucy commanded. "Breathe now!"

A gasp. A cry. And the baby began to wail. Gray skin flushed bright pink. Tiny arms pumped the air. Feet and legs churned.

"He lives!" Sheena laughed and cried. "Oh, thank you, dear Jesus!"

Lucy laid the baby in Sheena's outstretched arms and let out a deep breath.

It was done. The baby was born. Alive and safe. *Oh, God, thank you!* she prayed.

"'Tis a boy!" Sheena said. "A fine, lusty boy with his papa's bright red hair. We must cut the—"

"Where she is?" Rolf Rustemeyer shouted, plowing through the church door. Colleen clung to his hand and pointed at her mother. "Mrs. O'Toole? What happens to you? The little girl tells me—"

"The baby, I've had my baby!" Sheena was giggling now, kissing her squalling son on his forehead. "Rolf, cut the cord, and then run fetch Jimmy. I must show him this fine new boy of ours. What shall we name him, Lucy? What do you think?"

Lucy swallowed and glanced at Rolf. He was staring at her with a mixture of concern and admiration.

"You do this, Miss Cornwall?" he asked. "You bring this baby out?"

She shook her head. "It was Mrs. O'Toole—"

"Nonsense! I couldn't have done it without Lucy." Sheena took the German's hand and pulled him close. "Look, Rolf, look at my baby now. What do you think of him, eh? Isn't he grand?"

Lucy took a bit of baker's twine from her apron pocket and tied the baby's cord. Then Rolf slipped his knife from its holder on his belt. As he cut the cord, Lucy took off her apron and wrapped the baby in the soft white cotton. She had just slipped off one of Sheena's petticoats and begun to clean up when Jimmy O'Toole and five O'Toole children burst into the church. "'Tis a boy!" Sheena said as her husband knelt beside her.

"Glory be to God," Jimmy said. "Look, Will and Erinn, you've a new brother, so you have. And what do you think of him? Isn't he a wee thing? Sure you're a grand, elegant woman, Sheena. Why then I'm certain I've never been so happy in all my days."

"You've said that six times over, you silly galoot," she murmured.

"And each time I've meant it. Oh, Sheena, my love."

"Jimmy, Jimmy."

As the family clustered around Sheena, Lucy rose and took a step back. She could see the baby's small pink face, could remember her own daughter pressed against her breast. How long had she held the child? No more than a minute, it seemed. And then her mother had come and pulled the baby away.

"This is a child of sin," she had said. *A child of sin. A child of sin.*

Lucy twisted her damp fingers together. She hadn't meant for the soldiers to find her hiding there in the barn. Hadn't lured them. Hadn't made herself free to them. But they took her, and then her mother took the baby. The child of sin.

Whose sin? Lucy now wanted to ask as she stumbled out the door of the church into the September sunshine. *Forgive me, God! I didn't mean it to happen!*

"Miss Cornwall, you are very goot woman." Rolf Rustemeyer's voice stopped her on the road. "It is brave for you to help Mrs.

O'Toole. And before that you help Mrs. Hunter. Two babies in one day. This is very goot."

Lucy peered through the swirling clouds that filled her thoughts until she could see Rolf's shining hair and bright gray eyes. What was he telling her?

"Me, too," he said. "I help also, *ja*? First I carry Mrs. Hunter to her house. And then I cut the . . . how do you say it?"

Lucy looked into his broad, handsome face. "Cord," she whispered.

"The cord. We are the helpers today, you and me."

Lucy nodded.

"I think, you and me, we are much the same," he went on. "I am big German farmer, not talking goot English. People here are not wanting to be my friend, because they think I am not the same with them. Different, you know?"

"Yes," Lucy said softly.

"And you, too. You are different. Very quiet, not talking, baking bread every day. Not many friends. Why that is?"

She studied his face, the high cheekbones, the strong jaw. Didn't he know she was considered mad? Didn't he see how she sometimes struggled just to get through each day? Of course she had no close friends. People were wary. People were afraid.

"Here is what I think," Rolf said. "I think you and me are different. So, we are the same. You understand?"

"Yes," Lucy said. "I understand."

He smiled at her, a grin that lit up the morning. "Two babies in one day. In Germany, we say *wunderbar*. It means wonderful."

"*Wunderbar*," she repeated.

"*Ja!* You speak German very goot." He glanced at her. "Aha, now you smile. I never see you smile before this day. Maybe you think Rolf Rustemeyer is funny?"

"I think you are *wunderbar*."

He threw back his head and laughed. "You are *wunderbar!* I am *wunderbar! Two babies in one day is *wunderbar!*"

Lucy gasped as he took her hands and swung her around in a circle. Boots sending up puffs of dust on the dirt road, he danced a set of intricate steps. Then he kicked up his heels and whirled away.

"Two babies," he shouted as he jigged down the road. "Two babies and *wunderbar* Lucy Cornwall and a Christmas bride coming from Germany to marry with Rolf Rustemeyer! God is goot! God is very goot!"

Lucy sucked down a deep breath. She would have to hurry back to her shop. The oatmeal buns must be burned to cinders.

CHAPTER 2

ROLF looped his horse's reins over the hitching post in front of the mercantile and drank down a deep draft of cinnamon-scented air. As he exhaled, the crisp October dawn chilled his breath into a puff of white. More than a month had passed since the momentous day when two babies were born in the town of Hope. And today they would be making their first public appearance—at Lucy Cornwall's bakeshop. Rolf had been anticipating the moment.

He pushed open the front door with its string of jingling bells and stamped his boots on the mat. It didn't surprise him to realize he was the first customer of the morning. Though his large wood-frame house sat on a hill a mile from Hope, he usually was the earliest to arrive at the bakery for breakfast.

"Goot morning, Miss Cornwall!" He called his customary greeting as he stripped off his leather gloves and stuffed them into his coat pocket. "This will be a fine day, *ja*? The two babies come for everybody to see: Abraham O'Toole and Mercy Hunter. Goot names! I also have big news. Another letter comes to me from Germany!"

He looked across the cluster of tables, expecting to find Lucy bent over her oven or stirring a bowl of dough on the counter. Before the crowd arrived, Rolf was hoping to tell Lucy all about his plans for the coming Christmas—the big wedding he was preparing, the red roses he had ordered from a greenhouse in New York for his bride's bouquet, the pine tree he had selected to decorate his great room, and the set of very special holiday ornaments he was carving. He knew Lucy would listen quietly and then tell him how fine everything sounded. She could always be counted on for an encouraging word. Rolf noted a batch of steaming cinnamon rolls on the sparkling glass shelf, and he spotted a pitcher of milk beside it. But where was Lucy?

"Miss Cornwall?" Rolf called. "Where you are?"

He thought he heard a sniffle coming from behind the counter. Hooking his coat on the iron peg rack beside the door, he strode across the room and peered over the sheet of rolls. There, seated on the floor, was Lucy.

"You are praying?" he asked.

She looked up, her pretty cheeks flushed from the heat in the shop. "Excuse me, I was just . . ."

"No, is OK. I don't disturb you." He started to back away, but then it registered that Lucy was crying. An aching tenderness turned over inside his chest. "You are all right, Miss Cornwall? Maybe something is hurting you?"

She shook her head. "It's nothing."

"Why do you cry?"

She took the corner of her apron and blotted her cheek. Her voice was no more than a whisper. "I was remembering something."

"Remembering what?" Rolf peered down at her. Rosie Hunter had warned him not to be so blunt. She had done her best to teach him good manners along with her English grammar lessons. But Lucy was crying. Rolf felt sure he ought to know why.

"It's nothing," she said again.

He frowned. "You tell me you remember something. And then you tell me it's nothing. But if nothing makes you cry, it must be something."

Lucy blinked up at him. "Mr. Rustemeyer, you're crushing the cinnamon rolls."

He looked down. Sure enough, in leaning over the counter he had pressed the rolls almost flat. A layer of gooey white icing clung to his chambray shirt.

"*Ach, ich bin ein Dumkopf!* Stupid, stupid!" He rubbed at the icing with his hand, smearing it into the fabric. "Now, you will have to make more rolls, and is the day of the babies. Everybody is coming here! I help you. Tell me what I shall do, Miss Cornwall."

"It's all right." Her voice was soft as she got to her feet. "I have more rolls in the oven. And there'll be hotcakes and eggs."

"But I—"

"Good morning, Mr. Rustemeyer!" Pastor Elijah Book and his pretty wife stepped into the bakeshop. Mrs. Book was carrying their son. Rolf noted that the pastor's arm had slipped around his wife's shoulders in a gesture that bore witness to their love. These two, he thought, had truly been blessed by God. Rolf didn't know when he'd seen any couple so happy. Even their baby—who had begun his life as an orphan—reflected their intense joy. "And Miss Cornwall, how do you do? Isn't this a fine day the Lord has made?"

"Oh, Lucy, it smells heavenly in here," Mrs. Book said.

Before Rolf could explain about the squashed rolls, Salvatore and Carlotta Rippeto entered the room with a handful of their ten children in tow. Casimir Laski, the stationmaster, followed close on their heels. After him came the LeBlanc family, who ran the grain mill near the river. Then Ben Hanks, the assistant blacksmith, and his wife breezed in with Mother Margaret chattering about the threat of snow. Rolf barely had time to claim an empty chair before Jimmy O'Toole stepped into the shop and held up a squirming bundle of arms, legs, and bright red hair.

"I'd like you all to welcome Abraham Lincoln O'Toole," he announced as Sheena and the rest of their brood squeezed inside behind him. "My son is named for the late great emancipator of our country, and he's the first of the O'Toole family to be born on American soil. Say cheers, lad."

At that, Abe O'Toole let out a wail that nearly raised the roof. Everyone began to clap and call out congratulations as Rolf settled into his chair. He was hoping the O'Tooles would see fit to pass the baby around the room. At the very least, he ought to have the chance to hold the boy. It was he, after all, who had cut the cord—not that he should announce the matter at breakfast. He had managed to learn a *few* manners at Rosie's hand.

His teacher herself stepped into the bakeshop next, and behind her came Seth Hunter and their son, Chipper. It was the boy who carried their new baby.

"Here's Mercy," Chipper said, turning so everyone could catch a glimpse of the sleeping child. A wave of oohs and ahhs swept over the room. Rolf thought he had never seen a little girl so perfect. She had Rosie's dark brown hair, and her skin was as soft and pink as the petal of a rose.

By now the room was so crowded that Rolf felt obliged to offer the new mother his chair. He passed Chipper and the baby, and it was all he could do not to scoop both of them up in his arms. More than anything, Rolf longed for a wife and children of his own.

As he leaned against the wall, he thought about the letter burning in his pocket. A new epistle had arrived from Germany with the previous post—this one from Ingrid Volkart herself! And she had sent a photograph.

Rolf could hardly believe his blessing from God. The woman who was to be his wife looked exactly like the Christmas angel that had been painted in the frontispiece of his Bible. Her long hair was wound onto her head in a thick braid. Blond hair, she told him in her letter. Blond, like him! She had blue eyes, high cheekbones, and a pretty mouth he could hardly wait to kiss.

"Would you like a roll?" Lucy Cornwall asked, bringing Rolf out of his dream. She held out a plate piled high with sticky cinnamon buns. Rolf looked into her shining gray eyes, suddenly remembering the tears. She stared back at him for a moment before glancing away.

"I will take this one," he said. "And I will pay for all the others that I smashed flat."

"Never mind." Her voice was almost inaudible beneath the hubbub of excitement over the new babies. "It's nothing."

Rolf cocked his head as she slipped away to serve the others in the shop. The tears were nothing? The ruined rolls were nothing? Why did Lucy speak this way? Why did she seem so silent and alone even here among so many people?

Rolf studied the young woman as she made her way from table to table. He had heard some of the rumors people told about her. They said she was mad. They said she had tried to kill herself. He couldn't imagine such a thing. Lucy was sweet and kind and very gentle. And she was such a good cook! Rolf could appreciate that in a woman. In fact, he liked Lucy very much, and it bothered him that anyone would not think well of her.

"Your turn," Rosie said, appearing in front of Rolf and holding out her sleeping daughter. "Don't you want to hold Mercy?"

Startled, he looked down at the tiny baby. He could hear people chuckling around him. *The big German farmer*, they were probably thinking. *He wouldn't know how to hold a baby.*

"Of course, I hold her," he said, settling into a chair that had been vacated. They didn't know about his five little brothers and three little sisters. "Come to me, Mercy. *Wie geht's, mein süße Brötchen? Wie geht es Ihnen?*"

"What are you saying?" Rosie asked.

Rolf grinned. "What, you don't know German, Mrs. Hunter? Maybe I have to give you lessons."

"Tell me what you said to my daughter."

"I call her my little sweet bun," he said, patting the baby's bundled bottom as he cradled her against his shoulder. "Like Miss Cornwall's cinnamon roll, you know?"

"A cinnamon bun!" Rosie laughed as Sheena stepped to her side.

"And what of my wee Abraham?" Sheena asked. "Will you call him a sweet bun too?"

Rolf took the wriggly baby in his free arm and began to jiggle him against his chest. "Two sweet buns," he said, reveling in the warmth of the babies. *"Zwei süße Brötchens!"*

"Sure we know who to call in the middle of the night, don't we, Rosie?" Sheena exclaimed. "We'll send for this great galoot and make him rock our wee ones back to sleep."

Rolf laughed. In fact, he would gladly get out of bed for a chance to rock a baby in the night. Nothing could make him happier.

As the crowd in the bakery settled down to their rolls, hotcakes, and servings of fluffy scrambled eggs, Rolf held the two babies in his arms and gently rocked them back and forth.

To everyone's astonishment, Abe O'Toole dropped off to sleep as though he'd been given a tonic. And Rolf didn't mind that he was missing the chance to eat his cinnamon roll. For once, he would forgo breakfast.

He watched Lucy working as she always did—dishing out food, wiping the counters clean, pouring milk and coffee. No one helped her, but she didn't seem to mind. In the bakeshop, Lucy reigned as queen. So why didn't she smile? Why didn't she join in the banter as women told stories of their own babies and men discussed the coming winter?

To tell the truth, Rolf didn't usually think too much about Lucy Cornwall. He thought about eating breakfast, plowing, milking, eating lunch, threshing, chopping wood, eating supper, and getting a good night's sleep. Usually, his focus didn't waver much from the simple duties of his life. Oh, he liked to ponder passages he had read in the Bible or topics that Pastor Elijah had spoken about in church. Sometimes he worried a little about the weather. And lately, he'd been doing a lot of thinking about Ingrid Volkart.

But ever since the day the two babies were born, thoughts of Lucy had begun to slip into Rolf's mind. As the sun rose and the crowd began to file out of Lucy's bakery, he studied her again. He liked her cooking. He admired her efficiency. He appreciated her pretty gray eyes and rich brown hair. He respected her composure when she helped Sheena O'Toole give birth. So why didn't Lucy smile?

"You'll have to give them up now, so you will," Sheena said, taking her sleeping son from Rolf's shoulder. "But I'll be calling on you when he sets up a caterwaul, you hear?"

Rolf laughed. "I will come."

"It won't be long until you have babies of your own to rock," Rosie said. She lifted Mercy into her arms. "Any news from Germany, Rolf?"

"*Ja*, goot news!" He dug the letter from his shirt pocket. "Look, here is Ingrid Volkart."

As he held up the photograph, Rosie and Sheena gasped in unison.

"She's beautiful, Rolf!" Rosie cried.

"Blond hair," he said. "She comes on the boat very soon, and she brings with her two chests of bedclothes and furniture. She tells me she is very strong and smart."

"She said she was smart?"

"*Ja*. She goes to school, you know. And she likes to read books."

"Can she cook?"

"Every German girl can cook, Mrs. Hunter."

"But does she enjoy it? That's very important, Rolf, considering the pleasure you take in eating."

He chuckled. "I'm a big eater. Every day I thank God for Lucy's Bakeshop. What I am doing without Miss Cornwall?"

As he spoke, he glanced again at Lucy, who was gathering plates

23

from the empty table. For an instant, their eyes met. Then she dipped her head and hurried across the room with an armful of dishes.

"I starve, I think, without Miss Cornwall." He focused on the two women. "Thank you for bringing the babies. For me, this is great happiness."

"You're a fine man," Rosie said, bending to give Rolf a kiss on the cheek. "You're going to be a wonderful husband and father."

"And what an elegant wife to share your life with!" Sheena trilled as she headed for the door with Rosie. "I imagine before long we'll be visited with rows and rows of baby Rustemeyers!"

As the jingling bells fell silent, Rolf looked down at his uneaten cinnamon roll. Baby Rustemeyers. That was a nice thought.

Well, he would need to milk his cows before long. And take hay out to the pasture. And chop firewood. He picked up the roll and started across the room to the coatrack.

Her back to him, Lucy was washing dishes in a large metal tub. He didn't need to speak to her, Rolf realized. She wouldn't notice if he put his coins on the counter and hurried away. She probably wouldn't even turn.

He wondered if she was crying again.

"A very goot morning," Rolf said hesitantly. He paused at the counter as he fished in his pocket for money. "Everybody is happy with the babies."

Lucy nodded and continued to set dripping dishes on the table beside the washtub.

"Did you hold those babies, Miss Cornwall?"

She shook her head. "I was busy."

"Ja." He dropped the coins on the counter. "Well, I see you tomorrow."

"Good-bye."

He paused, suddenly aware that he was short of breath. "Miss Cornwall, why you were crying before? I wish you to tell me that."

"And I wish you to go away," she said, turning. Her eyes were filled with tears again. "Take your cinnamon roll, Mr. Rustemeyer, and go away."

He stiffened. "You are angry with me?"

"I'm not angry. I'm . . . it's nothing."

"Not nothing!" He came around the counter and took the wet plate from her hand. "Every morning I come here and eat breakfast and buy bread for my sandwich at lunch. And every day you work, work, never smiling. Now, this day, the day of the babies, you cry. To me, it is not nothing!"

"I'm very busy."

"Why do you cry?"

"I have to clean up."

"First tell me why you cry." He took both her damp hands and pressed them between his. "You give so much of yourself in this warm room full of food and happiness. But there is no happiness inside you. You have only tears and sorrow. Please tell me why."

She looked up at him, her eyes filling again. "I don't want to talk about it."

"But we are the same, you remember? You and me, we are alone, different from all the others in this town. I am your friend. Tell me why you cry."

Her lip trembled as she tried to speak. "Surely you know about me. Mad Lucy."

"I hear what they say. But I don't believe this."

"You should believe it. It's true!" Tears spilled down her cheeks. "Thoughts and memories sweep over me sometimes. They threaten to drown me, and I want to drown! I want to die!"

"No!" He squeezed her hands, horrified at her words. "You are goot woman, and beautiful and kind. We cannot have a happy town without Lucy Cornwall."

"You don't understand."

"Tell me!"

She stared up at him, her eyes in torment. "Don't you know? I had a baby once. A daughter. She was taken away."

"Who took her?"

"My mother. She had to do it. The baby was . . . she was . . ."

"Sick?"

"Born of sin."

Rolf stepped back. "You have a baby without a husband, Miss Cornwall?"

"I was . . ." She shook her head. "I was violated. Taken by soldiers during the war. Don't you know the story? I told the truth so that all the town could hear it, so there would be no more secrets, and I've tried to go on with my life since that day. Tried to live. Tried to become someone. And with God's help, I have. But sometimes all the hurt comes back. Blackness covers me like a curtain, and I can't find the way out. Don't you understand? I'll never be the same as I was before. I'll never be whole again."

Rolf stared at Lucy. He had heard the stories, but he hadn't wanted to believe them. It was too horrible to think of the gentle woman behind the bakeshop counter in such a way. She seemed pure and perfect. But she had been used by men—many men—and she had given birth to a baby. Rolf felt a glimmer of understanding.

"Today, when I knew the babies were coming," she whispered, "I could hardly bear it. My own daughter was so pretty and—"

"No, how can this be? This was a terrible thing. How can such a baby be pretty—"

"But she was! She was soft and sweet. I held her in my arms, and I loved her so much."

"Loved her? When she was born from what those men did to you?"

"But my child was—"

"Cursed. The product of a great sin. Better you don't think of the baby or those men. Better you put everything from the past out of your mind and think only about today. This day. The goot morning sunshine and the happiness of life here in Hope."

"I try!"

"Try harder, Miss Cornwall." He cupped her face in his hands, wishing he could tear the painful memories from her mind. "Think only goot things, *ja?* Think about happy days. You have goot bakeshop here. You make delicious cinnamon rolls. You keep all things very clean and pretty. You are goot woman! *Wunderbar!*"

He bent down and kissed her on first one cheek, then the other, fully and firmly, so she could not mistake him. "I like you, Miss Cornwall," he said. "Don't cry!"

Before she could respond and before he could consider the implications of what he had done, Rolf strode across the bakery. He lifted his coat from the rack, threw it over his shoulder, and marched out into the frosty morning. He had cows to milk.

><

Lucy sprinkled cinnamon-sugar across the sweet dough she had rolled out into a neat rectangle. She wondered if Rolf would come to the bakery this morning when she opened the shop for the breakfast regulars. It had been nearly a week since the day the babies were introduced to the town, since the day Rolf had held her hands and kissed her—but he had not returned.

Others were beginning to take notice. Seth Hunter had commented that it wasn't like the German farmer to go so many days without his morning rolls and his lunchtime sandwich. Yesterday Seth had announced that if Rolf didn't show up this morning, he was going to ride over to the Rustemeyer farm and check on him.

Lucy began to roll the dough into a long strip. The thought of something bad befalling Rolf twisted her stomach into knots. What if Rolf was sick? What if he'd had an accident on the farm? She had prayed and prayed for him, trying her best not to worry.

What if Rolf was staying away because he had kissed her? Or what if he felt he couldn't come near because he had learned the terrible truth about Lucy's past? What if she disgusted and revolted him?

"You haven't washed the windows this week, have you?" Felicity Cornwall stepped into the bakery and shook the snow from her shawl. She scanned her daughter thoroughly up and down. "Lucy, my dear, I can hardly see the lamplight through the glass."

Lucy began cutting the rolled dough into inch-thick buns. It was true. She hadn't washed the windows. The colder weather made that chore difficult, but she should have done it anyway. Her customers deserved clean surroundings.

"I'm sorry I missed seeing the babies the other morning," Mrs. Cornwall continued. "This cough plagues me so. I don't know when I've felt this terrible. I can hardly breathe. Oh, this prairie wind! Why did we ever leave Missouri? I would give my last penny to go back."

Lucy sighed. She had lost track of how many times her mother had rehearsed this litany. Next, she would be reminding Lucy of the land their family still owned in Missouri. Her mother had the deed but was convinced it was probably worthless now.

Mrs. Cornwall paused for a moment. "What are you wearing, Lucy? Not the apron with the hole!"

Lucy glanced down at the white patch she had carefully stitched to cover the charred spot where a coal had popped from the oven's firebox. Perhaps the apron did look bad. She shouldn't have worn it.

Mrs. Cornwall sighed and walked across to the dish rack. "Oh, well, I don't suppose anyone will notice." She began rearranging the cups and glasses Lucy had set there. "It's not as though you're making much headway socially, my dear. I do wish you could have brought yourself to dance at the harvest gathering last month. There are plenty of unwed homesteaders around here. Surely one of them would have you if you could just be more friendly."

Lucy slid the pan of cinnamon rolls into the oven and shut the heavy door. She picked up a handful of kindling and pushed it into the firebox. The last thing she wanted was a husband, she reminded herself. She knew what men expected from a woman, what they would do to fulfill their lusts. Never again would she submit to that kind of degradation. Though her heart constantly ached for her lost baby, she knew she would never bear another child. No, her life was here in her bakeshop. Alone.

"I was talking with Rose Hunter the other day in the mercantile," Mrs. Cornwall said, "and she told me about a young man who's homesteading near the O'Tooles'. I mentioned you, and Rose said she thought the two of you might make a good match. It's not as though he would have to know everything. Sometimes the past is better left unspoken. Are these all the eggs you have, Lucy? You're not going to feed much of a crowd with these. You can't just rely on the O'Tooles for eggs. They're Irish, you know, and . . ."

Lucy sighed as she stirred the white icing on the stovetop. Her mother had done her best to accept the Irish O'Tooles, especially now that her son, Jack, was married to one of them. Lucy adored Caitrin and regarded her as a sister, but Mrs. Cornwall continued to find small flaws with the family.

"They're bound to lose more of their chickens to coyotes the way they let them run free," she said. "Just like their children. I don't know how those O'Toole children have survived all these years. What they need is schooling. But then the Irish never have placed much value on education."

"Goot morning, Miss Cornwall." Rolf Rustemeyer burst into the bakery, flinging the door against the coatrack and marching straight to the counter, not even noticing Lucy's mother. "I am going to talk to you now. Better I say these words before the others come."

Lucy stared at him. Then her focus darted to her mother. "Mr. Rustemeyer—"

"No, don't make me stop. I am thinking many days about what I say to you in the bakeshop last week. And now I know I am wrong in what I tell you about that baby."

"Mr. Rust—"

"Is not bad baby. And you. You are very goot woman." He nodded once, as if that settled the matter. "The badness is with the men who attack you. With them is the sin. Not with you or the baby."

"Oh, I—"

"More words," he continued. "I am thinking very hard on the reason of your sadness, and I am coming to the answer. This is the way to find happiness for Lucy Cornwall: I am taking you back to the place from where you came, and we are finding that baby. Don't tell me no! I am deciding this matter in my own mind. Now, my harvest is in the barns. My cattle and hay can be brought to Seth Hunter's land for him to do the milking and feeding. I can take my chickens to Jimmy O'Toole. You will go in my wagon with me for the finding of your lost baby." He crossed his arms over his broad chest and grinned at Lucy. "And then you can be happy. *Ja?*"

CHAPTER 3

LUCY gripped the edge of the counter and stared at Rolf. He wanted to take her back to Missouri. Back to the place of torment from which she had barely escaped. She had promised herself never to go there again. Missouri had become the symbol of her attack, of months in an insane asylum, of the iron chains that had bound her. How could any place be more terrible?

But her baby! Rolf was promising to help find her lost child in Missouri. Did he mean it?

"You want to take my daughter away, do you?" Felicity Cornwall spoke from the back of the shop.

Rolf swung around in surprise. "Mrs. Cornwall! I am not seeing you in the bakeshop. *Ja,* I will take your daughter to find her lost baby."

The woman approached. "And what has possessed you to undertake this mission, Mr. Rustemeyer? What interest do you have in my daughter and her past?"

"Your daughter is my friend," Rolf said. "I see her very sad in these days, and I am thinking I can help her to find happiness."

"And what gives you the right—"

"Only caring." He smiled. "Lucy tells me you take the baby away after the birth. Where did you put the child, Mrs. Cornwall?"

"A lawyer in Sedalia handled the whole distasteful matter. I was

31

given to understand that he would place the child with a foundling home in Kansas City until a suitable family could be found to adopt it. Though I would have preferred that the baby had never been born." Her eyes fastened on Lucy. "At great expense, I bought my daughter an herbal remedy, a mixture she could have taken to rid herself of that sin. But Lucy refused to drink it. She is a willful young woman, Mr. Rustemeyer, and you can see how far her stubbornness has taken her."

Lucy swallowed, trying to force down the words of anger she wanted to shout at her mother. Of course she had refused to drink the potion! No matter how the child had been conceived, it was a living baby. Though the nine months of her pregnancy had been physically difficult and mentally overwhelming for her, Lucy was glad she had endured them. Glad she had brought the baby into the world.

"I do not think potions can get rid of sin, Mrs. Cornwall," Rolf said. "Only Jesus is doing that job."

"The child was conceived in sin. It should have been removed."

"Sin should be removed, *ja*. But not babies. The child of your daughter has no part in the sin that was done."

"What do you know about it? You weren't there. You have no idea what we've endured these past few years."

"This is true."

"My daughter has barely recovered her sanity. And now you want to take her back to Missouri to find the baby that was the cause of it all?"

"The baby was not the cause of it, Mama," Lucy spoke up, unable to keep silent any longer. "The men caused it. The soldiers."

"You caused it—you with your smart mouth and selfish ways! Do you think those soldiers would have come after you if they hadn't been lured to it?"

"Lured? I was hiding in the barn!"

"Listen to my daughter, Mr. Rustemeyer," Felicity said. "Do you see how she argues? She throws her words at me. I know she's partly to blame in what happened to her. She could have resisted, or hidden herself better, or run away—"

"I couldn't!"

"Don't contradict me, young lady. You lured those men, and then you insisted on bearing that baby. God visited his wrath on you for your sin!" She pointed her finger in Lucy's face. "Your madness is your own fault!"

Lucy could feel the blackness descending over her like a cloud filled with shadows and nightmares. She clutched the counter, trying to breathe, trying to see beyond the darkness. But her mother was right. She should have run faster, or hidden better, or screamed louder. She should have drunk the potion that would have torn the baby from her body. It was all her fault. Her torment. Her sin.

"Mrs. Cornwall, I do not think the madness is the fault of your daughter," Rolf said, stepping in front of the counter, his broad shoulders and massive chest blocking Lucy's view of her mother. "Look, I can see people coming down the road this morning for the breakfast at Lucy's Bakeshop. It's better you don't make your daughter cry anymore. She has enough tears already."

"Are you disputing me, Mr. Rustemeyer?"

"*Disputing?* I don't know this word. Me, I am not very goot with speaking English or understanding all the problems about your daughter. But this I know: God loves Lucy Cornwall. He wishes her to find happiness and peace. God gives to your daughter and me a friendship. From that friendship I make bravery to say to you that I will take your daughter in my wagon to Missouri and find her baby daughter. And that is all the words of Rolf Rustemeyer."

Lucy stared at Rolf's big back, hardly able to believe what she had heard. The black cloud lifted from her shoulders. A beam of sunlight slanted across the room. Lucy wanted to look at her mother, but at the moment all she could see was Rolf Rustemeyer's blue chambray shirt, black suspenders, and shaggy blond hair. And that was enough.

God loved her, Rolf had said. God wanted her to find happiness and peace.

Despite everything her mother had told her, Lucy knew Rolf was right. If she could just hold back the pain of her own memories and the words of accusation from her mother, maybe she could find that peace. Maybe she could taste joy. But how? How was it possible?

"Lucy cannot go to Missouri," Mrs. Cornwall said. "I won't allow you to take her."

"Where is the problem?" Rolf said.

"For one thing, you're an unmarried man. I won't have you carrying my unmarried daughter away in a wagon. What would people say?"

"I tell you this is nothing to worry about. I already have a wife who comes on the boat from Germany. We are marrying at Christmastime."

"I don't care about your Christmas bride. I care about my daughter's reputation. I do not want her to leave Hope. This bakery is her anchor. This town is her security. I am her strength."

"You?" Rolf shrugged. "Then you come with us. Keep your daughter safe from me."

"And you could take the deed to your land, Mama!" Lucy leaned around Rolf's shoulder, praying she had stumbled across the key. "You could take the deed with you to Missouri and see if the land is still in our family name. You've always said you wanted to go back to Missouri. This is your chance."

Felicity Cornwall's eyes narrowed. "We were Confederate sympathizers. That land is probably settled by Union families by now."

"But maybe not. You might be able to prove your claim to it, Mama. Think what that would mean for you. And for Jack and Caitrin! They would have more than just the local smithy to their names. They'd have Missouri land to inherit. Something to pass on to their children."

The older woman turned as the front door opened and several farmers sauntered into the bakery. Lucy could see her mother's lips working, tight and pinched. Despite her fears of Missouri and the past, Lucy felt hope soaring through her heart on golden wings.

Dear God, please let her say yes. Please let me find my baby. Please give me peace and joy. Oh, God in heaven . . .

"All right," Felicity said. "We'll go together."

"A fine plan!" Rolf gave a laugh as he turned and grabbed Lucy's hands, squeezing them so hard she thought her fingers might break. "We go to find your baby. And now, everything is happy!"

As he drove his team of horses eastward, Rolf listened to the conversation between the two women in the covered wagon bed behind him—if it could be called conversation. Mrs. Cornwall was doing most of the talking.

Never had Rolf heard such a stretch of words in his life. If Mrs. Cornwall felt an ache or gave a cough, she had to discuss it with Lucy for at least half an hour. If Mrs. Cornwall noticed a country church standing by the roadside, she considered it her duty to mourn to her daughter for another hour or two on the lack of good preachers, the need for better songbooks, and the wasteful ways in which pastors spent tithe money. Mrs. Cornwall preached sermons to her daughter on the shamefulness of modern fashions, on the absurdity of eating any food other than meat and potatoes, on the silliness of young people in the town of Hope.

"And as for the Hanks family," Felicity was saying as the wagon left the town of Lawrence and started down the road that led to Kansas City, "they certainly have been giving themselves airs of late, don't you think? It wasn't so long ago that Ben was our slave.

Now you should see him give Jack orders in the smithy! Why, the other day I heard him telling my son to make nails!"

"They had a big order for nails, Mama," Lucy reminded her in a voice as soft as milk. "They're for the new schoolhouse."

"But why should Ben order Jack to make them? Ben can't tell my son what to do. Ben is a—"

"No more, Mrs. Cornwall!" Rolf called over his shoulder, pulling the team to a stop on the side of the road. He'd heard more than enough out of Felicity Cornwall already. If she planned to start insulting Ben Hanks—one of the finest, most honest, most upstanding citizens of Hope—just because of his skin color, then Rolf would have to intervene. "Ben Hanks is goot man. He is helping me with all my farmworks—of shoeing the horses, making the wheels for my wagons, repairing my plow. Last summertime, he is coming all the way to my house—"

"*Is coming?*" Felicity cut in. "You must speak more clearly, Mr. Rustemeyer, if you hope for anyone to understand you. In the past summer, Ben *came* to your house. Not *is coming*. That's something that will happen in the future. I find it nearly impossible to know what you're talking about. You speak with such a thick accent, and your words are all mixed up helter-skelter."

Rolf could feel his biceps bunch up as he gripped the reins. "My apology."

"You mean to say, 'I apologize.'" She shook her head. "I thought Rose Hunter had given you some English lessons, Mr. Rustemeyer. Well, drive on. I can feel a storm coming. Oh, how my bones do ache! Lucy, fetch me that blanket. I'm quite sure it's going to snow, and we'll probably get mired miles from the city."

Rolf tried to calm his breathing as he watched Lucy rummage in the back of the wagon, looking for blankets and pillows to comfort her mother. He wanted to like Mrs. Cornwall, and he had prayed that God would show him her good attributes. But if truth be known, Rolf would like nothing better than to set Felicity

Cornwall off on the side of the road with nothing more than her wicked tongue and cold heart to keep her company.

"Rosie did teach Mr. Rustemeyer," Lucy said as she tucked a wool blanket around her mother. "Though I'm sure he has more to learn."

"That is obvious," Mrs. Cornwall said. "He butchers the language. It's a wonder anyone can understand him."

"Could I teach you English, Mr. Rustemeyer?"

Rolf had almost set the horses going again when Lucy's gently spoken words penetrated. Turning, he could just make out her eyes bright with hope beneath the canopy of the wagon.

"You teach me?" he said.

"Oh, I don't think so," Mrs. Cornwall began. "There's no use—"

"*Ja,*" Rolf spoke up. "Is goot for me to learn English."

He nodded at her. Lucy didn't give her mother a second glance as she stepped over the woman and climbed onto the front seat beside Rolf. Wrapping her shawl tightly around her shoulders, she slipped him a shy smile.

"Ben Hanks *came* to my house last summer," she said. "He came, she came, we came, I came, you came."

Rolf gave the reins a shake, and the horses started walking again. "He came to my house," he repeated. "She came. We came. I came. You came . . . you came to sit beside me, Miss Cornwall. I am happy for that."

"So am I," she whispered.

"But I think is very cold here on the front of my wagon."

"It's colder in the back."

Rolf chuckled. "A cold wind blows in the back, I think."

"A blizzard," Lucy said with a giggle.

"What are you two talking about?" Mrs. Cornwall called. "I can't hear you. I want to know what you're saying."

"We're speaking of the weather," Lucy replied. "Mr.

Rustemeyer, yesterday it *was* cold. Today it *is* cold. Tomorrow it *will be* cold."

"Not if you sit here beside me," he said in a low voice. "Is warm today."

"*It* is warm today."

"*It* is warm," he repeated. "I am warm. You are warm."

"We are warm." Lucy folded her hands together and let out a happy sigh.

❧

Though she could hardly feel her toes and she knew her nose must be bright red, Lucy was certain she had never felt so happy. For two days she had ridden beside Rolf Rustemeyer as snow dusted the roads and blanketed the prairie. They had discussed the steam issuing from the horses' nostrils, the iron gray color of the sky, the mystery of yeast, and the spelling of the word *rough*. Rolf had told Lucy all about his brothers and sisters in Germany, about his father's lumber business, and about his particular love for Christmas strudel. Lucy explained the best method of kneading dough, the reason green was her favorite color, and the way to grind cinnamon bark. And all the while, Lucy thought about the baby waiting for her at the foundling home.

She knew the little girl would be three years old by now, but in her mind she still envisioned the infant she had held to her breast so long ago. If she'd had time, Lucy would have sewn a new dress for her daughter. It would be wonderful to bring the child home to Hope in a gorgeous red velvet gown. But at least Caitrin had beckoned Lucy into the mercantile before she left and had given her a sack full of peppermint drops and a small silver comb. Wrapped in pink calico, the gifts awaited only the excited cries of their new owner.

"I don't know what I shall call my daughter," Lucy said as the first dwellings at the edge of Kansas City came into view. "She probably already has a name, you know. They've been calling her something there at the foundling home. But what if it's a bad name? What if it's not even a real name—like the one they gave Rosie Hunter when she lived there?"

"Which name will you like?" Rolf asked. "*Did* you like. *Are* you liking. *Ach*, I cannot speak the words!"

"Which name *do* I like?" Lucy said. "I like the name Hannah. It makes me think of the woman in the Bible who prayed to God for a child. Hannah was the mother of the prophet Samuel."

"Hannah is goot name."

"Shall I call my daughter Hannah?" Lucy glanced over her shoulder. She prayed her mother wasn't listening. "What if I'm not allowed to bring her home with us? I haven't spoken of the matter with Mama."

"Why she will not let you to take the baby?" His eyes searched Lucy's face. "Hannah is belonging to you."

"But our soddy is very small, and Mama has such trouble with her nerves. Children can be noisy. More than that, I keep thinking how Mama views my daughter. She sees her as sin and evil, not as a child. What if she makes Hannah feel worthless or—"

"As she makes you feel?"

"Me?"

"Can you not see this? The way she talks to you?"

"My mother has endured such trouble because of me. Jack had to forge chains to hold me, and the neighbors all taunted—"

"Your mama does not teach you the happy lessons. This I know."

"Happy lessons?"

"Because of your mother's teaching, you look all the time at the worries, the bad things that can come, the sadness in your life. But I say that around you is goot and happy things, too." He squared his shoulders. "Now I make decision. You teach me the English lessons. I, Rolf Rustemeyer, am teaching you the happy lessons!"

"I don't understand."

"Of course not. Is a language you never hear before today." He took her small gloved hand in his. "We practice. You say after me, *ja?* Snow is beautiful."

"Snow is beautiful."

"We are having fun journey to Missouri."

"We are having fun journey to Missouri." Lucy smiled. "We are having *a* fun journey to Missouri."

"Not correct my English now!" Rolf said sternly. "We do happy lessons now. English later. Say this: I am very smart woman. And also pretty."

Lucy stared down at Rolf's large hand covering hers. "I am a smart woman."

"Also pretty."

"Rolf, I've never been pretty. We should tell the truth in the happy lessons."

He frowned at her. "*Ja,* you are pretty, Miss Cornwall! Hair of brown like cinnamon. Face of white . . . like sweet icing. And eyes—"

"Like raisins?" Lucy couldn't hold back a giggle. "Do I look like a cinnamon bun to you, Mr. Rustemeyer?"

He reached up and touched her cheek. "When you smile, I see very beautiful woman. This is a happiness for me."

Lucy could feel her cheeks flush with heat. "But I'm not—"

"*Ja,* you are. Stop hearing the words of sadness, of no worth."

"The thoughts are in my head."

"Who is putting them there? Your mama?"

Lucy pondered the thought. "Maybe."

"God is not wanting proud people, Miss Cornwall. But he is also not wanting people with no hope or joy. You love your baby girl, but God loves his Son even more than that. Even so, he sends Jesus to die for you, Lucy Cornwall. And why is that? Is it because you are ugly and shameful and worth nothing? No, it is because God loves you, and he sees beautiful woman deep inside you.

Woman who can serve him. Woman who can be useful to him. Woman who has purpose to live on earth."

"Oh, Mr. Rustemeyer, if only I could believe that."

"Believe it!"

"It's not so easy. You view everything in such a simple way. For you, life is breakfast, lunch, and dinner. A big farm. Healthy livestock. Good crops. A roof over your head and a bed to sleep in at night. But for me, life seems terribly complicated. I feel things so deeply. I sense the sorrow in others. I know the meaning of pain. I feel the hurt and despair of the people I meet. For you, life is bright and hopeful. For me, darkness lies waiting just around the corner. And I don't believe all the happy lessons in the world can change that."

Rolf slumped over the reins as his team pulled the wagon down the streets of Kansas City. Lucy missed the warmth of his hand, which he had pulled away. His face was unmoving, his gray eyes quiet.

"Maybe you are right," he said finally. "Maybe I am foolish man to look always for goot. Maybe I walk over some people who are feeling the darkness you see."

"And maybe I look at the darkness too much." Lucy grabbed his hand and squeezed it. "You're right that God loves me and wants me to feel joy. I'm going to practice harder."

"*Ja?*"

"This afternoon, I'm going to see my daughter," she said. "I'm going to put my arms around her and hug her. And I'm going to put her in the wagon with us and take her back home to Kansas for Christmas."

Rolf grinned. "Hannah is her name."

"Hannah is her name. And she is *wunderbar!*"

✤

"I won't go into that place," Felicity Cornwall said. "I won't look upon that child, and I cannot understand your interest in her, Lucy."

"She's my daughter, Mama." Lucy dug in the bottom of her bag for the peppermint drops and the silver comb. "I'm more than interested in her. I love her."

"Well, I hope your curiosity will be satisfied. She was nothing much to look at as I recall the matter."

Lucy paused, images of her fear darting before her eyes. "Was she malformed?"

"She was only a tiny thing, all wrinkled and bloody. How should I know if she was malformed? I had no desire to touch her more than necessary."

Lucy lifted the calico-wrapped packet from her bag. "I love her, no matter how she looks."

"Well, don't expect the same of me."

"Mama, I'm going to take my daughter out of this orphanage and bring her home with me. I beg you to try to care for her."

"What? You'll not be bringing that child into my house. I agreed to come to Missouri so that you could find her. But I will never allow her to leave with us."

"Mama, that's what I've been planning all along! She's my daughter."

"And who is her father? A thief. A rapist. A Yankee."

"Please, Mama—"

"Ready now?" Rolf Rustemeyer's head and shoulders appeared in the opening under the canvas that covered the wagon. "Before we leave Hope, Rosie Hunter is giving to me the name of the woman who keeps these children at the orphanage. Mrs. Iva Jameson. We talk to her about Hannah."

His eyes flicked back and forth between the two women. Lucy took a deep breath and tried to calm herself. "Yes," she said, "I'm ready."

"Mr. Rustemeyer," Felicity said as Rolf helped Lucy out of the wagon, "don't think your motivations are a secret. I've seen the way you look at my daughter. I know what you've been telling her about me. You're trying to steal her away. You'd like nothing better than to have her and the baby, wouldn't you?"

"Mama!" Lucy clapped a hand over her mouth in dismay as her mother continued.

"Well, I can promise you that no matter what sweet words you use on my daughter, she will never leave me. She will be my support in my old age, and I will continue to be her strength. You cannot part us."

"I have no wish to take your daughter from you, Mrs. Cornwall," Rolf informed her. "My bride comes from Germany at Christmastime. Very soon I marry with Ingrid Volkart. I carry the photograph, you see?" He slipped his watch from his pocket and flipped open the gold lid. "Photograph of my wife is in my watch already. Is Ingrid I marry, not Lucy."

For some reason she couldn't understand, Lucy's eyes filled with tears as she stared at the beautiful blond German woman who was to be the wife of Rolf Rustemeyer. They would be a good match. A perfect partnership, with their common language and their shared dreams and their golden hair.

Rolf seemed so delighted at the prospect of his Christmas bride. How could Lucy wish anything but the best for him? Remembering to apply happy lessons, she lifted her chin and gave her mother the brightest smile she could muster.

"You see, Mama," she said, "Rolf has his own plans for the future. Come, Mr. Rustemeyer, let's walk into the orphanage, where my daughter waits for me."

Though she was trembling, she forced herself to turn and step away from her mother. Rolf marched along beside her, through the iron gate and down the long walk to the Christian Home for Orphans and Foundlings.

As he rang the bell, he looked across at Lucy. "You say this marriage to Ingrid Volkart is my plan," he said in a low voice.

"Yes," Lucy said.

"Why you say that?"

"Because you wrote the letter to your father in Germany. You asked him to find a bride for you. You planned it."

The door opened and a short, freckle-faced woman inquired of their names and their mission. As she led them into a carpeted sitting area, Lucy listened to the sounds of children playing in the distant rooms. Somewhere, far away, she could hear someone crying. A chill skittered down her spine as she wondered if this was her daughter.

Rolf sat down beside Lucy on the narrow horsehair settee and twisted his large fingers together. "I wish this marriage with Ingrid Volkart to be God's plan—not the plan of Rolf Rustemeyer."

"We make earthly plans," Lucy told him, her focus on the long hallway where she expected her daughter to appear, "but we must trust God with the result."

"Ah, Miss Cornwall!" A woman with a severely knotted bun stepped into the room and shook Lucy's hand. "And Mr. Rustemeyer. My name is Mrs. Iva Jameson, and I am the director of the Christian Home for Orphans and Foundlings. How do you do?"

"I do very goot, thank you," Rolf said.

"My assistant tells me you've come from Kansas about a child who was left with us here at the Christian Home."

"Yes," Lucy said. "My daughter."

"I've looked through our records, and I do have a file on the baby in question, Miss Cornwall." Mrs. Jameson lifted a single sheet of paper from a folder and peered down at it through wire-rimmed spectacles. "Three years ago, the child was brought to the home by a lawyer from Sedalia. He brought with him papers indicating that all parental rights had been terminated. Three months later, the girl was adopted by a man and his wife here in Kansas City. I'm not at liberty to give you their names." She looked up from her notes. "I'm sorry you won't be able to see her, Miss Cornwall."

CHAPTER 4

ADOPTED. Lucy stood staring at the woman in the orphanage, unable to move her thoughts past the word that had sentenced her to unfathomable loss.

"Come with me, Miss Cornwall," Rolf said, taking Lucy's arm. "We go to the wagon. Is better we find a hotel now, a place for you and your mother to rest."

"Wait," Lucy said. "Mrs. Jameson, I must see my daughter. Please, you have to tell me where she is. I need to know!"

"I cannot tell you anything. You signed release papers, Miss Cornwall. You agreed to give up your daughter. Someone else adopted her, and they are raising her as their own child. You must accept that."

"But I want her back. I gave birth to her. She's my daughter!"

The woman slipped the notes back into her folder. "Not anymore. Good day, Miss Cornwall. Mr. Rustemeyer."

As Mrs. Jameson set off across the room, Lucy started after her. But Rolf caught her arm, drew her back, and tucked her against his side. "Is all right, Miss Cornwall," he said. "Is going to be fine."

"No!" Lucy cried out. "I want her! I want my daughter. I didn't want to give her away. It was my mother. She hated the child. I've lived with the torment—and then the hope. And now—"

"Now is a new hour for looking forward—not back."

"I can't, I can't." Lucy sagged against him, feeling the weight of agony on her shoulders. "What is there for me ahead? A thousand batches of cinnamon rolls to bake and an aging mother who has never known a happy day in her life? Oh, God, help me!"

"God has goot plan for you, Lucy," Rolf said, holding her close. "He does not let you live so sad."

"I can't see his plan. I can't see any hope, any joy, anything."

"Come, we go outside and look at the snow. We thank God he is giving to your daughter a home and family, and we ask him which is now his plan for you."

Though she could barely make her feet move, Lucy allowed Rolf to help her out into the hall. The freckle-faced woman escorted them down the long corridor to the front door. As they stepped outside, she leaned over and touched Lucy on the arm.

"'Tis the Baker family has your daughter," she whispered. "John and Patience Baker. He's a schoolmaster, and they live on Oak Street."

Lucy paused and gazed into the woman's bright blue eyes. "You know my daughter?"

"I looked her up in our record book because I saw how sad you were. Don't tell Mrs. J, or I'll lose my position here at the home."

"No," Lucy said, "of course I won't. Thank you so much!"

She grasped Rolf's hand as they hurried down the sidewalk to the wagon. John and Patience Baker on Oak Street! Thank God!

⁂

"You will not go looking for that house, Lucy Cornwall." Mrs. Cornwall tugged on her gloves and settled her shawl around her shoulders. They had spent last night in a hotel, and this morning she had announced she was ready to conduct her own business. "The child has a home and family, and you are no longer her mother. It was a mistaken idea to come here in search of that baby in the first place. I never should have allowed it. I hold Mr. Rustemeyer responsible for the whole affair."

Rolf stood in the hallway of the hotel and studied the dejected woman inside the small room. He blamed himself as well. Like Felicity, he believed it would be a mistake for Lucy to look for the child's adoptive family. And yet he understood her sadness. She had been filled with such hope at the prospect of taking her daughter home to Kansas.

For the first time in his life, Rolf felt as though he had stepped outside himself and into someone else's heart. The ache he sensed was almost unbearable, yet he longed to take all of Lucy's pain and carry it himself.

"We won't be away long, Lucy," Felicity Cornwall continued. "I'm going to stop at the Land Office to check on the claim, and then I'll visit the bank to see how our account has fared since the war. After that, Mr. Rustemeyer will bring me back to the hotel. You are to stay here, my dear. Do you understand me?"

"Yes, Mama."

"Good. Now, don't do anything foolish. This news about the baby is no tragedy. On the contrary, you should be grateful. The problem no longer exists, and you can move forward with a clear conscience."

At that, Mrs. Cornwall pulled the door shut, leaving her daughter alone inside the room. Rolf shook his head as he walked down the corridor. He wished he could stay with Lucy. He didn't like leaving her alone, and he would prefer to spend as little time as possible with Mrs. Cornwall.

"A dreadful day!" Felicity exclaimed as they stepped out onto the sidewalk. "Can you believe this biting wind? I would swear I can feel it whipping right through my coat. Don't tell me you left the wagon tied up around the corner, Mr. Rustemeyer. Didn't you stop to think how miserable we would feel walking all this distance? I suppose not. Young people today think only of themselves."

Rolf gritted his teeth as he helped the woman onto the wagon seat and set his team in the direction of the Land Office. By the time they reached it, Mrs. Cornwall had complained about the disgraceful condition of the roads, the thick pall of smoke in the air, and the sorrowful state of her lungs. She voiced her certainty that she would die an early death from all her illnesses. As Rolf helped her up the long flight of steps into the building, he found himself almost hoping her prediction came true.

Rolf spotted a bench in a hallway where he could wait for Mrs. Cornwall to finish her business. As he brushed the snowflakes from his hat brim, he thought about Lucy. On the journey to Kansas City, he had seen a side of her that few people knew existed. She could be funny and lighthearted. She was warm and kind and generous. And she was trying her hardest to forge a path through the darkness that sometimes threatened to overwhelm her.

Rolf was beginning to understand that darkness. It crept toward Lucy from many directions. Some of it came from her mother, whose bleak view of life infected everyone and everything around her. Some of the darkness came from Lucy's past, from the terrible attack she had endured, from the loss of her baby, from the months in the mental asylum and the chains that had bound her. And some of the darkness was just Lucy's nature.

She saw and felt things more deeply than Rolf did. This meant her joys might be great, but so were her sorrows. In a way, Rolf felt grateful to God that Lucy was teaching him how to look beyond the simplicity of food, work, sleep, and family. Though Rolf didn't enjoy the feelings of concern and worry that beset him now, he was glad he could care in a deeper way.

And he did care. He cared about Lucy.

"You will not believe the incompetence!" Mrs. Cornwall sashayed out of the office and into the hall where Rolf was waiting. She had a sheaf of papers in her hand, a pen, and a bottle of dripping black ink. "Before they'll even look at my claim, they want me to fill out all these forms. This could take hours!"

Rolf stood and helped her down onto the bench. He took the forms, the ink, the pen, and set them beside her. Then he straightened, certain God was leading him.

"I shall return in two hours, Mrs. Cornwall," he said. "At that time, I am taking you . . . I *will* take you to the bank."

"Two hours!" She scowled at him. "Where are you going? What if I need you?"

"Your daughter needs me now."

"Lucy will be fine. She can't get into too much trouble in that small room. Don't worry about her."

"Goot-bye, Mrs. Cornwall." Rolf gave Felicity a nod. "I *will* come back later."

Before she could protest again, he strode outside and climbed onto his wagon. As he released the brake, he thought of all the things he wanted to say to Lucy. He wanted her to know how much he had come to care for her. He wanted her to realize that she had become beautiful and precious to him. He wanted her to smile again, to laugh, to practice her happy lessons. He wanted her to hope.

The snow was almost blinding as he drove his wagon back to the hotel and trotted up the narrow staircase to the room Lucy shared with her mother. As he knocked, the door swung open at his touch.

"Miss Cornwall?" His heart hammering, Rolf stepped into the room. In the dim light from the curtained window, he could see it was empty. "Lucy, where you are?"

And then, of course, he knew. She had put on her gloves and shawl. She had taken her calico-wrapped peppermint drops and silver comb. And she had gone to Oak Street.

Praying for God's help, Rolf bounded back down the stairs. "Oak Street?" he asked the man at the front desk.

"That way. You're runnin' behind, fella. The lady left without you."

Rolf tugged his hat down onto his brow and climbed back onto the wagon. Maybe it wouldn't be too late. Maybe he could stop Lucy. But what if she saw the child . . . if she disrupted the family . . . if she tried to take her daughter . . .

"Which is the house of John and Patience Baker?" Rolf asked a woman bundled to the nose in a knitted wrap. At the pointed direction, he jumped down from his wagon and ran up the sidewalk to the iron gate. It was a small brick home with a narrow yard and a deep front porch. Rolf could see the prints of Lucy's boots leading to the house in the freshly fallen snow.

When he rapped with the door's brass knocker, a housekeeper answered. "May I help you?"

"I look for . . . for Mr. Baker," Rolf said.

"He's with a guest at the moment. I'm sorry, but you'll have to come back later."

She started to shut the door, but Rolf held it open. "Mr. Baker is with Miss Lucy Cornwall, I think. I am her friend. I must see her."

The housekeeper stepped aside. "I shall inform the master of the house. And your name, please?"

"I am called Rolf Rustemeyer."

The woman nodded and set off across the foyer. Rolf stepped into the house and clutched his hat, aware of his muddy boots and the melting snow that dripped from the hem of his coat. And then he noticed a small face peering at him from behind the banister of a long, curved staircase. "Hello, little girl," he said. "How you are?"

She smiled, and it was Lucy's smile. "I'm fine," the child said softly. "How are you?"

"Cold. Is snow coming down outside."

"You talk funny."

"*Ja,* is because I come from Germany."

"Where is Germany?" The girl straightened and started down the steps.

Rolf grinned. "Far away across the ocean. Where I lived, it is tall trees and high mountains. And very beautiful rivers."

"Come this way, please, sir," the housekeeper said, emerging from the parlor. "Jenny, what are you doing downstairs? It's nap time!"

"But I'm not sleepy. Please let me go to Papa."

"Your father has visitors."

Rolf looked at the little girl with her shining brown hair and big gray eyes. She was dressed in a long white gown tied with a pink ribbon, and she clutched a pretty china doll in her arms. *Lucy's daughter*, Rolf realized. *Oh, liebend Gott, what shall I do?*

"Why not come with me?" he said to the child. "We go and visit your papa together."

Jenny gave a laugh of delight and clasped Rolf's outstretched hand. "You're nice!"

"*Ja,*" Rolf said. "I try."

As they walked into the parlor, he could see Lucy seated on a settee, her back to the door. Across from her sat a middle-aged man and woman. The woman was dabbing her eyes with a hand-kerchief.

"Papa, look, I brought you another visitor!" Jenny said.

At the sound, Lucy turned, and her focus fell on the little girl. She gasped. Rolf scooped the child into his arms and carried her across the room.

"I am Rolf Rustemeyer," he said, setting Jenny on her father's lap. "I am the friend of Miss Cornwall."

"Oh, we were just . . ." The man took his wife's hand. "Miss Cornwall says she has some news for us. She was telling us about her experiences in the war."

Lucy swallowed as Rolf sat down beside her. Her breath shallow, she stared at the child across the room.

"I tried, but I couldn't take a nap, Papa," Jenny said. "I'm too excited about Christmas!" She turned her bright gray eyes on the visitors. "We're going to ride on the train! We're going to see my grandma and grandpa."

"They live in Philadelphia," Mr. Baker explained.

"My parents." Mrs. Baker reached out and smoothed down the child's dress. "My father is a physician. Jenny's our only child, and they dote on her so. I'm sure you can imagine."

"We're sorry for the interruption, Miss Cornwall," Mr. Baker said. "You were explaining about the death of your father and the attack on your homestead. I believe you had mentioned the arrival of some soldiers?"

Lucy sat very still, gazing at the little girl. Rolf reached out and touched her hand. He could feel a tremor run through her.

"Soldiers," Lucy said.

"Please, Miss Cornwall," Rolf spoke up. "You don't need to—"

"The soldiers. It was a difficult time." Lucy's fingers tightened on Rolf's hand. "The war was difficult."

"Indeed," Mrs. Baker said. "When I think of all those lost in the fighting, I can hardly bear it." She lifted her handkerchief and began to dab at her eyes again.

"My wife is very tenderhearted in this matter," Mr. Baker explained. "Her brother was killed in Tennessee."

"Ach, this is bad news," Rolf said. "But now, all is peace again. We have much to thank God for."

"Yes," Lucy said, standing suddenly. "Yes, we do. I'm sorry I troubled you, Mr. and Mrs. Baker."

"But you're not leaving, are you, Miss Cornwall?" Patience Baker rose. "The tea will come up from the kitchen at any moment. And we're eager to hear what you wanted to tell us."

"I was mistaken," Lucy said, her voice shaking. "I shouldn't have come."

"But is there something we should know?" Mr. Baker was holding his daughter close. "Something from the war?"

"No," Lucy whispered. "Only that the war was difficult. But it's over now. It's over."

Before Rolf could catch her, she turned and ran out of the room. He stood for a moment, twisting his hat and gazing at the child in her father's arms.

"Give thanks to God for gift of your daughter, Mr. and Mrs. Baker," he said. "She is brought into the world at great cost and given at great sacrifice. Treasure her always."

The couple stared at him as realization dawned on their faces. "Yes, Mr. Rustemeyer," the man said. "We consider Jenny a precious gift from God. We intend to take good care of her all her life."

Rolf nodded. "And we do not trouble you again. Thank you. Good-bye, Jenny."

Setting his hat on his head, he hurried out of the parlor, through the foyer, and out the front door. He could see Lucy sitting upright on the wagon seat, her shawl over her head. As he climbed up beside her, he gently took her into his arms and held her close. Her body went limp against his shoulder.

"Again, you do a very brave thing," he said softly. "Now I have watched Lucy Cornwall bring one child into the world and let another one go. Never have I known such a woman as this."

As the horses pulled the wagon down the street, her sobs shuddered against his chest.

❧

Lucy sat across from Rolf at the table in the hotel dining room and listened to her mother's commentary on the day's events.

"And what do you think the land official told me then?" Felicity asked. "He said the claim is valid. The property is mine! At first I thought he might be mistaken. He didn't look bright at all, and

I've told you how much trouble he gave me with the papers I had to fill out. Did I tell you he wore spectacles? I don't care how poor my eyesight, I would never indulge in such frippery. Spectacles make a person look ridiculous, in my opinion. The man reminded me of an old tom turkey, with his wrinkled chin and popping eyes. But when he pointed out the notation in his book, I had no further doubts about the claim. The land belonged to my husband, and now it is mine. There's even a small cabin with a well nearby. Can you imagine such luck?"

"A blessing from God," Rolf said. He was buttering his fourth dinner roll. "And what is your plan for the land, Mrs. Cornwall? You will stay here in Missouri, or you will go back to Kansas?"

"Missouri will always be my home," she declared. "Yes, indeed, I've made up my mind to live here permanently."

"But, Mama," Lucy said. "What about—"

"You and I will have to go back to Kansas to pack our things, of course. Jack can load the furniture and chests. And I'll want to sell the bakeshop. With all of that to do, we might not be able to leave Hope before the start of the new year, which would be unfortunate. I wonder if Mr. Rippetto might be interested in buying the bakery. He has all those unmarried daughters, after all, and he ought to get some use out of them."

"You say you will sell Lucy's Bakeshop, Mrs. Cornwall?" Rolf spoke up, turning to Lucy. "You will not make the cinnamon rolls again? the bread for sandwiches?"

"Mr. Rustemeyer, don't forget you'll have your new wife to do your baking," Felicity said, dabbing crumbs from her mouth with a napkin. "And with all the children the two of you will be having, there will be no time for dallying in town. You'll have to be working in your fields from dawn to dusk."

"*Ja*," Rolf said. "Is true."

"Of course it's true. Lucy was only frittering away her time in the bakery anyway. When we move into our cabin here in Missouri, my daughter will have real work to do. We'll grow a vegetable garden and keep hogs. To my way of thinking, there is nothing finer than a rasher of fried bacon of a morning. I never did hold with that cinnamon roll nonsense."

"But I enjoy baking," Lucy said, summoning her courage. "Mama, I don't want to leave Hope. I don't want to sell the bakery."

"Lucy, what you want is irrelevant. I am your mother, and I consider it my duty to do what is best for you. Your behavior today—seeking out that child even though I had forbidden it—is all the evidence I need of your fragile condition. You do not need the responsibility and pressure of keeping up with a bakeshop. Why Rose and Caitrin dreamed up such employment for you is more than I'll ever understand."

"It's because I'm good at baking."

"This is true," Rolf added. "She is the best baker—"

"You stay out of this, Mr. Rustemeyer. You're the one who brought my daughter to the brink of insanity again. Dragging her all the way out here to find her daughter—what an ill-advised idea! And you'd have kept her outing this afternoon a secret from me, too, wouldn't you? If I hadn't noticed Lucy's wet boots and coat, I wouldn't have known about her foray to Oak Street. You ought to be strung up and shot. And as for you, Miss Lucy Cornwall, if you ever go anywhere without my permission again, I shall—"

"I'm twenty-two years old, Mama," Lucy said. "I'm an adult."

"And you have the mental functioning of a child. No, the best thing I can do for you, Lucy, is to take you out of Hope and bring you back to Missouri where I can look out for your welfare."

"I have friends in Hope!"

"Your Christian duty is to obey *me!*" Felicity pushed back from the table. " 'Honor thy father and thy mother that thy days may be long upon the land which the Lord thy God giveth thee.' You have no choice!"

Felicity tossed her napkin onto the table and paraded out of the dining room. Lucy stared down at her soup bowl. No matter how hard she tried, at this moment she could not remember a single one of Rolf's happy lessons. Instead, she could see only the roll call of losses in her life—her virtue, her daughter, her bakery, her home, her brother and his wife, her friends, her church. . . .

"Lucy, I do not want you to leave Hope," Rolf said. "I wish you to stay in Kansas."

She looked up into his warm eyes. "I must honor my mother. I have to obey her."

"That Scripture is written for children, Lucy. You are grown woman now. *Honoring* is not same thing as *obeying*. Children must obey, but you are not a child. You can honor your mother in other ways."

"But she's right. Sometimes I do childish things."

"Looking for your daughter is not childish. If this happens to me, I am doing same thing as you. How you think I know where to look for you? Is because in my heart I am with you."

Lucy stirred her soup, absorbing his words. "Jenny was pretty, wasn't she?"

"Beautiful. Like her mother."

"Patience Baker is her mother."

"This child has two mamas. One that gives her life. One that gives her a home. Is OK for you to be sad, Lucy. Is OK to think of Jenny and love her and pray for her. And is a very goot thing you do to leave her with the family who adopts her. What you did today was the action of a grown woman, not a child. This was done by a very brave and strong person. And this person is you, Lucy Cornwall."

Lucy nodded. It had taken all her strength to walk out of that house without revealing her relationship to the child. But she knew the Bakers loved Jenny. They were raising her in a Christian home, and they could provide a future that Lucy could never give her daughter. Jenny belonged to them now, and Lucy had to surrender to God's greater plan for the child. She would always love Jenny, always pray for her, always ache inside with the emptiness of her loss. But she would also thank God for the loving family he had provided.

"I have idea," Rolf said, setting his large hands on either side of his plate. "Big idea. Goot idea. This idea is taking care of all the problems, you will see."

"What are you talking about, Rolf?" Lucy asked. "What idea is this?"

"You wait. Tomorrow, I, Rolf Rustemeyer, am taking care of Lucy Cornwall, bringing great happiness and joy to you forever."

Lucy couldn't help but smile. If only she had the courage to tell Rolf Rustemeyer what happiness he brought her just by being himself.

༒

"*O Tannenbaum! O Tannenbaum!*" Rolf sang as he guided his team down the muddy streets of Kansas City. He had a deep baritone voice, and he enjoyed exercising it as often as possible—in the church choir, while he worked on his farm, and especially when he had an audience as pretty as the pink-cheeked Miss Lucy Cornwall sitting beside him on the wagon.

"*Wie treu sind deine blätter!*" he continued.

"O Christmas tree! O Christmas tree!" Lucy followed up in her own melodic soprano. "How lovely are thy branches!"

Rolf laughed. "Is very nice, we sing together, *ja?*"

"No, it is not," Felicity Cornwall said from within the covered wagon. "Christmas is still a long time off, and I'm not in the humor for carols. We have days and days of this miserable cold weather and bumpy road ahead. The last thing I want to have to put up with is your silliness."

Rolf glanced over at Lucy. For a moment, she seemed to shrink into herself, the veil of hopelessness slipping across her face. And then he heard the smallest sound.

"*O Tannenbaum,*" she sang softly, "*O Tannenbaum . . .*"

"How lovely are thy branches," Rolf joined in, keeping his voice low. Then he leaned over and whispered. "You are ready for the surprise I make for you, Lucy?"

She nodded and kept humming.

Rolf turned the team around a corner and pulled the wagon to a halt in front of the Christian Home for Orphans and Foundlings. "Here we are," he said.

Lucy stared at him. "But my daughter isn't here, Rolf."

"*Ja,* I think she is." He shrugged. "Maybe not Jenny. But maybe Hannah is here. Another daughter, you know? What you think about this idea I have?"

"Another daughter? You mean, you think I should adopt a child from the Home?"

"*Ja.* Get Hannah from here to take home with you, and then you will be happy forever."

Lucy looked down at her hands for a moment. "Rolf, joy is not something you or anyone else can give me. I have to trust God for that."

"But I think this baby can help."

"Maybe so." She lifted her head, and he saw a light flood her gray eyes. "Maybe God has a child just for me."

CHAPTER 5

W E DON'T have any babies available for adoption at present." Mrs. Iva Jameson spoke firmly, her hands folded at her waist. "I'm sorry to disappoint you, Miss Cornwall."

"What did I tell you?" Felicity said. "This is a foolish, foolish—"

"But I heard a baby crying yesterday," Lucy cut in. "When we were here to ask about my daughter, I heard a child crying down the hall. I'm sure of it."

Mrs. Jameson glanced away. "That baby is not adoptable. Moreover, it is not our policy here at the Christian Home to permit unwed women to take our children."

"I'm an adult, Mrs. Jameson. I own a bakeshop that brings me a good income, and I am perfectly capable of raising a child. If you have a baby here, I'd like to be given the opportunity to adopt."

"I told you before. That baby is not available."

"Why not?" Rolf asked. "Baby is here at orphanage house. Maybe that baby has no mama."

"The child is . . ." Mrs. Jameson paused, "unwell."

"Sick?" Rolf said.

"Crippled. She came from an impoverished family of thirteen children. A brother was tending her when she was inadvertently dropped."

"Dropped!" Lucy gasped. "Oh, how horrible!"

"The baby's back was broken. The spine crushed. Our physician has told us she will never walk. Of course the family could not care for her, and they signed her over to us." Mrs. Jameson motioned toward the door. "Again, thank you for stopping, Miss Cornwall—"

"I want to see her," Lucy said. "Please let me see the baby."

"What are you talking about, girl?" Felicity sputtered. "You can't take a cripple into our home! We haven't the money to care for a sickly child."

"Why shouldn't the baby have a mother's love and care?" Lucy said, turning on her. "Some of us have been given a difficult road in life, Mama. You know I've had a hard journey. Who better, then, to help this little girl on her own path?"

"This orphanage is better."

"No! Every child deserves a mother's arms and a mother's tender comfort."

"But she won't even be able to walk."

"I have goot idea," Rolf said. "I build wooden chair with arms, and Lucy's brother makes wheels out of iron. We can push the girl!"

"We?" Felicity spat. "You'll soon be married to your Christmas bride, Mr. Rustemeyer. It'll be Lucy and me pushing the cripple around. And what if Lucy has one of her spells?"

"I don't have spells, Mama," Lucy said. "I have a life. My life— with all its joys and sorrows. Why shouldn't I share it with someone who needs my love?"

"She's a cripple," Felicity said.

"Everyone's a cripple, Mama."

"What do you mean by that?"

"Each of us has a burden to bear. This baby's burden is her legs. Mine is the past. Yours is the bitterness you carry. And Rolf's is his loneliness."

"This is true thing," Rolf said. "Everybody has some troubles in life, Mrs. Cornwall. One kind or another. I think Lucy can make a very goot mother for this baby."

"My burden is bitterness?" Felicity asked.

"Yes, Mama," Lucy answered. "Bitterness."

"Well, I don't know about that."

"I know one thing for certain." Lucy turned to Mrs. Jameson. "I would like to take this baby and care for her myself. Please, ma'am, will you let me?"

"If you were married, perhaps we could consider it. But as it is, it is completely out of the question. I'm sorry."

Lucy nodded, understanding even as her heart was torn in two. And so her future was settled. She would move back to Missouri with her mother. She would never marry. She had lost her daughter, and more than that, she had lost her dream of ever loving a child of her very own.

❧

By the late November evening when Rolf's wagon team reached the bridge over Bluestem Creek, the farmer had whittled a sackful of wooden Christmas ornaments and studied the portrait of Ingrid Volkart until he had memorized her face. He had dug his wagon out of a four-foot snowdrift, he had spent more than a dozen nights under a wool blanket on the frozen ground, and he knew he had made the right decision.

"Oh," Lucy said softly, climbing out of the wagon bed and onto the seat beside Rolf. "Here we are. So soon."

At her words, Rolf dropped the reins and wrapped his arms around her. "Lucy, I go on this journey with you, and my heart is changed. I cannot let you return to Missouri. You must stay in Hope, stay with me. I ask you please this question. Can you marry with me, Lucy?"

For a moment, she said nothing. Rolf sat with his eyes closed and his heart beating so hard he was sure she could hear it. The team trudged along on the snowy trail from the bridge toward the mercantile as he waited for her answer.

"Why?" she asked finally, her voice fragile.

"Because I love you," he said. "This thing is never happening to me in all my life. The women I try to marry before, they are goot women, friends. But I do not love them. I only want a wife. Now, with you, Lucy, it is so different. I think about how we can talk together. How we can laugh and sing. I think about living many years with you, and this is what I want. But here is a strange thing. I am praying very much on this journey, Lucy, and I think God is wishing me to marry you. This is his plan for us."

Again, she said nothing. Rolf reached up and laid his hand on the shawl that covered her hair. Sliding it back, he ran his gloved fingers over the smooth curve of her head. He cupped her face and tilted it so he could look into her eyes.

"Say yes, Lucy," he whispered. "Say you love me, and you will be my wife."

"I love you," she said. "But I can't marry you, Rolf."

He tried to breathe. Tried to focus. All he could see was her beautiful face, her sweet lips, her tear-filled eyes. All he wanted at this moment was to hold her and kiss her and tell her every feeling that had built up inside him to the point of bursting. But she had said no. She wouldn't be his wife.

"Why?" he asked. "Because I am the big German, cannot talk goot English, eats too much, and is not so smart?"

A sad smile tipped the corner of her mouth. "Rolf, I think you are the most wonderful man on the face of this earth."

"Then why you will not be my wife?"

She looked away. "You already have a wife. You have promised to marry the German woman. You cannot break that vow, Rolf."

"I think about this woman on our journey. And I know I can never love her. Lucy, you are the one I love." He set his jaw. "Is the right thing."

"No." She sighed and leaned her cheek on his coat. "Even if there was no other woman . . . there's all the rest of it. All the reasons why I could never be your wife."

"You are talking about what those soldiers did to you? I think about that thing, too, and I already decide it does not matter to me."

"But it matters to me."

"Why? To me, you are perfect woman. What happened before is nothing." He swallowed hard, trying to think how he could explain to her the depth of passion in his heart. God had wiped clean any doubts. Lucy would be his bride, fresh and new, and he would cherish her forever.

"For me," she whispered, "the things that happened in the past changed how I feel. Rolf, I could never be a wife to you in the way you deserve. What the soldiers did was so painful and horrible. I can't imagine ever going through that again."

"But I love you, Lucy—"

"It doesn't matter." She was bent over now, weeping softly. "I'm sorry. I'm so sorry, Rolf."

He pulled the wagon to a halt beside the soddy that Lucy and her mother shared. Lucy's brother, Jack, and his wife, Caitrin, also lived there while he was building their house down the road. A lamp glowed in one paper-lined window. It was all Rolf could see.

"Lucy, Rolf—welcome home!" Jack called from the soddy door. "I heard the wagon. We were beginning to wonder if you'd ever come back. Where's Mama?"

"I'm back here in the wagon, stiff as a board." Felicity began to cough.

Rolf stared out through the iron-cold night as Jack and Caitrin greeted their family and began unloading the travel trunks. Lucy gave him a last glance as she climbed down from the wagon onto the frozen road.

"Good-bye, Rolf," she said.

He nodded once and set his team moving down the road toward his farm.

ઝ

While her mother spent the following days packing up the household belongings, Lucy reopened her bakeshop, and customers came pouring back in for her cinnamon rolls, fresh pies, fluffy muffins, and steaming loaves of bread. The only person who failed to make his prompt morning appearances was Rolf Rustemeyer. But Lucy knew he was planning a wedding. Rolf and his bride were to be married Christmas Day, less than two weeks away. Right after the woman's arrival from Germany.

The rest of the townsfolk were busy with preparations for the Christmas social, an event Rose Hunter had dreamed up. She confided to Lucy that she had missed so many Christmas celebrations while living in the orphanage that she was determined to make up for it now. Caitrin, Sheena, Rosie, and Lily cleared the mercantile of stock, while their husbands pushed back the counters so everyone could have room to mingle. Lucy volunteered to open the bakeshop during the social, and she filled her time in the preceding days making masses of cookies, cakes, and pies to feed the crowd. The late hours and busyness kept her thoughts from Rolf, she knew, and she was grateful.

The night of the social, Lucy dressed in the pretty red velvet gown she had sewn. She threaded a bit of lace through her hair, and she clasped a length of small garnet beads around her neck. Her father had given them to her one Christmas many years before the war, and she wore them only on very special occasions.

Though she knew Rolf's bride might appear at any moment, Lucy couldn't help wondering if he would come to the social. He never passed up an opportunity to eat good food, and there would be carol singing, too. As she began setting out the desserts, Lucy recalled how they had sat together on the wagon singing "O Tannenbaum." It was a memory she would cherish forever. She had tried to put him out of her thoughts, but she missed everything about Rolf—his warmth, his honesty, his strong arms. Even his appetite.

Next door in the mercantile, the crowd had begun to gather. Lucy heard the local band tune up their fiddles as cries of "Merry Christmas!" drifted through the air. A light snow began to fall, and she hurried to hang a string of jingle bells from her doorknob. Her breath misted in the chill air, and she waved at the festive crowd.

"I have hot cider in the bakeshop!" she called to the O'Toole clan, who had tromped over the bridge for the celebration. Little Abraham had been chosen for the role of baby Jesus in the children's play. At first, half the mothers in the community had protested that his red hair wouldn't do at all for the infant Savior. They favored Mercy Hunter in the starring role. The rest of the mothers wouldn't hear of a girl baby playing the part. And so, after yet another town squabble that had almost threatened to do in the entire social, baby Abraham was chosen by a coin flip.

Lucy smiled, thinking of the Savior himself and how none but a few poor shepherds had honored his birth. Hope, Kansas, had endured a greater flap over the matter than Bethlehem itself. Stepping back into her shop, she adjusted the pine swags she had hung from the curtain rods. The room smelled of cinnamon and nutmeg and vanilla. Hot coffee bubbled on the stove. Whether Rolf came or not, Lucy had made up her mind to enjoy herself.

"Oh, Lucy, everyone's here, and we can't find Stubby!" Rosie cried, hurrying inside and banging the door shut behind her. "He was going to be the donkey for Mary and Joseph to ride, but he's vanished. Have you seen him?"

Lucy reflected on the huge mutt who had wandered across the

prairie long ago and found a home with the Hunters. "He came begging at the window this morning."

"The last I saw him was at noon. He was asleep by the stove while I made lunch for Seth and Chipper. What are we going to do without our donkey!"

Lucy chucked and began to slice a pie. "I guess Mary and Joseph will just have to walk to Bethlehem."

"Goodness, Lucy, when you smile like that, you are just beautiful! You're going to come next door for the singing, aren't you?"

"I'd better stay here and tend the shop. You never know when someone hungry will walk in."

"Which puts me in mind of Rolf Rustemeyer. Where is that man, anyway? No one's seen hide nor hair of him since you came back from Missouri. What do you suppose he's up to?"

"Mr. Rustemeyer is a busy man," Lucy said, occupying herself with setting slices of chocolate pie on plates. "I'm sure he's getting ready for his wedding."

"I suppose so. Lily Book has the job of getting the church ready, you know. She told me it's what pastors' wives are supposed to do. Lily said the wedding is going to be beautiful. Did you know that before Rolf left for Missouri, he ordered roses to be brought in on the train?"

"Roses!"

"Red ones! Can you imagine? Well, I'd better go and tell them to start the play without a donkey." Giving Lucy a wave, she hurried out of the store.

Lucy knew the Christmas wedding would be lovely, but she put the thought of it out of her mind as people began drifting into the shop. Soon she was ladling out cups of cider and carving slices of cake. There was a momentary lull while the play took place next door, and then all the little actors rushed in as a group for their refreshments. Lucy had popped a huge bowl of popcorn for them. While their parents began singing carols in the mercantile, Lucy set the children to work stringing garlands of popcorn to take home as Christmas gifts.

"Chipper," she called to Rosie and Seth's son, "make sure the little ones don't touch the needles. Caitrin said they're brand-new ones from Kansas City, and they're very sharp."

She started around the counter toward the children just as Rolf Rustemeyer threw open the bakery door, stepped into the room, and set his fists on his hips.

"Miss Lucy Cornwall," he announced, "I make a decision."

"Oh, Mr. Rustemeyer," she said. She caught her breath, feeling the eyes of everyone in the bakeshop riveted on her. "Welcome to the Christmas social."

He looked around, seeming to notice the other people for the first time. "*Ja,*" he said. "Come. We go outside for talking."

"Outside?" But before she could protest, he strode across the floor, took her arm, and propelled her out the door into the snowy night.

"Lucy, this I say to you," Rolf began. He held her shoulders tightly clamped in his hands, as though he were afraid she might slip away. "Every day I am praying for God to lead me, and every day he is making my heart grow stronger. Lucy Cornwall, I love you. Even though you have turned me away, I cannot stop loving you. This evening, I make the decision to ask you again to marry me. I promise that I will be your husband in every way except the way that frightens you. All our children we will bring from the orphanage house. Next week, you and I will go to Kansas City and adopt the baby who can never walk. We will name her Hannah, and she will be our daughter. And this will be our family, a happy family, a family built by God."

Lucy stared at Rolf, her breath unmoving in her chest. "But you're going to marry Ingrid Volkart."

"God's plan is for me to marry with you, Lucy. When I try to follow my own plan and bring Ingrid Volkart from Germany, God lets me know it is wrong. Here is what I do not tell you when you first reject me. On the day you walk away from your lost baby in Kansas City, this is the day I know how much I love you. This is the day God shows me his plan. On this very day I write a letter to Ingrid Volkart, and I tell her that she should not come to America."

"But you never told me you had written to her."

"No, because Ingrid is not the only reason you refuse me that night. I know your feeling about marriage, Lucy. But I cannot stop my love for you. And so I come to you again."

Lucy stood ankle deep in swirling snow, her heart tumbling inside her chest. With his gray eyes confirming his words of love, Rolf caught her up in his arms and held her so tightly she could barely breathe.

"Say yes this time, Lucy," he murmured against her ear. "Say you will marry with me."

Lucy reached up and touched the soft golden hair that fell across his forehead. "I love you, Rolf."

"And?"

"And I think you're wonderful."

"And?"

"And . . . and I'll marry you."

"*Wunderbar!*" Rolf cried out. He threw his arms up in the air and shouted again. "Thank you, God! Look what I have here," he said. From his pocket he produced a small green sprig. "Is mistletoe, *ja?*"

Lucy caught her breath as Rolf slipped his arm around her, drew her close, and kissed her softly on the cheek.

At that, the door to the bakeshop burst open, and everyone swarmed the couple. "We were all watching through the window!" Chipper shouted. "Did you say yes, Miss Cornwall? Are you going to marry Mr. Rustemeyer?"

"How did you know what we were talking about?" Lucy cried as the children formed a ring around them and began to dance through the snow.

"Everybody knows how much you both love each other," Chipper said. "Mama says it's as plain as the freckles on my nose. So, what did you tell him?"

"Yes," Lucy said as Rolf caught her in his arms again. "I said yes!"

⤳

The Christmas Day wedding brought townsfolk and farmers from miles around. Lucy was nervous at first, but her focus soon centered on the man waiting for her at the altar in the front of the little white church. Wearing her mother's white wedding gown, she walked down the aisle carrying a bouquet of golden wheat and the fresh red roses Rolf had ordered from a greenhouse back East. He had gotten a haircut, she noticed, and he wore a black wool suit he had unpacked from the trunk he had brought with him from Germany. Lucy thought he was the handsomest man she had ever seen.

As she neared the altar, Lucy spotted her mother sitting on a bench at the front of the church. Felicity Cornwall wore a pale pink dress and the flowered hat that Lucy had given her for Christmas. Though she had briefly objected to the marriage, she soon changed her mind. Lucy had been correct about her mother's burden of bitterness, Felicity had confessed to her, and she did not want Lucy to bear a similar weight through life. Felicity also had abandoned her plans to move to Missouri. After all, she reminded Lucy, she would soon have a granddaughter to dote on.

After the ceremony, the congregation crowded into the bakeshop. Lucy had made her own wedding cake, and to her delight, everyone said it was the tastiest and most beautiful creation ever to emerge from her oven.

Later, Rolf's team bore his new bride home to the large wooden house he had built on his land. Lucy baked a batch of biscuits and fried a chicken, while Rolf built a roaring fire in each of the home's three hearths. After they ate, they sat down together on a couch in the great room.

"For our baby, I am making wooden roads up the stairs," Rolf said, taking Lucy's hand. "How do you call those?"

"Ramps," Lucy said. She loved the feel of her husband's strong, callused fingers woven through her own. "You're going to build ramps so we can push Hannah's chair up and down."

"*Ja,* I make them here in my house . . . *our* house." He gave her a shy grin. "And I will put them at the mercantile and the church, too. This way, maybe Hannah never knows she is different from the other children."

"It's not so bad to be different," Lucy said. "You taught me that."

"We are different. And now we are together. Look, I make something for you." He reached down and pulled a cloth sack from under the couch. "These I carve on our journey from Missouri. At first I tell myself I am making them for me. But soon I know in my heart I make them for you, for the hope I have for us. This is how God shows me his plan."

Lucy untied the twine bow and opened the sack. One by one, she took out a collection of small, painted, wooden Christmas ornaments. "They're beautiful!"

"In Germany," Rolf said, "we put these on the Christmas tree of married people. The angel shows that you and I wish for God to lead us in everything."

"Yes, we do. Always. And the house?"

"For protection. I promise to protect you always, Lucy." He stroked her fingers with his thumb. "Here is the rabbit for hope, and the teapot for visitors."

"Hospitality."

"*Ja.* And the bird is for joy, the fruit basket is for being generous, the Saint Nicholas is for kindness to others, and the flower basket is for goot wishes."

"What does the fish mean?"

"This is for the blessing of Christ."

Lucy picked up a delicately carved pinecone. "And this, Rolf?"

He fell silent a moment. "Is for the hope of many babies. But I tell you already we get our babies from the orphanage house."

"Yes," Lucy said. She picked up the small red heart. Only she could know what a great sacrifice Rolf had made in giving up his German bride for a woman who had said she could never truly be a wife to him. The man who had carved these ornaments had surrendered his own plans for a home filled with children. He had put God's plan first, and how Lucy loved him for that.

"This heart," she said, "must be for passion."

"And the red rose." He laid a petaled flower in her hand. "This is for true love. This rose, the love we have for each other, will live forever in my heart, Lucy. Is OK for me to kiss you?"

"Please," she said softly. "Kiss me, Rolf."

Their lips met, and Lucy felt as though she were blossoming inside. Like the red rose of love, she began to unfold in her husband's arms. First her fear fell away. And then her shame. Then her shyness and hesitation and even a bit of her modesty slipped aside. As they parted, she lifted a hand to her throat. "My goodness," she whispered.

Rolf chuckled. "Is a goot kiss because I love you."

"And I love you." She stood and took his hand. "Now, I have a gift for you, Rolf."

"For me?"

She picked up a lamp and led him toward the room where he slept. Though her own room was to be upstairs, Lucy pushed open his door and carried the lamp across the rug to the bedside table.

"What is this?" Rolf asked, gazing down at the white pillowcase.

Across it lay hundreds of red rose petals, scattered from Lucy's wedding bouquet.

"This is my gift to you," she said. "I give you this gift because I love you."

Rolf swallowed. "What do you mean, Lucy?"

"During our wedding, when Pastor Elijah spoke of God's will that a man and a woman should leave their parents, cleave unto each other, and become one flesh, I knew that's what I wanted for us. God is healing me a little more each day, and I know he brought you into my life as a gift and a blessing. Rolf, I want to be your wife in every way."

"*Ja?* Oh, this is *wunderbar!*"

Lucy realized that Rolf was blushing a bright pink as she slipped her arms around him and kissed his cheek. "Merry Christmas, my love. Merry Christmas."

My mother used to make big batches of these cinnamon rolls and deliver them to my sister and me when we lived at a boarding school in Kenya. Sometimes I think they were my primary sustenance! I loved them, and I'm so pleased to share the recipe with you. I imagine it's much the same as the recipe Lucy used in her bakeshop.

—Catherine Palmer

Cinnamon Buns

Dough:
2 pkgs. yeast
½ cup sugar, divided
1 cup warm water (105–115° F)
1 cup milk
½ cup shortening
1 tbsp. salt
2 eggs, slightly beaten
6 cups flour

Filling:
½ cup sugar
4 tsp. cinnamon

2–4 tbsp. softened butter or margarine
½ cup raisins (optional)
½ cup pecans (optional)
½ cup chocolate chips (optional)

Glaze:

1 cup confectioner's sugar, sifted
2 tsp. milk
1 tsp. vanilla

Dissolve yeast and ¼ cup sugar in water. Set aside.

In saucepan, scald milk (don't quite boil it but heat till it's bubbly around the edges). Add shortening, ¼ cup sugar, and salt. Stir until shortening is melted. Cool until just warm to the touch. Add yeast mixture. Add eggs; stir well. Add 3 cups flour; stir until mixture is smooth and well blended. Add 3 more cups flour, or as much as is needed to make a soft but easily handled dough.

On a lightly floured surface, knead dough until smooth and elastic, about 5 minutes. Place dough in greased bowl, turning to grease top. Cover with a clean cloth and let rise in a warm, draft-free place until double. Punch dough down and let stand 10 minutes.

Roll dough into 15x10-inch rectangle. Spread with softened butter or margarine. For filling, combine sugar and cinnamon and sprinkle evenly over dough. If desired, sprinkle optional ingredients over the cinnamon-sugar mixture. Roll dough up from long side, jelly-roll fashion; pinch edge to seal. Slice into about fifteen 1-inch slices.

Arrange slices in a greased 13x9-inch baking pan. Cover and let rise again until doubled in bulk.

Preheat oven to 375° F. Bake rolls about 20–30 min. They should be lightly browned both top and bottom. Cool in pan on wire rack for 5 minutes; drizzle with glaze.

A NOTE FROM THE AUTHOR

DEAREST FRIENDS,

So many of you have written to me asking for further stories about the characters in my series A Town Called Hope. I thank you for following these characters, who are so dear to my heart, from book to book.

When requests for Lucy Cornwall's story continued to arrive in my mailbox, I decided she would make the perfect heroine for a Christmas story. Clearly, Lucy is a woman who has endured much—a woman for whom the healing and transforming power of Christ's love is very real. She grew out of the depths of my own pain, and I pray that God can use her story to reach out to others.

If this novella has been your first introduction to the town of Hope, Kansas, I encourage you to read the stories of its growth from a single, small soddy into a bustling community. In *Prairie Rose*, you'll meet Rosie Mills and Seth Hunter, whose love flourishes despite their suffering from great loss. In *Prairie Fire*, you can watch villain Jack Cornwall change as the flames of Caitrin Murphy's passion—and God's love—tame him into a true gentleman. And *Prairie Storm* introduces the town preacher, Elijah Book, whose tumultuous relationship with Lily Nolan can only be calmed by the love of Jesus Christ.

Thank you for sharing with me in the joy, faith, and love of the town called Hope. May God bless you richly!

Catherine Palmer

ABOUT THE AUTHOR

Catherine Palmer lives in Missouri with her husband, Tim, and sons Geoffrey and Andrei. She is a graduate of Southwest Baptist University and has a master's degree in English from Baylor University. Her first book was published in 1988. Since then she has published more than twenty books and has won numerous awards for her writing, including Most Exotic Historical Romance Novel from *Romantic Times* magazine. Total sales of her novels number more than one million copies.

Her books include the series A Town Called Hope (*Prairie Rose, Prairie Fire*, and *Prairie Storm*); *Finders Keepers*; and novellas in the anthologies *Prairie Christmas, A Victorian Christmas Cottage, A Victorian Christmas Quilt, A Victorian Christmas Tea*, and *With This Ring*.

Her original HeartQuest series, *The Treasure of Timbuktu* and *The Treasure of Zanzibar*, is being re-released as the Treasures of the Heart series. The first two books are now titled A *Kiss of Adventure* and A *Whisper of Danger*. Also look for the brand-new third book in the series, A *Touch of Betrayal*.

Watch for Catherine's first mainstream novel, *A Dangerous Silence*, available early in 2001.

Catherine welcomes letters written to her in care of Tyndale House Author Relations, P.O. Box 80, Wheaton, IL 60189-0080.

REFORMING
SENECA JONES

⁊

Elizabeth White

In loving memory of my paternal grandparents
Roy Seneca Cook and Nina Josephine Jones Cook
To my parents, who taught me to trust God

❧

CHAPTER 1

Fort Kearny, Nebraska
November 1860

A nnie Fitzgerald wanted to go home. She wanted to mur-
der her older brother, Micah. She wanted to take a hick-
ory stick to her younger brother, Cane. She wanted to
punch the stationmaster right in his beaky nose. In fact, she reflected, if she had been there when the Lord created men, she'd
have advised him that the world would be much better off if he'd
just skip straight to the female of the species.

Annie made sure the casual observer would never suspect the
turbulent emotions churning beneath the bosom of her neat, if
shabby, blue traveling dress. She regarded the unfortunate Mr.
McCabe of the oversized proboscis with calm gray eyes. Clasping
her gloved hands with ladylike precision upon the rough counter,
she politely repeated his words to make sure she'd heard correctly.

"My brother Micah is away until *Christmas?*"

Mr. McCabe shrugged apologetically. "At least. He said to tell
you he was sorry, but his business was urgent. Washington, you
know."

*Washington. Bunch of Yankee politicos trying to run everybody's life.
Interfering in my life.* Under less frightening circumstances, Annie
would be willing to admit that there were equally as many southern
politicos as northern ones stirring up trouble in Washington.

Now, though, she wished desperately that she were back home
in Alabama, where life was, if not particularly comfortable, at least

familiar. During the long trip north and west, the weather had gotten steadily windier and colder, the landscape flatter, and the vegetation more sparse. Her fellow travelers had been friendly but laconic to the point that Annie longed for a chatty southern conversation about something other than wheat farming and gold mining.

But after her parents succumbed to a summer cholera scourge, she'd been forced to sell the patch of rocky northern Alabama dirt she and Cane had inherited. Even if she'd been of a mind to farm it, she didn't know how, and Cane was too young to run it. Unable to come home for the funeral, Micah had offered to bring his younger siblings to Fort Kearny, where he was stationed with the U.S. marshall's office. The money he sent, plus the proceeds from the land sale, had just barely covered stage fare and the other expenses of moving.

Of course, her widowed neighbor, Frank Beesom, had offered marriage—for the third time. But Mr. Beesom had six unruly children, and Annie would sooner hog-tie herself to a mule and a plow for eternity than consign herself to being an unpaid nanny for that mob.

Turning from the stationmaster's sympathetic gaze, Annie squeezed her eyes shut and tried to pray. Mama and Daddy had at least taught her to trust God before passing to their reward. Oh, how she still missed them, especially now!

Her parents had sacrificed mightily so she could earn her teaching certificate. She had been able to modestly add to the family income, as long as she lived under her parents' roof. A single woman couldn't survive alone, though. Particularly with a high-spirited twelve-year-old brother like Cane to supervise.

Heavenly Father, Cane deserves at least the same education I got. She'd counted on Micah to help her make sure that happened.

But Micah had apparently been detained while on an important mission. Micah would probably be frantic with worry over his brother and sister, and he would return as soon as he could. But for now the responsibility appeared to be Annie's alone, for an indefinite period of time. What on earth was she going to do? No place to stay, little money left after the long journey west, and no prospects of a job.

Feeling the tears stinging the backs of her eyelids, Annie pinched the bridge of her nose and swallowed hard. In a fort this size, someone was bound to need a hired girl.

Straightening her shoulders, Annie turned with sudden decision. "Mr. McCabe, do you know of any—" She stopped when she saw the station manager's eyes bug out, as something outside on the street caught his attention.

"Awck!" squawked McCabe.

"What's the matter?" Annie turned to look out the window, but she saw nothing except a big horse tied to a hitching post in front of the saloon across the street. Then her gaze followed the upward direction of Mr. McCabe's pointing finger, and she felt the blood leave her face in a rush. "Cane!" she shrieked. Picking up her skirts, she took off for the door.

By the time she got outside, a crowd had collected on the front porch of the station, and she had to push her way through a wall of broad, blue-uniformed shoulders of cavalry officers, the fringed buckskins of prospectors, and the flannel and homespun of farmers and their wives. Huffing in frustration, she finally got through and nearly tumbled down the uneven steps leading to the dusty street.

"Cane!" she shouted again. "Get down from there!"

Hands to her mouth, she watched her little brother teeter on the sloping roof of the saloon. It appeared he had climbed out a second-story window with the intention of jumping onto the horse below. He was going to kill himself. And if he didn't, she was going to do it for him.

Her God-fearing parents had given their younger son the name Canaan, after the Promised Land. But over the years, more and more people had shortened it to Cane. Spelling notwithstanding, the name of the original troublemaker seemed to fit the boy much better.

Cane was good at pretending not to hear his name when he was called. He skidded another couple of inches closer to the edge of the roof. The horse below, unaware, stuck its nose into the watering trough nearby.

Annie realized that another knot of men had gathered outside the front door of the saloon, as if to watch a circus. She advanced into the street, gesturing wildly. "Somebody go up there and get that child off the roof! Hurry!"

But her words were drowned out by a collective roar from the crowd now lining both sides of the street. She felt like a Christian martyr in the arena.

"Hey, lady, get back out of the street!" shouted a young man leading a big chestnut mare out of the stable next to the Overland office. "The Pony's due any minute!"

"What pony?" She kept her eyes on Cane, who had suddenly started jumping up and down like a monkey. "I have to get my brother! He's going to fall!"

But just as she reached the center of the street, she realized that part of the noise emanated from a cloud of dust boiling toward her from the west end of town.

"Look out! Here he comes!" someone in front of the saloon shouted.

For the first time, Annie took her attention from her daredevil brother. She froze.

Straight toward her galloped a brown-and-white paint mustang. Its rider wildly waved a black hat over his blond head with one hand and held on to the reins with the other. He stuck like a burr to the saddle, and he was going to run right over her! By now the thunder of hooves was deafening; whichever way she moved the rider would swerve and hit her. She'd never been so frightened in her entire life. She shut her eyes.

She felt a rush of wind and motion as the horse swept behind her, so close that her skirt was snatched sideways, exposing a froth of white lace petticoat. Staggering, Annie saw the mustang make a skidding turn and come back toward her, slowing, but still at a gallop. Whooping, the rider cut one flamboyant circle around her, then another, each time flourishing that dusty black hat above his head. She could see a glint of bright blue eyes beneath the mop of sun-streaked hair falling across his forehead. A broad grin split his face.

He was *laughing* at her! He bowed to the gathered crowd, who cheered and whistled at his outrageous performance. Kneeing his horse to a walk, he leaned over and caught Annie by the waist just as she managed to unlock her knees.

She found herself pulled up from behind and plunked sideways across the saddle in front of the rider, held firmly in scandalous proximity to a dusty, buckskin-clad chest. She squirmed wildly. "L-let me down! Are you insane?"

She heard him chuckle. "Prettiest welcome party I've had in a long time. Good thing I'm ahead of schedule—plenty of time to transfer the *mochila*."

"What's a mo-mokeela? Never mind," she said hastily, refusing to be sidetracked. This lunatic evidently wasn't going to voluntarily let go of her. "I suppose this is your idea of a joke, but my little brother is about to fall off that roof over there—" She pointed at Cane, who had hunkered down to watch the show from his vantage point on the roof. He looked in no imminent danger, so Annie relaxed a fraction. "I've got to get him down before he hurts himself."

"That big kid up there?" Annie could feel the rider shift to look over her head. "Looks to me like he's having a pretty good time."

"He's only twelve, and he's horse crazy. He was just about to— listen, I'm not going to argue with you. Let me down off this horse this instant or I'll have you arrested." She made herself look up at him and found her tormentor to be young, entirely too good-looking, and possessed of a long dimple creasing one ruddy cheek. She hardened her heart. "This instant," she repeated.

"This instant?" he mimicked her Alabama drawl. "I'm not in such an all-fired hurry as that."

"Hey, Seneca," called the man who had led the horse from the Pony Express stable earlier and was waiting impatiently a few yards away. "I need the *mochila* so I can head out. You can do your spoonin' after we make the transfer."

Seneca? What kind of silly name was that? Annie tried again to jerk out of his arms. Her reputation was going to be in tatters, and she had been in town less than an hour.

"Here now, be still," protested the rider, clicking his tongue and guiding the now placid horse toward the stable. "You're gonna make Becky nervous."

Annie had drawn in a breath to lambaste him, but a laugh bubbled out instead. "Your horse is named *Becky*?"

"Sure." He gave her another wicked grin, his eyes sparkling with mischief. "Named after the girl who gave me the best kiss I ever got. 'Course," he forestalled her outraged response, "I could change her name to yours, if you want."

The implication left Annie speechless.

"See," continued Seneca imperturbably, "I think we can work out a little deal here. You give me the best kiss I ever got, and I'll help you get your brother off that roof. Shut up, Rusty," he said to the other Pony Express rider, who was bent double laughing at his friend's antics. "Go get your own girl."

Annie had never in her born days imagined herself in such a situation. The daughter of hardworking, Bible-believing parents, she had been reared to expect masculine respect and protection. Her father had impressed upon her that if she comported herself as a Christian lady, she would be treated as such. So far her experience—even in the last grim six months of uprooting herself and Cane, moving into alien territory—had proven her father right.

As far as she knew, women of godly character did not bestow indiscriminate kisses on heathen cowboys. Was there something about her—the way she looked or dressed—that had invited such unwanted attentions? Was it her precipitate and unladylike charge into the middle of the street?

She felt the top of her head and realized with horror that her bonnet had flopped down her back by its ribbons. Oh, mercy, what immodesty!

As Annie groaned and started to struggle again, she happened to look upward. She was horrified to see that Cane was back on his feet again, apparently disinterested in his sister's encounter with the Pony Express rider now that the acrobatic stunts were over.

Annie involuntarily looked at the mobile mouth hovering hopefully above hers. His teeth were white and mostly straight, and there was a golden stubble along the clean line of his jaw. She wondered what it would feel like. Her stomach did a back flip. She'd never kissed a man before.

No, I'm not giving in! Not even to get Cane off the roof!

She stiffened her posture as much as was possible in this mortifying position. "I'll have you know, Mr. . . . Mr. . . . ."

"Jones," he supplied helpfully.

"Jones." She gave him a baleful glare as she tried to straighten her bonnet. She was going to frighten him as much as he frightened her. "My older brother is a U.S. deputy marshall, and I assure you, the man who insults and harasses me will wind up in front of a preacher with a shotgun at his back and a ring on his finger."

"Sweetheart, I wish you'd make up your mind," Seneca said in feigned confusion, while slyly tugging the bonnet off her head again. "You're balking at giving me a kiss, and now you want to marry me? I'll have to think that one over. My calendar's pretty full these days—"

"That's *not* what I meant, you heathenish reprobate!"

Up went the straight, dark blond brows. "Becky, would you listen to that jawbreaker? She sounds just like a schoolmarm I had when I was a kid. Here, if you're worried about your reputation . . ." He quickly wrapped the reins around the pommel and brought the black hat up to shield their faces. Before Annie could protest, Seneca covered her lips with his, effectively stealing the breath right out of her body.

Mercifully, it was over before it had much more than begun. At least, that was what Annie told herself when Seneca Jones jerked his mouth from hers and plopped his hat back on his head. Shaking, she looked up at him as he hurriedly took up the reins and with a kick of his heels headed the horse across the street toward the saloon.

His smiling mouth was now a grim line that made him look older somehow. "What's your name?" he asked as he pulled Becky to a halt.

"Annie Fitzgerald," she mumbled, humiliated. Had she actually participated in that kiss?

He nodded. "OK, Annie Fitzgerald. Here's some advice. Go home. I don't know where you came from, and I don't know who this big bad brother of yours is, but you don't belong here. You can't keep your little brother from roof walking, and you can't seem to stay out of the street. People will take advantage of you." He held her gaze. "Go home."

Despair scoured Annie. She'd allowed this man to take her first kiss. Still, there was something oddly steady in his gaze that broke the strong reserve she'd built.

"I can't," she blurted, folding her hands primly in her lap, as if she sat in someone's parlor rather than in the circle of Seneca Jones's arms. "My parents are dead, and there's no place to go back to. I brought Cane out here so my brother Micah could take charge of him, but—but Micah's gone, and I don't know—"

"Micah Fitzgerald is your brother?"

Annie nodded. She wouldn't have thought him capable of it, but Seneca sat quietly for a full minute, sucking on his bottom lip and staring over her head.

Finally he sighed and gestured upward, where Cane's brown eyes and shock of wheat-colored hair were visible now, upside down, below the edge of the roof. "Hey, kid," Seneca called.

"Hey, mister!" Cane replied eagerly. "That was some great ride."

"Thanks. You want to come give me a hand putting Becky in for the night?"

Cane nearly tumbled over the edge of the roof. "Sure!" His voice scaled two octaves in his excitement. "I'll be right down." His freckled face disappeared.

Seneca smiled at Annie, who wasn't sure whether to be grateful or aggravated. She frowned, to be on the safe side. "You hurt Cane, and I'll—"

"I know, you'll get the deputy marshall after me."

"No. I'll come after you myself with a load of buckshot."

"I'm so scared," he said dryly. "While Cane's occupied, why don't you walk down the street and introduce yourself to Reverend Edwards. He's real good at taking in strays."

The teasing glint in Seneca's eyes took the sting from his words. Annie nodded gratefully as she slid to the ground. Talking to a pastor was just what she needed right now.

She'd never been so confused in her life.

⤳

Seneca Jones had never been so tired and hungry in his life.

He leaned over the stall door, watching as Cane Fitzgerald curried Becky, who had her nose buried blissfully deep in a manger full of hay. The boy had apparently been well taught, for his movements were sure and soothing, and he talked nonsense to the horse in that splintery adolescent drawl that showed evidence of soon becoming a deep baritone.

"You got a horse of your own, kid?" Seneca asked idly, thinking that if a woman's big gray eyes hadn't sidetracked him, he'd be enjoying a meal and a hot bath—not necessarily in that order—over at Mrs. McCabe's boardinghouse. But he supposed he had a responsibility of sorts.

Seneca wasn't big on responsibilities unless they had to do directly with his own welfare. On the other hand, he had a soft spot for women with dark red hair and dainty ears. And lips like elderberry wine. He hoped the preacher would talk her into going back to Dixieland where she belonged, because he wasn't sure he could stay away from her, and—all that teasing about shotguns and rings aside—Seneca had no intention of getting himself roped and tied anytime soon.

"No, sir," Cane answered Seneca's question, laughing as Becky blew out a mouthful of hay and turned her head to affectionately nuzzle his neck. His cheek rested close to the mustang's satiny shoulder while he bent to pick the rocks out of her forehoof. "Just my pa's plow horse. Don't even have him no more, 'cause we sold him to help pay the stage fare."

Sir? The hair lifted on the back of Seneca's neck. *How old does this kid think I am?* Still, Seneca nodded amiably. "Well, you're doing good. If you don't mind mucking stalls, I can see that Mr. McCabe gives you a job as a stablehand."

The boy straightened, shoving a hank of straight, coarse hair out of his eyes with his forearm, his face alight. "You think he'd take me on as a rider?"

Seneca chuckled. "Do your job and keep your nose clean, and maybe in a few years . . . you got to be at least fifteen before they'll talk to you."

Cane's bony, expressive face fell. "I'll be fifteen next summer." He went hurriedly back to Becky's pedicure.

Which was a good thing because it was all Seneca could do to keep a straight face. "Ahuh. Well, like I said, stay out of trouble, and we'll see."

Seneca's stomach complained loudly, and weariness settled over him like a soggy blanket. Seemed like the relays got longer and colder with each ride. The weather on the plains—always unpredictable—had worsened with the approach of winter. Come to think of it, the chill in the barn was just about unbearable.

Yawning, Seneca stepped back, pulling up the sheepskin-lined collar of his buckskin coat, then shoved his hands deep into its pockets. "Hey, kid, you just about done there? I'll take you over to Mrs. McCabe's and buy you a meal for your trouble."

"That's the boardinghouse for the Pony Express riders, ain't it?" Cane gave Becky a final pat, dropping her hoof and adjusting her blanket. He gave Seneca an eager grin as he pushed through the stall door. "I bet y'all got some stories to tell!"

"Yeah, but don't you believe half of them," Seneca said dryly, leading the way back out into the frigid late afternoon. He and Cane walked along the boardwalk lining the street, toward the Pony Express office and boardinghouse. Activity on the street had slowed down considerably since his show-off ride into town. People liked a spectacle, and he was always happy to oblige, but it had scared the bejeebers out of him to ride up on a woman standing like a statue in the middle of the street. He'd ridden circles around her, not to frighten her but to teach her to watch where she was going.

Seemed like Seneca himself had been the one to learn something in the encounter with Cane's sister. He had a sinking feeling the lesson was going to have some long-lasting effects, and not all of them pleasant. Seneca glanced at the youngster slouching along beside him, trying to look both self-assured and devil-may-care. A sudden insight brought his brows together in a frown. *Do I look that way to other people?* The mental question was addressed to nobody in particular, but he had an eerie feeling that somebody was looking over his shoulder. Somebody bigger and with a whole lot more authority than Seneca Jones.

Shrugging off the thought, Seneca lengthened his stride and hurried up the front steps of a two-story building with a broad railed porch. A line of muddy boots paraded in a neat row beside the door. Without knocking, he stuck his head in the door and shouted, "I'm home, Mrs. Mack! Where are you, beautiful?"

With a cheerful "halloo," a lovely and comfortably plump woman in her early thirties appeared in a back doorway. She bustled forward, drying her hands on her apron and beaming a welcome. "Seneca! I heard you'd ridden in earlier. You're usually over here scavenging before the dust settles in the street. Where have you been?"

"Making a new acquaintance," he said, tugging a suddenly bashful Cane into view. The boy took off his battered brown felt hat and stared at the polished wooden floor, his face bright red. "Want you to meet a new *compadre* of mine. This is Cane Fitzgerald, late of old Alabam'."

"Welcome, Cane, welcome," said Mrs. McCabe with a smile. "You boys come in and shut the door before you heat up the whole outdoors."

Seneca headed for the fireplace, where he stood warming his hands and reveling in the aromas of coffee and bread emanating from the kitchen. The first meal after a "Pony" run came close to Seneca's idea of heaven. He looked over his shoulder at Cane, who had stopped just inside the door. The boy was gawking at the huge room, with its two long tables with benches on either side, the clean-swept floor, and the wide, many-paned windows that let in the pale afternoon sunlight. This room and his eight square feet of space in the bunkhouse had constituted Seneca's home for the past nine months; in fact, he'd lived here longer than any other place since he'd left the orphanage in St. Joseph when he was about Cane's age. The McCabe family and the other riders *were* family to him, and he was proud of his position as top rider of this outfit.

"Rusty's gonna have a tough run," he commented, shrugging out of his coat and gloves as he at last felt warmth seep into his fingers. "Coming up for a storm out west."

"I worry so about you boys out there," said Martha McCabe as she handed Seneca a blue enameled tin cup full of coffee. "The Blackfoot are still stirred up about whites coming into their territory and killing the buffalo."

"I wouldn't be scared of no Injun if I had a horse like Becky," put in Cane, finding his voice as he joined Seneca by the fire. "She could outrun anything on the prairie, I bet."

"Not far from the truth. She's an Indian pony herself."

"Do the riders always take their own stock on the runs?"

"Hardly ever." Seneca shook his head, smiling. "It was a bet."

"Seneca Jones!" Mrs. McCabe, who had been setting two places at one end of the table closest to the fire, looked up with a disapproving frown. "You know gambling is a sin!"

"See, Mrs. Mack, I asked the preacher about that, and he couldn't find anywhere in the Bible that said 'thou shalt not teach your friends not to doubt your ability.' " Seneca winked.

Mrs. McCabe gave a skeptical snort. "I'm pretty sure it *does* say that 'pride goeth before a fall.' "

Seneca laughed. "Anyway, I rode Becky on the first leg, left her at the relay station, and picked her up on the way back. Beat Peewee Malone's best time by three hours."

The good woman looked much less than satisfied but recognized the uselessness of arguing scriptural admonitions with Seneca. He'd learned to evade censure in the hard school of a mission orphanage. Giving up on the unrepentant object of her lecture, Mrs. McCabe turned to Cane. "Well, young man, where's the rest of your family?"

"Ain't nobody left but me and my sister Annie. Oh, and Micah. But I don't remember him, 'cause he left home when I was a baby."

"You poor dear," Mrs. McCabe crooned as she headed for the kitchen, where she began to rattle lids. The tempting aroma of bean soup wafted in, making Seneca's stomach groan in anticipation. "Is Micah Fitzgerald your brother?" she asked, returning with two steaming crockery bowls, which she set down with a basket of corn bread. "Come, boys, sit down. Eat your fill before the rest of the crowd comes in for supper."

"Yes, ma'am," Cane answered politely, eagerly taking a place across from Seneca. "Thank you, ma'am. You know my brother?"

"I certainly do, and a finer example of manhood you wouldn't want to meet. Present company excepted." Mrs. Mack nodded at Seneca, who removed his hat and sailed it at a peg near the door. It landed neatly. He picked up his spoon, smiling at Cane's awed whistle. Mrs. Mack, standing at Cane's shoulder, cleared her throat. "Seneca, would you like to return thanks?"

He felt his face flame. He hated to pray aloud, and she knew it. She must be punishing him for the gambling joke. "Er, how about the kid saying grace?" he mumbled. "Guest and all . . ." He looked pleadingly at Cane, who blinked, startled.

"Me?" His bony shoulders lifted and dropped. "Sure, why not?" Cane bowed his head, as did Mrs. McCabe, and Seneca rolled his eyes in relief. "Dear God," began the boy conversationally, "thank you for bringing me and Annie to Nebraska. Thank you that I get to be a Pony Express rider one day. Thank you for this food and the hands that prepared it. Please keep Micah safe until he gets back." Cane scratched his freckled nose as if he were taking mental inventory of thanks and needs. Apparently satisfied that he had covered all contingencies, he popped the table with the flat of his hand. "Amen." He looked up and grinned at Seneca. "Annie's gonna be sorry she missed this." He began to ply his spoon with gusto.

"Where is Annie?" Mrs. McCabe plopped into a rocker beside the fire and picked up a skein of yarn and a half-finished sock dangling from a pair of knitting needles.

"She's gone to talk to the preacher," Cane said around a mouthful of soup and corn bread. "Annie's real religious."

Seneca watched Mrs. McCabe's expression light with interest. She was a very religious woman too. Gave him a hard time every Sunday morning at meeting time. "Oh, that's wonderful!" she exclaimed, glancing slyly at Seneca. "Have you met Miss Fitzgerald, Seneca?"

"Oh, he met her all right," Cane butted in while Seneca's mouth was full. "Kissed her smack on the lips in the middle of the street."

"Seneca Jones!" The stationmaster's wife straightened in horror, a knitting needle pointed at him like a sword. "Tell me you did not do that!"

"OK, I'll tell you, but last I heard, lying is a sin too."

"Sure 'nough, he did," insisted Cane, despite a dirty look from Seneca. "Come flyin' in on that paint mustang and rode two circles around her." Mrs. McCabe's mouth opened and closed as if she couldn't think of an appropriately scandalized reply. Enjoying her full attention, Cane tipped his chair on its back legs and continued. "Annie was real mad when he snagged her around the waist and pulled her up on the horse with him."

"I should think so," Mrs. McCabe finally managed to get out, glaring at Seneca. "I hope she slapped him silly."

Cane scratched his head. "Actually, I think she kind of liked kissin' him."

Seneca pushed his bowl away, his appetite gone. Martha McCabe was looking at him like he was the fattest turkey in the barnyard the night before Thanksgiving. His goose was cooked for sure.

But a reprieve came in the form of the McCabes' youngest child, five-year-old Evangeline, who burst through the front door, panting. Her mop of silver blond curls stood up every which way; her little red wool coat was buttoned one off, with the collar sticking up around a green scarf; and mud caked her black ankle boots. "Mama!" she gasped. "Oh, Mama! Papa's bringing home the prettiest lady with the reddest hair you ever saw! She's gonna be my schoolteacher, and Papa says she can stay here with us. Come look!"

CHAPTER 2

ANNIE followed Lloyd McCabe's tall, straight figure up the steps of the boardinghouse run by his wife, wondering why the Lord had suddenly taken to answering her prayers backward and inside out. She wanted so much to honor her father's dying wish that Cane be educated and given the opportunity to go to college. At first, the job that had fallen into her lap when she went to visit Preacher Edwards had seemed like a boon sent directly from heaven. Fort Kearny's only schoolteacher had recently married and moved away with her husband, and the position was open to a qualified applicant.

Annie's letters of reference more than qualified her, as did her cultured southern speech. She had worked hard to eliminate any traces of the bad grammar and sloppy diction so prevalent among her neighbors and relatives. In fact, the minister had all but done a holy dance when he realized the hordes of school-aged children now running wild on the town streets would be under the control of a competent teacher come next Wednesday.

Lloyd McCabe, who also acted as the town's school superintendent, had sealed the deal. Head spinning from the suddenness of it all, Annie found herself not only gainfully employed but also in possession of a room for herself in the McCabes' boardinghouse and a bunk for Cane with the Pony Express riders.

It was this last that caused Annie to question the Lord's attention to detail. On the walk over from the Pony Express office she had had time to consider all the ramifications of putting her impressionable young brother in company with rowdy tumbleweeds like Seneca Jones.

And there he was in the McCabes' dining room, seated across from Cane, as if her fretting had conjured him out of thin air. She might have known he'd be sprawled at the table like a king on a throne, regarding her with a hint of that ridiculous dimple creasing his cheek. She ignored him and smiled at Martha McCabe's eager welcome.

"Oh, Miss Fitzgerald, you can't imagine how glad we are to have you here! The mister and I have five young ones ourselves, and I declare I can't keep up with their schooling and run the boarding-house, too."

Annie smiled at the little blond moppet attached to her mother's skirt, her index finger stuck in her rosy mouth. "I've met Evangeline. She seems to have quite a vocabulary for her age."

"Oh, dear me, yes," sighed Mrs. McCabe. "The child's tongue is loose at both ends. Which is exactly why she needs to be in school."

Evangeline, sliding toward the table and Seneca, removed her finger from her mouth with a loud pop. "Are you a princess?" she asked Annie seriously. "'Cause if you are, you can marry Seneca. He's the prince."

"Only princess I'm marrying is you," said Seneca, curling one arm around the child and tickling her under the chin. He gave Annie a sideways look, and for the first time she noticed the uneasiness in the blue of his eyes.

She could not contain her blush, which deepened when she noticed Mrs. McCabe looking at the two of them very oddly. She jerked her gaze from Seneca's and leveled a disapproving frown at her brother. "Cane Fitzgerald, where are your manners? Didn't Mama teach you to remove your hat when you come indoors?"

Startled at the sudden attention of everyone in the room, Cane coughed violently as a corn-bread crumb went down the wrong way. "I, uh, forgot." Recovering, he grabbed his hat by the brim and tossed it at a row of pegs studding the wall by the door. It collided with several others already hanging there and knocked them to the floor. He winced. "Oops."

"Cane!" Annie exclaimed. "What is the matter with you? Go pick those up right now."

"All right, all right." Cane slouched to obey, grumbling. "Seneca did it; why can't I?"

"I might have known," Annie muttered, then smiled brightly at Martha McCabe. "Mrs. McCabe, do you need some help in the kitchen? I'm a fair hand at buttermilk biscuits, if I do say so myself."

"Oh, please, dear, call me Mrs. Mack, like the boys do—or better yet, just Martha. I can see we're going to be great friends."

"All right. And I'm Annie."

She unbuttoned her coat and hung it by the door with her bonnet, surreptitiously watching as Seneca helped little Evangeline remove her outer garments, his tongue stuck in his cheek as he wrestled with the tiny black buttons of the red coat.

"Evvie, let Seneca alone," admonished the child's mother over the sudden hubbub of four other riders, three stablehands, and the remaining McCabe progeny arriving for supper. The scraping of chairs across the hardwood floor, the racket of conversation and laughter filled Annie with an unexpected sense of belonging, as if she'd suddenly inherited a whole new family. The activity of carrying steaming baskets of corn bread and chilled crocks of butter, and replenishing the soup, made her feel welcome as no amount of deferential treatment would have done.

She couldn't help noticing that Seneca didn't seem to mind Evangeline's adoration at all. When Evangeline brought him a book to read to her, he laughed and moved to the rocker, where he pulled her onto his lap. "You read it to me," he suggested, then listened drowsily as she "read"—mostly made up, as far as Annie could tell—a convoluted tale of a prince and a frog and a pair of magic geese.

At last Annie was able to sit down with her own bowl of thick, nourishing soup, next to Martha at the end of the table closest to the kitchen door. Lloyd McCabe sat opposite, supervising his three middle children and discussing current events with the other men.

Martha proudly introduced her four boys, in descending order of age, as Josiah, Daniel, Benjamin, and Jack. She then pointed out each of the Pony Express employees by name. Annie listened politely but feared she'd have to have a review lesson at a later date. Her gaze kept wandering to the sweet tableau by the fire. Evangeline had fallen asleep midstory, her rosy cheek snuggled against Seneca's chest as he snored gently with his blond head tipped against the back of the rocker. The book was opened upside down across his knee.

She couldn't have said why the sight touched her so.

"He's a sweet boy, but trouble incarnate," said Martha thoughtfully.

Startled, Annie turned to find her new friend observing her with hazel eyes bright with concern. The milky-fair skin of a redhead betrayed Annie once again. "Who?" she mumbled into her coffee cup, as if she didn't know.

Martha pushed her dishes back and folded plump arms on the table. "I realize our acquaintance is short, Annie, but I can tell you're a good girl." She sighed. "I've seen you two looking at each other." Martha laughed when Annie opened her mouth to protest. "And Cane told me what happened when Seneca rode in this afternoon. It's not at all out of character for him, you know."

"I don't know what you mean," Annie said stiffly.

"I think you do. Seneca is the kind of handsome, rootless fellow who can make a girl feel like she's the center of the universe, then waltz off with someone else in a heartbeat."

"I was crossing the street to get my brother off the roof of the saloon when Mr. Jones nearly galloped over me. Then he reached down and grabbed me. I certainly didn't *want* him to kiss me." Annie twirled her soup spoon in agitated circles inside her bowl.

Martha gave her a dry look. "I'll take your word for it. I just wanted to warn you not to take anything Seneca says seriously. He'd rather flirt than eat, and he's got some—well, some very bad habits."

Annie had no intention of taking Seneca Jones seriously or otherwise. Still . . . "You let him close to your own daughter."

"There's a big difference between a five-year-old and a beautiful young woman," Martha said evenly, refusing to drop her gaze. "I can't break confidence and tell you more than that. Just, please . . . be careful."

Annie doubtfully eyed Seneca's innocent profile, the protective curve of his arm around the sleeping child. Then her troubled gaze moved to her brother, who was trading jokes with one of the McCabe brothers. *He* was the one she worried about. Annie knew she could control her own emotions. Her resolve firmed to make sure Cane grew up to be the godly sort of man her father would have been proud of.

Seneca Jones or no Seneca Jones.

❧

Waking to the light of a watery dawn seeping through the bunkhouse window, Seneca yawned and stretched, easing his stiff muscles one by one as he lay in bed. He was always a little slow getting started the morning after returning from a run, and the frigidity of the room made him more than reluctant to poke his nose out from under his pile of blankets. Apparently the fire had died during the night.

It was his first winter back in Nebraska since a five-year stint as a cowboy along the Chisholm Trail for a Texas-based outfit. Seemed his blood had thinned considerably during his sojourn in warmer climes. He thought of southern Annie Fitzgerald, with her delicate skin and flimsy cotton dress. She was going to be one frosty magnolia if she didn't find herself some wool petticoats somewhere.

The thought of Annie made him stir restlessly and consider braving a shave with the icy water in the washbasin. Maybe he could con Martha into boiling him some water for a bath.

"Hey, Jones, you gonna sleep all day?" he heard from the doorway. Bowlegged Billy Eakin stood there, dressed in his Sunday-go-to-meetin' best, with a jaunty bandanna tied under his prominent Adam's apple and a wide grin on his equally wide mug. "I know you ain't much on religion, but I thought you might want to know there's already a pot goin' on who gets to escort that pretty new schoolmarm to church."

Seneca scowled and sat up, looking around. For the first time he noticed the unnatural silence of the still-dim bunkhouse. No snores, no grunts and grumbles, no coarse jokes. No riders or other hands. Nobody but him.

In the normal way of things he'd have had plenty of company sleeping in on Sunday morning. Irritated him to no end—those hypocrites pretending interest in church just to impress a red-headed schoolteacher. He lay back down and pulled the blanket over his head. Not him, no sirree.

But like a mustachioed angel—or demon, Seneca wasn't sure which—Billy clapped his hands and rubbed them together loudly. "Me, I figure I got a better shot than anybody else, bein' as I'm right there ever' Sunday. Miss Fitzgerald seems to set a good bit of store by church attendance."

Seneca grunted.

"'Course, Peewee Malone thinks he's got the upper hand, since he won that fancy carriage and pair of bays from Major Applegate last week."

Seneca threw back the blanket and glared at his best friend, who returned his look innocently. "Peewee Malone is a snake in sheep's wool."

Billy grinned. "You mean wolf."

"Wolf, snake—same thing," Seneca said irritably. "You come in here and wake me up to inform me a fellow I couldn't care less about is going to church. Well, I happen to think that's a very good thing."

"Well, OK." Billy shrugged. "Just saying." He turned to go, tossing over his shoulder, "Miz Mack made griddle cakes for breakfast if you want some."

Ten minutes later, dressed in his usual denims and a clean red flannel shirt, and sporting a cut on his chin where he'd shaved with the icy water, Seneca strolled, whistling, into the dining room. All activity halted, every eye riveted on him.

He sat down unconcernedly at his place at the table closest to the fire and helped himself to a plateful of hotcakes. Gradually conversation in the room returned to normal, and Seneca rubbed his hand under the back of his collar where embarrassment stung his neck. So what if he decided to get up and get dressed on a Sunday morning? Was that such an earthshaking event? He dumped half the pitcher of syrup on his cakes and forked himself a couple of sausage links. He was hungry, that was all.

Halfway through his meal, he looked around and found her at the other table, seated between Evangeline and Peewee Malone. *Annie.* She was listening attentively to Evangeline's prattle and evidently trying to ignore Peewee's equally ignorant blather. She had pushed away her plate and leaned her elbow on the table, her cheek against the heel of her hand. She had on a soft yellow dress and looked like a painting he'd seen in a gallery in St. Louis once.

Seneca would never have admitted it to a soul, but he had a weakness for beautiful pictures.

Then Peewee touched Annie's shoulder to get her attention, and Seneca found himself on his feet, skirting both tables. He stopped behind Cane, who sat opposite Annie amidst the interchangeable McCabe brothers, whose names he could never keep straight in his mind.

"Hey, kid." He teasingly thumped Cane's ear, and the boy looked around, face alight with hero worship.

"Seneca!"

"Since you're up early, you interested in going for a ride?"

"Sure!"

"Absolutely not."

Seneca's gaze slid to Annie, who regarded him with great displeasure. He gave her his most practiced cocky smile. "Why, good morning, Miss Fitzgerald. I didn't see you sitting there."

"I'm sure you didn't," she bit out. "You're not taking my brother anywhere."

"But, Annie, there's plenty of time before church," objected Cane. "It's barely seven o'clock."

"You're not getting all dirty before we meet most of our new neighbors," Annie said firmly. "We want to make a good impression."

"Hmm, that's a real holy attitude," said Seneca. He thoughtfully stuck his fingers in the front pockets of his jeans. "Last I heard, Jesus kind of frowned on going to church to impress people."

To his surprise and horror, he saw tears shine in those big gray eyes. "That's not what I meant," she choked.

"Jones, you are way out of line," growled Peewee, getting to his feet.

Digging in deeper, Seneca sneered at his perennial rival. "Oh, and I suppose your motives are pure, too. I've seen you drooling over Miss Fitzgerald's shoulder for thirty minutes, hoping to sweet-talk her into riding to church with you."

Peewee snarled and made as if to leap over the table, but Annie jumped up, dabbing a knuckle against each eye. "Cane and I are riding to church with the McCabes in their wagon," she said, giving Evangeline a wobbly smile. "I hope both you *gentlemen* will come as well, and I promise to—to pray for you."

She picked up her plate and cup and walked into the kitchen, leaving Seneca feeling about two inches high. Still, he winked at Cane. "How 'bout we take that ride this afternoon?"

"Yes, sir!" Cane beamed.

"Quit calling me *sir*," Seneca growled. Without another word, he stalked over to the door, grabbed his hat and coat, and went outside to cool his burning face.

Women!

❧

The McCabe family took up the whole of one homemade pew midway back in the sanctuary of the Freewill Community Church. The house of worship somehow held its own just two doors down from the Gold Digger Saloon and Dance Hall—the roof of which Cane had so recently explored in his quest for acrobatic fame.

Evangeline insisted on sitting next to Annie, which put quite a squeeze in the seating arrangements. Before the second hymn had been sung, however, the five-year-old squirmed her way into Annie's lap and promptly fell asleep.

Annie rested her chin on top of the child's soft curls and tried to concentrate on Reverend Edwards's message concerning the upcoming Thanksgiving season. It was based on Ephesians 5:20: "Giving thanks always for all things unto God."

Instead, she found herself praying, as she'd promised to do, for Seneca Jones. She closed her eyes. *Oh, Lord, what an aggravating, cocky, selfish . . .*

No, that wasn't the way to go about it.

She'd prayed for a job, and the Lord had graciously provided almost immediately. Thanks to Seneca Jones. It had been his suggestion to see the pastor, which had led to her being hired to teach in the school. On the other hand, she might eventually have had the job through her acquaintance with Lloyd McCabe. Maybe.

She sneaked a look up two rows and across the aisle, where the rider in question sat beside his friend Billy Eakin. Billy's broad face was serene as he attended to the sermon. He was a true believer, Annie was sure. His gentleness and joyful demeanor radiated the love of Christ.

Seneca, on the other hand, looked like he'd been given a jar of garlic-stuffed pickled eggs for breakfast. He had his Pony Express Bible in his hand, as did the other men, but he didn't even bother to open it to the passage being discussed. His blue green eyes were practically crossed with boredom.

And why did she care what color his eyes were, anyway?

Oh, Lord, please bring him to the foot of your Cross. Help me put up with him without getting angry again. And please keep him away from Cane.

Annie wasn't a fool. Seneca Jones was just the sort of wild, good-looking hero-type who would lead Cane into all sorts of trouble. She'd seen Cane's eagerness when that fight almost erupted at the breakfast table.

Over me! Even now she could hardly believe it had happened. To be fair, Seneca hadn't responded violently when Peewee Malone threatened to attack him. But he had certainly started it with his barbed remarks about hypocrisy.

Me? A hypocrite? She pushed the thought away. Certainly not. She remembered Martha's warning and almost laughed aloud. There was absolutely no danger of falling under the spell of Seneca Jones. Annie had high standards. She wanted a husband who loved the Lord as much as she did. Not a man who held his Bible closed in church and scowled over his shoulder every five minutes.

Suddenly, a pair of hot blue eyes caught hers, and her stomach took a dip.

Certainly not.

>—

Seneca twirled his thumbs round and round, studying the men seated in the pew in front of him. Pete Gilchrist, never before seen in daylight without a hat, was discovered to have a bald spot in the center back of his head. Bob Haslam's neckline looked exactly like the southern border of the state of Texas. The collar of Jake Vincent's brown plaid wool shirt kicked up on one side, making him twitch every time it tickled his jaw. Seneca thought about reaching up to smooth it down, but he'd already drawn enough snickers for one morning.

Stuck in church with nobody to talk to, nothing else to do, unhappy with his own thoughts, Seneca gave his attention to the white-haired preacher standing behind the homemade oak pulpit. Preacher Edwards still had the slightly dazed expression that had come over him when he realized his congregation had swelled to nearly twice its normal size. Pony Express riders had to take an oath of morality that, in reality, rarely affected their lives. Seneca certainly never took it very seriously.

"Do you want to be a child of light?" the preacher asked, pausing as if he expected a verbal answer from his congregants. "Then, as the book of Ephesians says, put away all the things of darkness— drunkenness, sexual immorality, impurity, greed. Obscene stories, foolish talk, and coarse jokes. Don't be fooled by those who try to excuse their sins, because God's terrible anger comes on those who disobey him."

Well, isn't that just delightful? thought Seneca, folding his arms and snatching a look over his shoulder at Annie Fitzgerald. *God's gonna squash Seneca Jones for dallying with a pretty girl.*

Annie's eyes were closed, her chin nestled against the top of Evangeline's head, but he knew she wasn't sleeping. She had the look of a praying Madonna. He faced forward again, her peaceful face limned on his brain. *A child of light.* That's what Annie was. Not just a pretty girl. She loved her brother enough to travel thousands of miles to see him cared for. She believed in her principles enough to stand up to the ridicule of a smart-aleck rider.

After her reaction to being kissed earlier, he'd expected prunes and prisms. But he'd watched her carefully last night during supper, while pretending to listen to Evangeline's nonsense. Annie was a servant. She didn't come in expecting everybody to wait on her like most pretty women he knew. And she seemed to genuinely enjoy the McCabe kids.

Seneca squirmed. He'd gotten into the habit of flirting with everything in skirts. It was a rude awakening when a woman refused to flirt back.

As he pondered the mystery of Annie, Seneca found his thoughts reflecting, mirrorlike, on himself. He mentally reviewed the preacher's list of sins. It pretty much described his life. For the first time in his life, Seneca felt the dirt of all that disobedience. Like a man holding a lamp coming into a dusty and unused room, his spirit choked at the sight. He leaned over to prop his elbows on his knees, looking at the floor between his fancy, scrolled-leather boots.

"Let us sing psalms and hymns and spiritual songs among ourselves and make music to the Lord in our hearts," continued the preacher, joyfully thumping the pulpit with his fist. "We should always be thankful to God the Father for everything, in the name of our Lord Jesus Christ."

Be thankful? Seneca couldn't remember the last time he'd given thanks for anything spiritual. Going to church brought back childhood memories of tight, scratchy clothes, slicked-down hair, and a bottom numbed from prolonged contact with backless wooden pews. Of angry-faced, hard-boiled preachers who resented wild orphans unable to contribute anything to the church or the community. Of a long-ago funeral service where he was too big to cry and too young to understand.

Seneca squeezed his eyes shut. He must have missed something. How did one get from being the object of God's anger to being a child of light?

➤

Shivering in the midafternoon shade of the Pony Express barn, Annie perched on top of the split-rail corral fence, while Martha leaned next to her. The two women had cleaned up the monumental mess after Sunday dinner, then wandered outside to watch Seneca teach Cane the running mount for which the Pony Express riders were famous.

Cane, who had been horse crazy since he could walk, already knew the basics of riding. He had spent every spare minute after his chores were done pestering the daylights out of any neighbor who had a saddle horse and would let Cane get on it.

Annie sighed as she watched her younger brother eagerly mimic his teacher's movements. In a just world, Cane would have a horse of his own by now. But their father had died before accomplishing his intention of providing mounts to transport Annie and Cane the five miles to the school where she taught.

"How much longer is Mr. Jones going to be here?" Annie asked. "Before his next Pony Express run, I mean."

"Depends on the weather and the progress of the Pony through the mountains in the western division," Martha answered, fidgeting with her knitted scarf. She seemed uncomfortable with inactivity, even on Sunday. "Two runs a week come through here, but the riders usually have eight or nine days' rest between rides.

That's why we have several riders lazing around at any given time."

"You mean he'll be here until next *Wednesday?*" Annie couldn't keep the dismay from her voice.

Martha laughed. "I'm afraid so. But then, remember, he'll be gone for the same amount of time."

Annie watched Seneca run like an Indian alongside the pinto named Becky, grab the saddlehorn, and hop nimbly into the saddle. When he was safely astride, she remembered to breathe. "So he—the riders live half the time here and half the time . . . where?"

"The next home station to the west is Willow Island. There are three swing stations in between. Once in a while, in an emergency, he's had to go farther, do a double stretch." Martha clapped her hands and shouted as Seneca galloped in a wide circle around the big corral. The compact little mustang responded to every pressure of his knee, swaying and turning like a ballet dancer. "Seneca's probably the best rider in the division. He carried the news of Lincoln's election. Made his part of the run in less than four hours."

"I see." Annie saw more than she wanted to. Seneca Jones could have been a circus rider. He was obviously showing off for Cane, who jumped up and down waving his hat, his breath making puffs of condensation around his head. Even Annie couldn't contain the shivers of excitement that raised the flesh of her arms and made her heart pump like a locomotive engine. She forgot how miserably cold she'd been, perching on the fence in the open air, protected only by a pair of gloves and a coat borrowed from the eldest McCabe son. She hardly noticed when one of Martha's younger boys called from the back door that Evangeline had awakened from her nap and wanted her mama.

Annie watched the perfectly conformed, powerfully muscled horse pound around the far side of the corral. Seneca gradually pulled her to a canter, then a trot, and finally to a dainty, mincing walk. Clearly Becky knew that she was the focus of attention and reveled in it. Just like her master.

With a salute of his quirt, a western riding crop that Annie suspected was more for show than use, Seneca reined in and dismounted in front of Cane.

"Can I try now?" Cane asked, taking the horse's reins and eagerly patting her neck.

"Sure, just get a good running start and hop on. Do exactly what I did."

Annie blurted, "Cane, I don't think you should—"

"Let him try," Seneca interrupted. "Becky's too good-mannered to let him get hurt."

"Which is more than I can say for you," she retorted. He merely grinned and turned away to give the girth a final check before Cane led the mare away. "Be careful," she called after her brother, who also seemed inclined to ignore her.

Annie watched as Cane clicked his tongue, and Becky moved smoothly into motion. He trotted along beside her several paces before he grasped the pommel, bounced once as Seneca had taught him, and swung lightly into the saddle. He rode around the corral, waving jauntily to Annie as he passed her.

"See? The kid's a natural." Seneca had moved to stand beside her, one elbow slung over the rail so that the fringe on the sleeve of his buckskin jacket brushed her skirt. He poked the brim of his hat back with one finger and looked up at her. "All that fussing for nothing."

Annie slid to the ground and was gratified to find that Seneca wasn't as tall as he looked on horseback. Her lips were on a level with his chin. Quietly she said, "You will oblige me, Mr. Jones, by desisting from subverting my authority."

He wrinkled his nose and leaned closer. "Would you mind saying that in English, Miss Fitzgerald?"

She could see tiny green flecks of devilment in the blue of his sparkling eyes. Ooh! She would *make* him take her seriously. "Maybe I should say it in Swahili, which is probably closer to your native language. My brother is going to grow up to be a gentleman, not some horse wrangler. And I won't have you countermanding everything I tell him."

He leaned back against the fence again, folding his arms across his chest. "Is that right?"

"That's right."

"Well, see, that's gonna be a mite inconvenient when Cane's working in the stable before and after school."

"What do you mean?" Annie had been grateful when Mr. McCabe had offered to pay Cane a dollar a week as an assistant stablehand. That would at least buy his books.

"Mr. McCabe assigned me the job of training and supervising your brother until I leave on my next run."

"He didn't!"

"He did." Seneca's expression was suddenly warm and sympathetic. "Look, Annie, I understand your concern, but Cane is not a baby or even a little boy anymore. Any man who's gonna survive in this country has to be proficient—see, there's a word for you! — with horses." He gave a wry little shrug. "He might as well learn from the best."

Perhaps, Annie reluctantly admitted, he had a point. She watched Cane canter around the corral on Becky, already happier than she'd seen him since the death of their parents. It was just so hard to know what to do when she had to make all the decisions herself.

She gave Seneca a doubtful look. How could he be so—so self-confident about *everything*? "I won't object," she said, "on one condition."

He rolled his eyes. "What's that?"

"If Cane even remotely comes to any harm under your supervision, I'll come after you—"

"With a load of buckshot," he finished for her. He gave her a mocking two-fingered salute.

"And another thing."

Seneca sighed. "What now?"

"I have not given you leave to call me Annie."

He grinned, then put two fingers to his lips and gave an ear-splitting whistle that brought Becky toward him at a gallop. Cane delightedly hung on for dear life, grabbing the pommel when the horse skidded to a stop before her master, one leg bent in a comical simulation of a curtsy.

"Maybe you're right," said Seneca thoughtfully. "I should call you Princess, so I won't get Annie here confused." He stroked the mare's glossy neck and whispered something in her ear that made her whicker and nuzzle his face, for all the world as if she were kissing him.

Cane looked confused. "You changed Becky's name to Annie?"

Seneca chuckled. "Ask your sister."

CHAPTER 3

ANNIE avoided an encounter with Seneca Monday morning by the simple expedient of slipping into the kitchen at dawn, where she wrapped a cold cinnamon bun in a napkin and put it into her pocket for later. She wanted to walk down to the schoolhouse and inventory the classroom, making sure of her supplies before the children came to her on Wednesday.

However, she could not quite erase him from her thoughts. She found herself rehearsing all the ways she would have answered his teasing remarks yesterday, if she'd only had time to *think*.

Lord, why does that lazy, mocking smile scramble my brain so? He doesn't treat anyone else that way.

After humiliating her in front of her brother, he'd gone whistling off to the stable, with Becky and Cane trailing behind, like the Pied Piper leading the children of Hamlin Town. She hadn't seen hide nor hair of Seneca the rest of the day. She'd have assumed he'd disappeared into the bowels of the dance hall, except for the fact that it was closed down in deference to the Lord's Day.

So she'd spent the entire evening—while cutting down a dark blue wool dress Martha had outgrown after Evvie's birth—foolishly wondering who he was with and what name he'd be giving his horse next.

She wished a week from Wednesday would arrive *now*. Then

Seneca would be gone for a blessed week and a half. *I'm wishing my life away, Lord. I'm sure that doesn't please you either.*

Annie pulled her breakfast from her pocket and absently began to eat as she quickened her step. Even Martha's old hooded cloak and sturdy boots failed to keep out the bitter cold. As soon as she received her pay, she would have to begin replacing her inappropriate southern wardrobe.

She looked up at the steel gray sky, wondering how heavy those clouds would have to get before it snowed. The hills of north Alabama received a good snow once or twice a year, but rarely before Christmas. Thanksgiving wouldn't arrive for another week, and here it already looked like a bitter storm was on the way. She prayed that Micah was somewhere safe and warm.

Though she hadn't seen him since she was still in pigtails, Micah stood in her memory as the brother-hero of her growing-up years. Even after he'd left home for service in the U.S. cavalry, he had continued to write and always included whatever offering of monetary help he could afford.

Their aging parents had come to depend on his contributions, and Annie lived for his letters describing such faraway places as Sacramento, Salt Lake City, and St. Joseph. Micah had always been a quiet, laconic young man, but his letters were newsy and cheerful. When he left the army to take a job with the marshall's office, his communication with home became less frequent. Annie had almost lost track of him, until upon the death of their parents he offered to bring his younger siblings west.

Annie's trust had been badly shaken when she arrived in Fort Kearny to find Micah gone. Her initial anger that he'd failed to meet them as planned had, over the last couple of days, given way to real concern. Floating another prayer for her older brother heavenward, Annie hurried on.

The one-room schoolhouse stood on the westernmost end of town, protected on two sides by the enormous, impregnable walls of the stockade. The school faced the road leading to the gates, and the east side adjoined a thriving saddle-making enterprise. For many years, classes had been conducted in the church building. Three years ago, however, the hardy homemakers who had accompanied their husbands to the busy outpost had convinced the military to invest in a separate building for the education of their offspring. Built of sturdy, seasoned cedar transported from the edge of the Platte River, it looked, Annie decided, like it would last at least another hundred years.

Annie stopped at the gate in the whitewashed picket fence surrounding the schoolhouse and surveyed her new domain. A pleasurable wave of ownership brought tears to her eyes, and she found herself smiling.

Silly, because she had no claim to the property itself. But the children who gathered here would be *her* students. Every morning she would ring the brass bell mounted in the yard. She would write upon the blackboard and sweep the floor and tend the woodstove whose black, cast-iron chimney poked through the roof.

She pulled the heavy key given to her by Mr. McCabe from her pocket and, pushing through the gate, crunched across the frozen grass of the yard, and entered the building.

An hour later she heard a noise at the door and looked up, startled, from studying the textbooks she had found on the teacher's small desk at the front of the room. The door swung inward and a familiar figure in a shallow-crowned black hat, buckskin jacket, and denims stood silhouetted in the gray morning light.

"Seneca! I mean, Mr. J-Jones!" Annie slammed Plutarch's *Lives* shut. Not that there was anything wrong with preparing herself to teach ancient history. "What are you doing here?"

"Good morning, Princess," he said cheerfully. "I came to see if you need firewood."

"No, I'll be f-fine."

"Your teeth are chattering," he observed, his boots echoing

loudly on the bare plank floor as he strode toward her, dodging student desks and chairs. "Don't you want me to start you a fire?"

"I can do it my—"

But he'd already pulled open the door of the stove and begun laying a fire. Which she would have done already if she hadn't lost track of time while reading about those scandalous Sabine women. She pulled her cloak higher around her neck. It really was cold in here. She stared, fascinated by the ripple of muscle visible through the supple leather of Seneca's jacket as he worked. She'd assumed the Pony Express riders would be skinny little fellows, but Seneca appeared quite . . . sturdy.

Rattled, Annie blurted, "Where were you last night?" Appalled at the forwardness of her question but unable to call it back, she gripped her fingers together atop the desk and examined the patches in Josiah McCabe's left glove. Out of the corner of her eye she saw Seneca shrug, his back still to her.

"I went to see the preacher."

Annie blinked. "You went to—?"

"I had a question. There." Seneca gave a final jab with the poker and closed the door of the stove. He brushed his hands together, dusted the knees of his pants, and stood up in one lithe move. He looked at Annie, who was still a bit slack-jawed, and a hint of his dimple appeared. "Come over here closer to the stove." He drew up a tiny first-grade-sized chair. "Your throne, madam."

Annie sat where she was, regarding him distrustfully. Beside him were both warmth and danger. Like any fire, it could protect her or consume her. *Lord, here's the first real temptation I've had in a long time. He's so attractive, but even Martha has warned me away from him. What do you want me to do?*

There was something different in Seneca's eyes this morning, and she couldn't put her finger on it until she moved to sit in the little chair. She'd expected him to crowd her, touch her in some way. Instead, he leaned against the edge of the teacher's desk, watching her settle her skirts and extend her hands to the stove.

"Thanks for letting me stay," he said, and the deep note of humility in his voice caused her to look up again, startled.

"Thank you for the fire," she said, uncertain how to answer. "I was c-cold."

"Don't you want to know what the question was?"

"I'm not sure. I don't know you well enough to—" She swallowed. "We shouldn't even be alone here together."

"That's true. But I wanted to talk to you, and I couldn't in front of—" He restlessly took off his hat and turned it round and round in his gloved hands. Annie got the feeling he rarely sat still for any length of time unless he was asleep. She half expected him to jump to his feet and start to pace. But he blew out a breath and kept his distance. "I needed first to apologize to you for taking advantage of you the other day."

"Which—?"

"You'd never been kissed, had you, Annie?"

Annie's shoulders went back. "Mr. Jones—"

"Oh, for pete's sake, don't call me 'Mr. Jones' in that schoolmarm tone of voice!" he burst out, then bit his lip. "I mean—can't we just be a couple of friends who call each other Annie and Seneca? Nobody around here stands on ceremony."

"Maybe that's why women aren't safe in the streets!"

He winced. "See, I'm trying to say I'm sorry, and you're not helping at all!"

"So you're forgiven. Now let's talk about something else."

"No, I want you to know I really don't go around kissing every girl who crosses my path. You were just so doggone pretty—"

"How did you know it was my first kiss?" Annie interrupted, her face flaming. "Was it that bad?"

"Aw, Annie!" He tossed his hat onto the desk and crouched in front of her, taking her hands. She tried to jerk them away, but he

119

held fast. "I know an innocent when I see one, and I could shoot myself because I hurt you. You know how the preacher talked yesterday about making excuses? Well, that's what I was doing when I was needling you. Trying to make myself feel better by making you look bad."

The last thing Annie had expected from Seneca Jones was blunt honesty, particularly coupled with repentance. She stared at him, very much aware of his hands encircling hers.

"I forgive you," she said again, this time in a very small voice. She decided true forgiveness required a frightening degree of intimacy.

"Thank you," he said quietly.

There was an awkward silence while Annie stared at the crease Seneca's hat had pressed into his shiny tousled hair. She'd never had a man kneeling at her feet before. She cleared her throat. "So what was your question?"

"Question?" He looked up, a naked vulnerability in his eyes that shot straight to her heart.

Oh, Lord! she begged. *Keep me safe!* "You said you asked Reverend Edwards a question."

"It had to do with getting out from under the wrath of God. You know, in the sermon yesterday morning."

Annie tried to remember. "I thought he was preaching about Thanksgiving." She laughed. "Funny how two people can listen to the same message and hear totally different things."

"I was watching you and Billy. You both seemed to be comforted by those verses, but they just made me mad. And then scared. And then sad. 'Cause I know how far away I am from being good enough to go to heaven."

"Seneca." Annie hesitated, blushing at the sound of his name coming out of her mouth. "You can't *be* good enough to get to heaven."

He scratched his head. "Yeah, that's what the preacher said. I don't quite get that yet, but if I spend enough time with you and Billy I'll eventually figure it out."

Annie knew how much courage it took for Seneca to admit his confusion, but something in his tone and the way he looked at her struck a chord of dismay beneath her breastbone. "This is awfully sudden, Seneca. You've known me for less than two days, and I'm not what you—I can't—" She floundered, wondering if she imagined the ardent expression in his eyes.

"Yes, you are what I think you are, Annie Fitzgerald. I know your brother Micah well. He chased off a band of Indians that cornered me on my second Pony Express run last spring. Once we got back to the fort, we spent a good bit of time together, and he bragged on his little sister and brother back home in Alabama. I thought he was making it up until I met you." He looked away. "I would never have kissed you—insulted you like that—if I'd known who you were. Then once I'd done it, something made me test you a little. To see if it could really be true."

"I was so awful to you," Annie whispered. It had never occurred to her before how powerful a witness for Christ her own actions could be.

"No, you weren't." He touched her chin, almost reverently. "I saw the same thing in your face that I see when Billy looks at me sometimes. Sort of a—a sorrow, I guess you'd call it." His voice lowered to a kind of fierceness. "I *hate* that look, Annie, and I'm not gonna put it there ever again."

"Are—are you saying you want to change to please *me?*" Annie asked incredulously. Her body was warm as toast, but she began to shiver violently.

"I know I'm not good enough for you now. But with God's help I'm going to straighten out. Quit cussing and flirting and drinking and gambling. And anything else that makes you unhappy."

"Seneca, you can't—oh, please don't say that!"

"I can do anything I put my mind to. You'll see." Seneca

squeezed her fingers and stood up. "Let me build up the fire, and I'll leave you alone to study or whatever you were doing. Cane's waiting for me to help him in the stable, so I've got to get back, anyway."

Annie watched helplessly as he stoked the fire, then picked up his hat and dropped it back on his head. With a smile and a little wave, he was out the door, leaving Annie seated on her "throne," feeling like the princess whose frog had just turned into the court jester.

"Oh, my." She put her hands to her mouth and gave a breathless little laugh. *"Oh, my."*

⌘

Seneca's "reformation" lasted through Wednesday, when he discovered that Peewee Malone had taken off toward Mud Flats with his best saddle.

Cane was the one who had saddled Peewee's horse. "He told me you wouldn't mind," the boy said, backing up a step when Seneca picked up a twenty-pound feed sack and chucked it at the tack room wall.

Seneca slammed his hand against the worktable in the barn, causing a pile of broken harnesses to jump. "How could you take his word for anything?" Seneca demanded. "The man would lie to his dying granny!" He let loose a string of cuss words that made Cane blink. "That saddle was made by Israel Landis himself! The best saddle maker in St. Joseph."

"I'm sorry, Seneca. I was just trying to help."

Uneasily, Seneca looked around to make sure Annie wasn't anywhere in earshot. "I know." He sighed. "Look, don't tell your sister. . . ." Cane wrinkled his forehead. "Never mind. You mucked the stalls yet?"

"Yes, sir."

"Don't call me *sir*."

"But Annie said—"

"Just—" Seneca tipped his hat back and looked at the ceiling. "Just don't. All right?"

"Yes, si—all right. Can I do anything else?"

"Naw. Doesn't school start this morning? Your sister will be expecting you." Seneca picked up his carbine rifle and cleaning kit and carried them into the bunkhouse, Cane trailing like a puppy. Seneca dropped into a straight chair by the fire and started to take the gun apart. He looked up when Cane stood there shifting from one foot to the other. "You still here?"

"Aw, school is for babies," Cane said, taking up the poker to violently stir the fire. Sparks jumped onto the rug.

"Here, quit that, you're gonna burn the bunkhouse down." Seneca hastily stood up and stomped out the sparks. "What's the matter with you, kid?"

Cane jammed his fingers into his back pockets and hunched his bony shoulders. "How old were you when you started riding the cattle trail?"

"Too young." Seneca sat down again and picked up the barrel of the rifle. He stuffed a swab into it with the steel rod. "Didn't have anybody who cared about me the way your sister cares for you."

"Were you an orphan too?"

Seneca nodded. "My folks were killed by Indians on the way to California when I was eight years old. Right outside of Seneca, Kansas, which is how I got my name. I finally ran away from the orphanage and tagged along with a bunch of cattlemen headed back to Texas."

"Texas?" Cane's face lit up. "After I ride the Pony awhile, I think I might go there. I hear there's horses all over in Texas."

"Horses and cows and not much else." Seneca propped the gun across his lap and began to polish the wood of the stock. "I got homesick for the prairie."

"Seems to me there ain't much up here but sky and grass," Cane muttered. "Ain't even no snow. Annie said it would snow."

Seneca gave him a droll look. "You want to see snow? Just wait a few days and you'll be so sick of snow you'll wish you were back in Alabama." Realizing he'd been neatly sidetracked, Seneca leveled a finger at the boy. "You do what your sister says and go on to school. Learning things will make you a better horseman."

"I don't see how that follows." Cane gave Seneca a mutinous look from under his brows. "You're doing all right without it. So's my brother, Micah."

Seneca sighed. He couldn't deny that he was perfectly happy with his life. And he could hardly blame the boy for not wanting to molder away in a classroom when most of the boys his age were out hunting or ice fishing on the river. "Tell you what. Go on to school and I'll take you hunting this afternoon."

"You will?" Cane grinned in delight; then his face fell. "I don't have a gun."

"I'll find you a gun. Now get to school."

⪜

Thwack! Ca-chunk!

The rhythmic sound had been thudding outside the school-room window behind her desk for the last twenty minutes, and Annie had had about all she could stand. She thought she knew what it was, and she was going to take care of it this instant. It was difficult enough to teach fractions, even without distractions.

"Students, I want all of you to get out your readers while I step outside for a few minutes."

Cane and Josiah McCabe looked at one another and snickered. Annie ignored them and pulled on her cloak and gloves. Taking a deep breath, she stepped outside into the snow that had fallen like a deep blanket during the night. She sank nearly up to her knees, soaking her skirt and her stockings. "Grrr," said Annie.

Stepping in a set of widely spaced boot tracks, she waded around to the back of the building. Sure enough, there was Seneca Jones, chopping away at an enormous pile of wood. He had finished a neat stack already.

"*What* do you think you're doing?" She planted her hands on her hips.

He paused with the ax high above his head, looked around, and gave her an engaging grin. "Annie! Is it recess already?"

"*No*, it's not recess! It's only nine o'clock. I'm trying my best to teach arithmetic, but you're making such a racket none of us can think!"

"Oh." The ax dropped to his side. He tipped his hat back. "I'm sorry. I figured with this snow you'd need lots of wood."

Annie's irritation vanished at his genuine chagrin. "We do. I mean, I appreciate you doing this, but could you come back when school's over?"

"Mr. McCabe has asked me to ride back to Summit station later today to deliver a telegram message to the keeper there. I wanted to get your wood chopped before I go."

"You're leaving?" Annie felt a stab of totally unnecessary disappointment. She strove to appear casual, but he must have taken it for eagerness.

He frowned. "I'll be out of your way 'til tomorrow morning."

"I didn't mean . . ." Annie sighed and clasped her hands behind her back. Who would have thought he could be this sensitive. "Seneca, what am I going to do with you?" A reluctant smile tugged at her lips.

He instantly grinned. "Invite me inside for cocoa?"

"How did you know—?"

"I saw Josiah toting it out of the house this morning. I can smell chocolate a mile off."

Annie tilted her head, trying not to laugh. "I suppose we could take a short recess." With a pang of guilt, she watched his face light. She really shouldn't encourage him.

"I'll have the boys finish your wood after school." He swung the ax one more time, leaving it stuck blade down in a thick piece of log.

Annie turned around to slog her way back to the front door but found herself scooped up and held above the snow drifts in Seneca's arms. She squealed and clutched his neck.

"Little thing like you could get stuck for days in snow like this," he said, his breath puffing above her head as he retraced his own steps.

"Put me down," Annie ordered breathlessly. "I'm already wet to the knees."

"When are you going to get some decent winter clothes?"

"When I—when I get paid."

"Must be hard to find boots that small."

Annie stuck out her foot in its down-at-heels high-button shoe. She looked up to find Seneca's eyes not on her feet but on her lips. Her heart skipped into her throat. "I had the older boys shovel the front walk. You can put me down."

"The steps might be slippery." He walked up them carefully and bent his knees to open the latch without dropping her.

But Annie popped Seneca on the shoulder with her free hand before he could get the door open. "Wait, Seneca."

He stopped, startled. "What?"

"You can't carry me in there like this. Can you imagine Evangeline not telling her mama?"

"What if she does?" He looked down at her, his mouth quirked.

"Seneca," she said, trying to keep her voice patient but insistent, "I could lose my job."

His mouth opened as if to argue; then he sighed and gently set her down. "I'm sorry. I didn't think." Then, with an irrepressible wink, he reached around her to open the door. "Howdy, boys and girls," he said cheerfully. "Look who I found making angels in the snow!"

The entire class looked around, and twenty-two mouths fell open as Seneca strode into the room behind their teacher. The students laughed and clapped their hands, while Annie blushed and whispered fiercely, "You're embarrassing me!"

"Seneca!" Evangeline McCabe, Annie's youngest student, jumped out of her seat and ran to Seneca with her arms high. He swung her up into his arms, smiling as she patted his wind-reddened cheeks with both hands. "You came to see me!"

"Sure did. I heard you had cocoa on the stove."

"Mama sended it." She squirmed to get down and did a little jig of excitement. "Miss Fitz said we could have it when we finish our 'rithmetic."

"Settle down, Evvie," Annie said mildly as she draped her outer garments over a chair by the stove to dry. "Everyone, fetch your cups from your lunch packs. Mr. Jones, why don't you read the children a story while I pour the cocoa?"

"I have a better idea," he replied, removing his hat and plopping it on Evvie's head. She giggled and whirled like a ballerina. "Since I'm the guest of honor—" he grinned when Annie rolled her eyes—"I think I should be read to."

"Oh, you do?" Annie shook her head. "Very well, Sir Lazy-bones. The children have been taking turns reading *The Pilgrim's Progress* aloud. Cane, it's your turn to begin, so you may give up your seat to Mr. Jones and stand here by the fire."

"Aw, Annie—I mean, Miss Fitzgerald—," he groaned at her reproving look, "do I have to read today?" His words were directed at his sister, but his gaze was on the loose-limbed rider standing hip-shot just inside the door.

Frowning, Annie was about to reply when Seneca ambled over to Cane's desk at the back of the room and jerked a thumb upward. "You do if you want to borrow my gun to go hunting. Don't want any ignorant hunters out on the prairie." Seneca walked over to pluck the dog-eared book from Annie's hand and opened it to a center page. After perusing it quickly, he handed it to Cane, who had reluctantly followed his hero to the front of the room. "Looks like a great story," said Seneca. "Let's hear it." He sauntered back to Cane's chair, sat down, and casually crossed one ankle over the other knee as if he spent every day of his life ensconced in the hallowed halls of academia.

While her students quietly lined up to have cocoa ladled into their tins, Annie listened to her brother stumble over John Bunyan's elegant, heavily spiritual prose. But her attention was woefully splintered by the presence of one charming, smooth-talking rider. How could he so easily manipulate people—herself included—with just a few words and a confident demeanor? It was downright frightening.

When the children had all been served, Annie filled her own cup and took it back to Seneca, who looked up with a smile and whispered, "Thanks." But he seemed engrossed in the adventures of Christian the pilgrim, Cane's reading having grown smoother and more expressive as he went along.

Annie returned to her chair, which she pulled close to the stove in order to let her skirts dry. They listened to Cane read for nearly an hour. When he began to get hoarse, Annie took pity on him and interrupted. "Surely Mr. Jones is ready to take over now."

But Seneca blinked, stretched, and jumped to his feet. "Nope, I've got to get over to Summit before dark. Which reminds me." He scanned the faces of the older boys along the back row. "You fellows need to build Miss Fitzgerald a woodshed and take turns getting to school early to chop for her. Who wants to start tomorrow?"

Josiah McCabe raised his hand. "I will, Seneca."

Not to be outdone, Cane volunteered for the next day, and before she could draw breath, Annie knew she'd have wood in the pile beside the front door every day for weeks to come. Bemused, she sat with her chin in her hands, watching as Seneca organized his troops.

"I'll be back tomorrow by noon," he said quietly, carefully placing his empty cup on her desk, before slipping out the door.

Annie reluctantly pulled her thoughts together and began to write spelling words on the blackboard, one list on the right for the smaller children, one on the left for the older crowd. How many m's were there in *tomorrow*? She paused with her back to the class, smiling ruefully to herself. How she was going to concentrate for the rest of the day was anybody's guess.

≻

Seneca's normal route was to Willow Island station, seventy-five miles to the west of Fort Kearny, where he would stay overnight, meet the eastbound Pony rider, and ride back for a ten-day rest.

Occasionally, however, Lloyd McCabe entrusted him with interim delivery of local messages that arrived by telegraph. Fort Kearny currently being the end of the telegraph line before Salt Lake City, news was fresh and exciting. Political dickering over the slavery issue as new states were added to the Union made improved communication with the west coast critical in nature. If California came in as a slave state, the balance of power in Washington could shift irreversibly.

The owners and operators of the Pony Express took their place in the political scheme very seriously. Determined to win a multi-thousand-dollar government contract for a new central mail route, Russell, Majors, and Waddell had poured money none of them had into the operation of the Pony Express—mostly, Seneca knew, to prove that the route was just as viable as the longer but more dependable southern route.

Most of the riders couldn't care less themselves about the political intrigue that fueled their jobs. Seneca, however, was aware of the historical significance of his last ride west, carrying the news of Lincoln's election. Seneca's stint in the southern state of Texas had not changed his conviction that the United States of America should stay just that—*united*.

He wondered if southern-born and -reared Annie had any opinions on the subject. He'd ask her about it tomorrow when he saw her again. He'd never before wondered what went on inside a woman's brain; he assumed all they thought about was snaring a husband and spoiling a man's fun. But there was something about Annie that invited conversation, a brightness and softness to those gray eyes that drew him to protect her and share himself with her.

As he carefully guided Becky along the familiar wagon tracks to Summit, Seneca fingered the telegram in his pocket. Regular Pony Express mail was carried in one of the four locked cantinas attached to the *mochila*, which was thrown over the saddle and sat upon by the rider. But McCabe, a sober expression drawing down his heavy brows, had handed Seneca this message and had urged him to get it to Summit before dark and return with an answer on the morrow.

He hoped it didn't carry more news of impending war.

God, he began uneasily, looking up at the overcast sky, *if you're up there listening, I'm sure you've got an ear out for Annie. And maybe you even care about me. So would you take care of whatever's in this note and give me a chance to make up to you for all my mistakes? Some good news would go a long way in proving to me you're real.*

He leaned forward and urged Becky faster with his heels. The sooner he got to Summit, the sooner he could get back to Annie.

CHAPTER 4

GIRL, he's playing you like a one-string banjo," said Martha McCabe, as she folded a huge lump of sourdough bread dough in half and thumped it a good whack with one fist. "Don't you go moonin' over Seneca Jones, or you'll wind up an old maid with a broken heart."

Annie, who was supervising Evangeline's kneading of her own bit of dough, wiped a smudge of flour off the child's button nose and sighed deeply. "I know. But I don't seem to have any control over my feelings, Martha."

"Nobody said you could control your feelings. It's your actions you got to watch out for."

Annie squirmed on her kitchen stool. "He hasn't done anything really outrageous in over a week. And he said he wants to take me to church tomorrow."

"Going to church doesn't make you a Christian any more than standing in the kitchen makes you a soup ladle. And you know it." Martha picked up her rolling pin and gestured for emphasis. "Don't think you're going to marry him and then change him. It doesn't work that way."

Remembering the floating sensation of being held above the snow in Seneca's arms, Annie's heart pinched painfully. "Of course, you're right." She sighed. "It's just that Cane's never been such a good student." She absently pinched off a bit of the sweet dough and popped it into her mouth. "Who's Becky, anyway?"

Martha gave her an odd look. "Why, you know that's his horse's name."

"Yes, but he said . . . there's some girl he used to know . . ."

"I don't know of anyone except—" Martha suddenly laughed. "His mother's name was Rebekah, I believe."

"Ooh, that—!" Annie picked up Evvie's dough and squished it in her fist. "I never knew such a tease in my life!"

"That's exactly what I'm talking about," declared Martha, planting floury fists on her ample hips. "You can't tell when he's serious and when he's pulling your leg."

Evvie looked up with enormous blue eyes. "Teacher, if Seneca pulls your leg does that mean you're gonna get married?"

Annie met Martha's sparkling hazel eyes and fell to kneading the little lump of dough with fierce concentration. She couldn't speak for fear of bursting into giggles.

Evvie leaned closer to Annie, tugging her sleeve. "Are you gonna answer me, or is it none o' my biz-a-niss?"

Laughter escaping, Annie pulled Evangeline onto her lap and tickled her. "If I ever need to worm information out of anyone, I'll certainly call on you, Miss Nosy Rosy."

"My name's not Rosy; it's Evvie," giggled the child, squirming down from Annie's arms. "Mama, can we bake my bread now?"

When all six loaves of bread, including Evvie's little biscuit-shaped lump, were set near the stove to rise, Martha dusted her hands and shooed Annie and Evangeline from the kitchen. "While I get the Saturday wash started, why don't you ladies take my coffee grinder down to the blacksmith to get it fixed and see if my big kettle's ready to bring home yet."

Annie helped Evangeline fasten her little red coat, then swung her new dark blue cloak around her own shoulders. Lloyd McCabe had advanced her a small sum, enabling her to buy the hooded cloak, a pair of heavy boots, and a length of blue-and-brown plaid wool for a winter dress. She and Martha had spent the evenings after supper cutting and fitting the fabric to Annie's petite figure, then used the time together sewing by the fire to become better acquainted. By the end of the week, the two women, despite nearly ten years' difference in age, were fast friends.

As she and Evvie stepped onto the front porch, Annie reflected that Martha probably knew everything there was to know about each of the Pony Express riders and stock tenders under her husband's supervision. It wasn't that she was a Nosy Rosy; Martha simply cared enough about people to really listen when they talked.

Annie had found herself sharing her own intimate thoughts and concerns with her new friend. She didn't fear betrayed confidences, because Martha never spoke out of turn. Therefore, her warning about Seneca certainly gave Annie pause.

Evangeline, on the other hand, was a fount of information, whether one wanted it or not. As they walked the short distance from the boardinghouse to the blacksmith shop, swinging hands, Evangeline dipped sideways to look up at Annie. "You know what, Teacher?"

"What Evvie?"

"I bet if you was to marry Seneca he wouldn't be so sad."

"Sad?" Annie frowned and squeezed Evvie's mittened hand. "What makes you think Seneca is sad?"

"I was up in the loft playing with the kittens when he rode in yesterday, and I heard him tell Billy he was gonna get drunk."

Annie stopped, bone frozen by a chill that had nothing to do with the wind all but pushing them down the street.

"Seneca don't never get drunk 'less he's real sad," Evvie added, tugging Annie along. "Come on, we're almost there!"

Annie followed, her brain whirling with questions. She had noticed that the usually garrulous Seneca was very quiet at the evening meal last night. And he had disappeared with three other Pony Express employees afterward, with barely a glance in Annie's direction. She had put it down to weariness after a hard and fast ride. But now that she thought about it, it was past noon and she hadn't seen him at all today. Had he been sleeping off a hangover?

Annie had seen enough abusive drunks in her short life that she had no intention of yoking herself to a man with an addiction to strong liquor. Furthermore, Scripture says "Be not drunk with wine, but be filled with the Holy Spirit."

Martha had warned her that Seneca had "bad habits." The thought of those blazing blue eyes blurred with drunken confusion, a stagger in the lazy, long-legged swagger, saddened Annie and made her almost physically ill.

As she and Evangeline battled the wind and dodged drifts of snow that had blown across the boardwalk after being cleared by shop owners earlier in the day, Annie's temper began a slow boil. How dare Seneca Jones talk of "straightening up"—make deliberate assaults on her heart—and worst of all, set himself up as a role model for young boys like Cane and Josiah—when he had no intention of holding himself to any sort of moral standard?

With the coffee grinder clanking against her skirt in agitated rhythm, Annie skidded along the walkway, heedless of Evangeline's squeals of delight every time they skated across a patch of ice. Annie prayed angrily with every step. *Just wait until I see him, Lord. Didn't you say to be righteous in anger? I'm so glad I never agreed to let him court me.*

Suddenly it occurred to her that Seneca had never actually *asked* to court her. He had teased her, picked her up in his arms, even kissed her, but never said one word of serious commitment. But he would have, she was sure, if she'd given him half a chance.

Wouldn't he?

"Teacher, you passed the blacksmith shop!" Evvie protested, yanking on Annie's hand.

She came to a precipitate halt and looked over her shoulder. "Oh, fudge!" she muttered and turned around to retrace her steps.

Unfortunately, her boot heel found an icy patch that cost her her balance and sent her sliding downhill on her derriere, the coffee grinder scalloping exquisite designs in the snow-lined walk.

Evvie shrieked with laughter and hopped after her like a red-coated snow bunny. "Teacher, wait! I wanna slide, too!"

Arms flailing, Annie skidded helplessly and managed to stop only when she plowed feetfirst into a snowdrift directly in front of the blacksmith shop. Her cloak had flapped open like bird wings, her skirt was rucked up to her knees, and her black worsted stockings—as well as the seat of her drawers—were frosted with damp snow.

Laughing hysterically, she tried to get up but couldn't find purchase for her hands on the ice. She managed to turn over onto her stomach and push to her knees but slipped again and fell with an "Oomph!"

"Evvie," she gasped, "come give Teacher a hand."

But though she heard Evangeline giggling, it wasn't a little red mitten she saw dangling before her nose; it was a large, fringed, buckskin glove. Beyond it was a pair of well-made snakeskin boots. They looked just like Seneca's boots.

"Take my hand, Princess," he said. "But you might want to let go of the coffee grinder first."

Humiliated, Annie dropped the handle of the device and reached down to make sure her limbs were properly covered. How much had he seen?

"Annie, you're going to catch pneumonia if you don't get up out of that snowdrift." His voice was amused and tender. "I'm not looking."

"Grrrr," said Annie. But she had no choice. She let him grab both her hands. He pulled her to her feet in one smooth motion and balanced her with an arm around her waist when she nearly toppled again.

"You seem to be having a hard time adjusting to the snow," Seneca observed, tucking her against his side as he guided her carefully through the doorway of the smithy.

She looked up, and his eyes sparkled beneath the brim of his hat. He didn't look sad at all to her.

"I'll get used to it," she said. Relieved to see that Evvie had already skipped inside and stood as close to the forge as Tab Gorman, the smith, would allow, Annie took the coffee grinder from Seneca and stepped out from under his arm. The smithy was warm, dimly lit, and smelled of horses, grease, and metal. Annie hadn't had a reason to come here before, so she looked around with interest, taking in the long worktable on one end. On the wall above it were displayed the hammers, tongs, clamps, and other tools of the blacksmith trade unidentifiable to her untrained eye.

She didn't notice that Seneca had disappeared until a sudden burst of male laughter from the far end of the long, barnlike building jerked her head around. One of the voices sounded extremely young, almost like Cane's. He was supposed to be helping the McCabe boys collect enough buffalo chips to provide fuel for the boardinghouse and station through Sunday, which was of course a day of rest.

Annie edged past the forge and anvil, where the massively built Mr. Gorman worked patiently to form horseshoes for Seneca's horse. Peering into the shadows illuminated by a couple of kerosene lamps set on barrelheads in the corner, Annie tried to identify the four men seated on an odd collection of chairs and stools around a low plank table. It was obvious that a card game was in progress.

The blond head of a fifth man, standing with his back against the wall behind the table, Annie easily recognized as Seneca's. She had barely taken note of the cigar clamped between his white teeth when she realized that his gloved hand rested on the shoulder of her little brother! Cane held a handful of cards, the backs of which sported risqué pictures of ladies of dubious gentility. Cane was hatless, flushed, and seemed to have been seized by a sudden and violent fit of coughing.

Horrified, Annie rushed to her brother and pounded him on the back. "Cane! Sweetheart, are you all right?"

Tears streaming down his cheeks, Cane gasped a huge lungful of air and fell to coughing again.

Annie glared up at Seneca, who had stepped back to observe Cane's asphyxiation without any noticeable signs of distress. He plucked the cigar out of his mouth and blew a puff of smoke over her head.

"Do something!" she demanded, angrily waving the smoke away.

"Short of pumping him with the bellows, I think he's gonna have to recover on his own," Seneca observed mildly. "Just move back and give him room to breathe."

Annie looked to the remaining three card players for help. She recognized a couple of stablehands and Peewee Malone, who had returned just that morning from his Pony run.

At her pleading look, Peewee wiped the grin off his face, folded his cards, and scooped up the rest of the offensive deck, stuffing it in his shirt pocket. "He'll be OK, Miss Fitzgerald. Just a little too much—" he caught Seneca's straight gaze and faltered—"too much cigar smoke."

Since Cane did indeed seem to be recovering on his own, his breathing returning to normal, Annie's concern seesawed into rage. "What on earth are you men thinking?" She spoke to them all, but her gaze found Seneca. There was a slight curl to his mouth and an unreadable glint in his blue eyes, though he did not defend himself. "How dare you corrupt a young boy with your gambling and indecent pictures and—and—filthy weed!"

Cane looked around at her and managed to croak, "Annie, Seneca didn't—"

"Didn't know you'd be sticking your dainty nose outside the house on your day off," Seneca interrupted, flicking the ash off the end of his cigar. He put his hand on Cane's shoulder again—hard.

"Ow!" the boy yelped, flinching.

Annie momentarily forgot her other grievances. "Cane, have you hurt your shoulder?"

"Nuh-uh," he said, casting a "help me" look up at Seneca. "I just ran into a door in the dark this morning. In the stable," he added, at her skeptical look.

Suspicions thoroughly roused, Annie frowned at Seneca, who sighed and shook his head. "Time to fess up," he advised Cane.

Reluctantly, Cane pulled his right arm out of his coat sleeve and unbuttoned his shirt enough to slide it off his shoulder.

Annie gasped. A livid purple-and-blue bruise covered Cane's collarbone from his neck to his shoulder and halfway down his chest. "What on earth?" She reached to gently touch him but paused when he ducked away from her and yanked his shirt and jacket back into place. Again her gaze found Seneca. Somehow she knew this was his fault. "Who did this?" she demanded.

"Not who. What." Cane stood up between her and Seneca, and Annie suddenly realized that her brother was looking her in the eye. When had he gotten so tall? "It's just the kickback of the gun I've been using. Seneca's been teaching me to hunt. You knew that."

"Yes, but—I didn't know it was going to knock your arm half-way off. Surely you could find a less dangerous gun—"

"Must be a buffalo gun to make that big a bruise," interjected Peewee, shooting a malicious look at Seneca. "I got a big 30-aught shot-gun that—" He stopped, eyes narrowed. "Come to think of it, I haven't seen that gun since I got back! Jones, you didn't steal my gun while I was gone and let that wet-nose kid play with it, did you?"

Annie watched Seneca hook a thumb in his belt and smile lazily. "You mean the way you stole my best saddle and came back with it all to pieces because you didn't fasten the rigging rings right? No, as a matter of fact, Billy loaned us his deer rifle."

Peewee was now on his feet. Annie nervously stepped back, pulling Cane with her. Seneca was perfectly calm of face, but she could sense tension in the set of his broad shoulders and the whiteness of his knuckles. There were evidently deep-seated resentments between these two men.

Lord, she prayed, *please don't let anybody get hurt. What can I do to bring peace?*

"You're a liar," said Peewee deliberately, smiling a nasty smile when Seneca's eyes narrowed to flinty slits.

"What? That you took my saddle without asking, or that nobody messed with your two-bit gun?" Seneca jerked his head at Cane. "Go see how Becky's shoes are coming along, will you, kid?"

Cane opened his mouth to refuse, but a look from Seneca sent him slouching reluctantly away from the table.

Peewee let loose a string of expletives that made Annie's eyes widen.

Seneca glanced at Annie. "Malone, there's a lady present."

Peewee didn't seem to care who his audience was. "I saw that saddle at Landis's first, Jones, and you know it. He didn't have no right to sell it out from under me."

"You'd just blown all your money in a card game, and I happened to be flush." Seneca shrugged. "You lost out."

"Well, I'm sick of losing to you. If Miss Fitzgerald don't want to see your pretty face smashed in, she'd better sashay over to the other end of the building." Malone executed a sarcastic bow in Annie's direction. "Maybe then she won't be so excited about kissing you—"

Annie screamed when Seneca's fist launched, exploding with a crack of both knuckles and jaw. Blood spurted everywhere.

"Stop them!" Annie exclaimed to nobody in particular, but the three stablehands immediately took sides, two rooting for Seneca, the other evidently a pal of Peewee. She looked around for help, the sound of flesh connecting with flesh and the iron smell of blood turning her stomach. To her relief, Tab Gorman, alerted by Cane, had thrown down his hammer and nails and come running. The fight was over in seconds, though it seemed to Annie to have lasted for hours.

She stood with her fists knotted in her skirt, watching as Peewee fell back against the table, bleeding from the nose, his dislocated jaw already swelling and purpling. The blacksmith did a quick once-over, handed the short-statured rider a less than pristine rag to sop his nose, and then turned to Annie. "Are you all right, Miss Fitzgerald?"

She was shaking like a blancmange. "Never mind me. Shouldn't we notify the law?"

Gorman scratched his wide, flat nose. "No cause to put anybody in jail, I reckon. They was just working out a difference of opinion. Seneca, you want me to call the doc?"

"Not unless you want him to come take care of this barnyard fowl," he said with a contemptuous jerk of his head toward Peewee, who gave a muffled snarl. Seneca laughed. His face was perfectly white, except for the bruising, and he held his right hand cradled in his left, but he managed a short bow in Annie's direction. "Miss Fitzgerald," he said through his teeth, "please forgive this barbaric display of ill manners." His eyes promptly rolled back in his head, and he crumpled in a heap at Annie's feet.

❧

Seneca came to in Doc Tucker's little office, the pain in his right hand making him wish he could go back to the blessed darkness of oblivion. Then he heard Annie's soft, drawling voice and wished he were dead and out of his misery. He kept his eyes shut.

"Is it broken?" she asked, referring, he assumed, to his hand.

"Appears to have messed up several fingers and cracked his

knuckles," Doc replied in what Seneca deemed to be entirely too jovial a tone.

"Poor boy," Annie said, gently brushing the hair back from Seneca's forehead. He decided he would endure worse pain than this for her sweet touch.

"These young bucks and their arguments," Doc said gruffly. "Bring it all on themselves and waste my time. At least they didn't get to guns this time."

"G-guns?" Annie repeated. "They've fought with guns?"

"Well, not these particular two. But it happens all the time."

Seneca decided it was time to make his presence known. He opened his eyes.

Doc grunted. "Well, if it ain't Lazarus come back to life," he said, referring to the biblical character Jesus raised from the dead. He examined Seneca's pupils. "How you feelin', boy?"

"Like I rammed my hand into a cast-iron wall," Seneca muttered. He sat up, avoiding Annie's eyes. He could tell she was watching him anxiously. How embarrassing to have fainted like a schoolgirl right in front of her. "But at least I can still ride." He examined his misshapen hand, which Doc had wrapped with bandages and packed in ice.

A dubious expression on his craggy face, Doc sat back, took off his spectacles, and began to polish them. "I reckon you could, but it's gonna hurt some 'til them bones knit. I pushed 'em back together best I could. I can give you a dose of laudanum—or a little trip over to the Lucky Lady for a fifth of whiskey would help."

"No. I can stand it." Seneca finally allowed himself to look at Annie. In her wide eyes he saw endless questions. "I don't drink anymore."

Doc shrugged and got to his feet with an arthritic grunt. "All right, but you ought to at least sit still for a while. Don't want you keelin' over in the street." He looked at Annie, who had also risen as if to leave. "Can you keep an eye on him for me, Miss Fitzgerald?

I got to walk back to the smithy to check on Seneca's punchin' bag." With a twitch of his gray mustache that passed for a vinegary smile, Doc picked up his black bag, jammed his hat on his head, and hobbled out of the office.

Annie reluctantly sat down again. Seneca noticed that her bonnet was hanging down her back, and her russet hair had escaped from its snood to fall in coppery waves around her face. She stared at her gloveless hands clasped in her lap.

Seneca cleared his throat. "How's Peewee?"

Big gray eyes lifted to soak him in remorse. "His face will never be the same," she said tightly.

"Wasn't too pretty to start with." He tried for a joke, but she bit her lip and looked down again. "Annie." He sighed, the throb of his hand forgotten. "I didn't steal his gun. He *did* take my saddle, which I paid for this summer, fair and square, in St. Joseph." When she turned her face, he could see the delicate working of her throat above the high curved collar of her dress. *Oh, God, don't let her cry.* He tried again. "Peewee insulted you. I couldn't let him get away with that."

"What he said was true. I behaved like a strumpet, allowing you to kiss me in the middle of the street." She blinked, and one tear rolled loose.

"That was not your fault! It was just a joke—" Seneca stopped, Annie's white face telling him he'd just stepped wrong.

She jerked to her feet again. "I know it was a joke for you," she choked, "but it was my first—"

"Annie, don't leave, let me explain—" *Heaven, help me,* he prayed. "Please, Annie . . ."

She hovered in the doorway, her back to him. "How can you possibly explain what you've done to my brother and me? You've drawn Cane into gambling and—and licentiousness. You've ruined my reputation—" She whirled, fixed him with blazing eyes.

"And what you've done to yourself! I heard about your drinking binge last night."

"What are you talking about? I told you I quit drinking!"

"Evvie said—"

"Evvie said what? You'd take the word of a *five-year-old* over mine?"

"She was up in the loft when you told Billy you were going to go get drunk."

"I said I *felt* like it, but I never—"

"Didn't you tell me you'd be back by noon yesterday? I waited—couldn't help wondering . . ." Annie bit her lip.

Seneca stared at her, an absurd resentment warring with an equally ridiculous jubilation that his actions mattered so much to her. "You wouldn't believe me if I told you," he muttered.

"You're right. I probably wouldn't. Seneca, you mix me up like a—like a deck of cards! You're dangerous, and I can't trust you. I've got to get Cane out from under your influence before it's too late."

She was openly crying now, and Seneca felt like joining her. But he'd had enough humiliation for one day.

"Fine," he gritted. "I've been condemned and hanged without a trial. See you later, Princess." He flopped back onto Doc's examining table and slammed his eyes shut. He winced when the front door crashed hard enough to make the table vibrate.

"Annie," he whispered. "Oh, Lord God, what have I done?"

❧

That night Annie let herself out the front door of the church, where she had just spent a quiet hour in earnest prayer. She wrapped her arms around a column on the church's porch, resting her forehead against the cold wood. She had never felt so young and unsure in her life, even while she had been bearing sole responsibility for her parents' burial.

Decisions weighed heavily on her tonight—mainly how to deal with Cane. Martha and Lloyd, bless them, had agreed that the Pony Express riders' bunkhouse might not after all be the most suitable environment for an impressionable youngster and had suggested that Cane move in with Josiah and Daniel. Lloyd had also offered to keep a fatherly eye on Cane.

Cane had resented the slur on his manhood and protested loudly, but Lloyd had advised Annie to be both firm and patient. "Boys will be boys, Annie," he'd said, "but you want to nip defiance in the bud."

She stood now in the frozen blackness of the Nebraska night, tipping her head back to scan the limitless expanse of the heavens beyond the walls of the stockade.

"Oh, Jesus, are you there?" she whispered. "I trust you with my life. But this adventure is not going well. Cane hates me. And Micah's gone. And I—" she faltered as a star winked at her, almost mockingly—"I think I'm in love with Seneca. Because if I weren't, his actions wouldn't hurt me so much." Shame burned in her cheeks. "How can I love a man like Seneca Jones? Do you love him too? That's a silly question. I know you do. So would you save him, Lord? Not for me, but for his sake, and for the sake of Jesus who died for him."

She hugged the post, feeling lonelier than the distant moon and empty of tears. Empty of everything.

"Please, Lord."

CHAPTER 5

THANKSGIVING came and went, while Annie daily fed reading, writing, and arithmetic into young minds already full of mischief and imagination. She especially delighted in her students' coming awake to the world outside the stockade walls. The arrival of news articles from California made the boys wild with gold fever; catalogs had the girls sighing over fashions back East; and news from the South sparked lively discussions about states' rights, unity in government, and slavery.

"One day Nebraska will be a state, too, and you-all will be the ones making decisions about how things are run," Annie told them one afternoon in mid-December.

The blank looks she got made her sigh. At the moment, sledding and skating were much higher priorities than civics lessons. She closed her book and stood up with a smile. "But meantime, let's enjoy the break in the weather and go home early!"

Loud cheers greeted this announcement, of course, and Annie soon found herself alone in a deserted classroom. She erased the blackboard, smiling over Evangeline's crooked script version of Ephesians 5:1-2: "Be ye therefore followers of God, as dear children; and walk in love, as Christ also hath loved us." She was a bright little thing, already reading well above her age level, but neatness was low on her list of priorities.

Annie stacked her books precisely in the center of her desk in the order she would need them tomorrow. She put the essays she had just collected for grading in a portfolio to take home.

Home. A tiny room in a boardinghouse. No kitchen or parlor to call her own. Just a bed, washstand and chest, with a hook behind a curtain for her two dresses.

No family except Cane and Micah, who was somewhere miles away on the Nebraska prairie.

No husband.

As she opened the stove to bank the fire so the coals would live through the night, Annie swallowed against a sudden lump of tears. Since she had become part of the community inside the fort, there were several men paying court to her. Marriageable young women were in such short supply in a military post that she could have long since attached herself if she so desired.

But she did not desire. She wanted a man with the vitality and joy and chivalry of Seneca Jones. She wanted Seneca, she admitted to herself and to the Lord.

But she did not want his undisciplined approach to God. She did not want to wonder what he was up to at all hours of the night. She gave the fire a desolate jab with the poker, making it flame again despite her intention of putting it to rest.

Lord, I'm just like this fire. Just when I think I've forgotten him, something reminds me of his eyes or his smile, and it starts all over again.

"I saw the kids running loose early, so I came to walk you home."

She turned, and there he was, just like he was every day when he wasn't gone on a run. He made sure she didn't have a chance to overlook him. After the fight with Peewee, Lloyd McCabe had gotten the two of them together and made them shake hands. There could be no strife in such a close-knit enterprise as the Pony Express. Both men had apologized to Annie in subdued voices for

146

distressing her. She had accepted, hoping for a more personal word from Seneca.

He had since behaved as if the fistfight had never happened. And when he spoke to Annie, it was in a deferential tone that was somehow more distressing than any number of unasked-for kisses.

She would have to give him credit, though, for honoring her request that he stay away from Cane. He took care of his job at the station, rode when he was required to, and looked after Annie with a quiet solicitousness that filled her with despair because she could not trust it.

"You didn't have to come for me," she said, swinging her cloak over her shoulders and picking up her portfolio. "It's not even dark outside." Her treacherous heart banged against her ribs when he took her elbow to make sure she didn't slip on the hard-packed snow.

He smiled down at her. "I'm glad you let them out early. They'll be skating and sledding down the bluff out onto the river."

She wistfully shaded her eyes against the glare of the sun on the diamond-bright snow and listened to the shouts and whistles and giggles of the children running down to the river. "I never learned to skate."

"Me either. Kind of hard to do on horseback."

They both laughed at the mental picture of Becky slip-sliding across a frozen pond, then walked on in companionable silence.

At least Annie assumed it was companionable until she caught Seneca casting her a troubled sideways glance. She lifted her chin. *I'm not going to ask him what's wrong.* Despite her disappointment in him, she longed to know his heart. But Seneca was more dangerous than any prairie fire.

Suddenly his gloved hand slid from her elbow to her wrist. "Come this way, Annie." He tugged her behind him down a cleared path between the parsonage and the dry goods store. It led into what was, during the warmer months, Jens Nordemann's cornfield. Now the dry stalks stuck up like frosty coatracks, which Seneca and Annie dodged as they plowed through the lumpy white-covered earth.

"Where are we going?" she panted, struggling to step in his tracks without tumbling headfirst into a drift.

"You'll see."

Moments later they reached the edge of a garden, which gave onto an open snow-covered field. Beyond were the wooded bluffs diving down to the icy Platte River below. Annie stared in wonder at the beauty of the scene, one gloved hand to her mouth. The one Seneca was not holding.

She could see the children some way down the river, cavorting in the snow and on the ice, their laughter ringing like music in the distance. Across the river, beyond the cottonwoods and willows dripping with tendrils of ice, the endless prairie stretched into a cerulean sky. Annie shivered at its purity, its coldness, and its unbreakable distance.

She looked and looked, until Seneca squeezed her hand.

"Are you too cold? We can go back now."

"No . . ." She looked at him reluctantly. The tenderness in his eyes took her off guard. "Oh, Seneca."

"You are the most beautiful woman I've ever seen," he said simply. "You probably think I say that regularly." He shrugged and looked away. "Maybe I used to. But I never met anybody like you before. I never wanted to be good before, to do right and please God. I've seen how the other men look at you, and it makes me do crazy things. Like lighting into Peewee that time." A grin tugged at his mouth. "I wasn't mad about the saddle so much as I was mad about him sitting by you in church that Sunday."

"Seneca . . ."

"No, let me finish." He chewed the inside of his cheek as if thinking and jiggled her hand. "Boy, this is hard. I'm gonna have to ask you to wait for me a little while, because I don't have a house, and I can't afford to support both you and Cane, and I know you want him to—"

"Seneca!" Annie jerked her hand away in astonishment. "Are you asking me to marry you?"

"Well, sure."

Her mouth fell open as she stared into eyes as pure blue as the sky, full of hope and tenderness and everything she'd ever wanted to see in the face of the man she loved.

But it was all wrong.

"But I don't know you!" she whispered. "You tease and joke and carry me around and k-kiss me, but you won't let me see what's really inside you." He frowned, but she blundered on, dying inside. "Something has been bothering you since you got back from that trip to Summit station. Maybe you *didn't* get drunk that night, but if you even talked about it there must have been—"

"I'd just heard some rumors," he said easily, stepping back from her. But his expression was veiled again. "Nothing you need to worry about."

"Oh, I see." Annie did see. She folded her arms inside her cloak. "Seneca Jones, you are afraid. You're afraid somebody's going to get past that cocky facade and realize you're not king of the world. So you don't open up to anybody. Not me, not the preacher, and certainly not God." She reached for him and shoved at his chest. "Well thank you very much, but I don't want half a man or half a marriage. I love you and I want it all!" she shouted. Her voice dropped and carried clearly in the crisp winter air. "Or nothing."

She turned and walked with as dignified a tread as she could muster through the deep snow. Back to the boardinghouse. Back to warmth.

Back to emptiness.

༈

Seneca wasn't drunk.

No, he assured himself, he was only slightly corned.

He left the back room of the Gold Digger, where he'd been playing poker since midnight, and wandered outside for a breath of fresh air. The inside of his nose instantly froze, but when he reached to pull up his muffler, he realized he'd left it in the saloon, along with his hat.

Muttering to himself, he fumbled in his shirt pocket for a cigar and stuck it between his teeth. He tried for several minutes to light it, then gave up and simply rolled it around in his mouth as he meandered down the street.

Eventually he was going to have to go back to the bunkhouse and go to sleep. But he wanted to make good and sure he wouldn't somehow run into *her* before he did.

Afraid? He would laugh if the idea weren't so ludicrous. Afraid of whom? A little pint-sized, redheaded Alabama schoolteacher named Annie Fitzgerald? *Ha!* The day he was afraid of a woman would be the day . . .

"She loves me." He said it out loud and stopped, swaying, still staggered by the sound of those words. *I asked her to marry me. What else does she want?*

He looked around, as if to discover the answer to his own question, and found himself in front of the church. Craning his neck backward so he could see the purity of the cross on the roof outlined against the starry velvet sky, he whispered it again, "What else does she want?"

"*I want it all . . . half a man, half a marriage . . .*" Annie's words tried to find purchase in his murky brain, but it was as if some demonic force stole their import away. Tired of trying, he lurched forward and wrapped his arms around one of the porch columns. Security. The world stopped reeling, and he slid to the ground.

God. He knew that some of Annie's problem was wrapped up in

God. Religion was a woman's concern—he'd decided that a long time ago. What it had to do with a man and a woman falling in love with one another he had yet to figure out. He'd tried being good to please Annie, and the result was nothing but trouble. Nobody appreciated his efforts, least of all the object of his affection.

"God, what do you think of me?" he asked, half facetiously, looking up at the entrance to the sanctuary. All was quiet, except for the faint tinkle of music from the saloon.

"Seneca!"

He almost thought it was the Almighty answering audibly. Then he realized somebody had grabbed his shoulder and said his name again. An agonized adolescent whisper.

"Josiah!" Seneca said. "What're you doin' out this time o' night?"

"Seneca, you gotta go get him!" Josiah's round face, white and scared, swam into Seneca's vision. "I told him not to do it, but he went anyway, and he took the preacher's mule!"

"Who? What are you talkin' about?"

"Cane! He said he was gonna break into Ardis Towne's woodshed."

Seneca's stomach, already queasy, took a dive and roll. He didn't have to ask what the attraction was in that shed. Everybody knew old Ardis had a private stash of homemade corn liquor that would take the paint off the side of a barn. It was cheaper than saloon stock and convenient for men whose wives wouldn't let them anywhere near the Gold Digger.

"Josiah, you need to go get your pa." Seneca knew he wasn't in any shape to ride clear out to Ardis's place.

The boy shook his head so hard his ears fairly flapped. "Nuh-*uh*! Pa'd skin me alive for bein' out this late."

With an exasperated sigh, Seneca extended a hand. "All right. Help me up, then go get into bed. You boys ever pull a stunt like this again, and I'll personally skin you *both* alive."

"Phew! Thanks, Seneca." Josiah tugged Seneca to his feet, then darted down the alleyway from which he'd appeared. A moment later, Seneca saw him flit across the street and fade into the shadows beside the boardinghouse.

Seneca shook his head and rubbed his bleary eyes. He wished he were going home to bed himself. It had been a long night.

Apparently it wasn't over yet.

>

Annie was wakened from a sound sleep by a muffled thump, as of a body hitting the floor, just outside her room. The thump was followed by a soft, agitated knock upon her door and a tense whisper.

"Annie! Open up—I need you!"

Cane. What was he doing up at this hour?

Struggling out from under the covers, her feet hit the icy floor, and she fumbled for the flannel dressing gown flung across the end of her bed. Gray light seeped through the gingham curtains at the single window. An hour or so before dawn, Annie surmised.

She yanked open the door and gasped.

"Shhh!" Cane grabbed her arm and clapped his hand across her mouth.

Wide-eyed, Annie looked down. In the semidark hallway Seneca lay facedown upon the floor at her feet, his hands clenched into fists above his head. The seat of his jeans was torn and bloody, his legs slightly drawn up in obvious pain. Horrified, her gaze went back to Cane, who suddenly broke into silent sobs, tears pouring down his red, dirty face.

Her brain froze for half a moment while she pictured all the wild and violent things that could have brought about such an awful scene. She blinked, then bent to gently touch Seneca's rumpled hair and feel for a pulse in his neck. She nearly fainted with relief when it throbbed against her fingers.

"Cane," she said quietly, continuing to stroke Seneca's head as she looked up. "Listen to me. Quit crying now. You've got to help me get him off the floor, then go get Doc Tucker." Cane only knuckled his eyes. "You hear me?" she said more sharply.

Her brother hiccuped and nodded.

Between them they managed to get Seneca into Annie's room, where they laid him facedown on the bed. He gave a muffled groan, then relaxed. He had fainted.

"Don't you want to know what happened?" Cane could hardly get the words out because his breath hitched on every word.

She gave him a grim look as she moved to her washbasin to wet a rag. "Later. Go for the doctor."

Annie had made Seneca as comfortable as possible while still keeping her eyes from the area of his wound. She had also quietly wakened Martha McCabe, because she knew this whole situation was more than she could handle on her own.

Martha wasted no time on reproaches or questions, which Annie would in any case have found unanswerable. Clad in a surprisingly frilly pink dressing gown, her dark hair hanging in a braided tail down her back, Martha took one look at Seneca's recumbent form and shooed Annie from the room. "Send the doctor in right away," she instructed before firmly shutting the door in Annie's face.

Annie paced for fifteen minutes, wringing her hands, then finally thought to build a fire in the family sitting room. Hot water might be needed. Dawn spread fingers of gold across the hearth rug. She was sitting alone by the fire, rocking furiously, wondering why Martha didn't come out and tell her if Seneca was dead or alive, when Cane burst in, the doctor stumping behind him.

"He's in Annie's room," Cane panted. "This way."

He darted past, but the doctor paused long enough to peer at Annie over his spectacles. "Can't you keep that boy out of trouble?"

A heated reply trembled on Annie's tongue, until she saw the twinkle in Doc's faded blue eyes. "Which one?" she said with a sigh.

He chuckled and followed Cane into the hall, where she heard the murmur of voices—old, young, and feminine—exchanging information. Just before the door shut again, she heard another deep groan. Seneca.

On her feet, Annie clutched the afghan she'd pulled off the back of the rocker and put around her shoulders.

Martha and Cane appeared in the doorway, Cane's right ear firmly in her grasp. "Tell your sister what you've been up to tonight," she said grimly.

Instead, Cane's nose pinkened as he struggled manfully against more tears. "I promise I won't do nothin' like this ever again," he choked out, "if you'll just let me move back in the bunkhouse with Seneca and the other riders."

Annie's knees buckled so that she folded into the rocker again. "Cane, what have you done?"

The boy glanced at Martha, who gave him a mother-look as she let go of his ear. She snorted and stomped toward the kitchen. "I'm going to start us some breakfast. But I'm listening," was her parting shot at Cane.

"Mr. McCabe treats me like a baby," he began, edging toward Annie, awkwardly stumbling on the edge of the rug. Still an adolescent boy, despite his height and roughening voice.

"Mr. McCabe is *kind*," she said evenly. "Were you running away?"

"Not exactly. I was just having fun." Cane collapsed onto the hearth at Annie's feet, all knees and elbows. "Grady Nordemann bet me I couldn't get a bottle out of Mr. Towne's woodshed and drink it by myself."

"A bottle?" Annie scrunched her nose. "You mean a *whiskey* bottle?" Cane sheepishly nodded, and she felt like she'd been punched in the stomach. "You wanted to be like Seneca."

"I *do* want to be like Seneca. But he said he don't drink no more. So I don't neither."

The utter, naive stupidity of that statement made Annie want to scream. *Lord, my Father, how do I deal with this?* "Cane," she said carefully, "if you want to follow someone, then follow Christ."

He grimaced. "That's exactly what Seneca said."

"When did he say that?"

"After he cussed me a blue streak on the way back here."

Annie shut her eyes. *Oh, Lord, please . . .* She couldn't even articulate her need. *Groanings too deep for words.* The Scripture suddenly pierced her. *Father, I need . . . Holy Spirit, pray for me.*

"Cane—" She took a deep breath—"will you do that? Will you learn to follow Christ like Pa wanted you to?"

"I want to," he muttered, studying his hands. "I know I been stupid."

"Everybody falls short of the mark, honey. Even Seneca. Even me."

"It's my fault Seneca's hurt."

"How did it happen?" Annie blushed, trying not to picture the embarrassing nature of Seneca's wounds.

"Seneca caught me before I actually got into the woodshed. He was trying to help me back over the fence, but Old Man Towne's dog started barking, woke him up, and he come out with a gun. Put a load of buckshot into Seneca before I could pull him over after me."

Buckshot. In the—er—posterior. Short of lead poisoning, Seneca would not die, but oh, the humiliation for a rider of his caliber. Grounded and forced to recover, lying facedown, for days. Maybe weeks.

There were a thousand other questions she wanted to ask, but she was distracted by the awareness of Seneca in her room. She couldn't even get dressed until they moved him.

She affectionately squeezed Cane's shoulder and bent to look him in the eyes. "What you did tonight was very wrong, for lots of reasons, and you'll have to pay the consequences." He gave her a jerky nod but held her gaze. She felt her eyes tear up again. "But, Cane, I want you to know that any restrictions I put on you are there because I love you so very much."

He blinked, looked away, and swiped his nose. "I'm sorry," he whispered.

Annie sighed. "I know you are. Go on and see what Martha has for your breakfast." Martha, she suspected, would give Cane the verbal scrubbing he needed.

When Cane was gone, she sat for a while, rocking and praying. Had her brother been scared deeply enough that he would change his behavior from now on? Could she risk continued proximity to Seneca—both for herself and for Cane? Should they both move to the other end of town?

Maybe I should go home to Alabama after all. Wonder if Frank Beesom's married yet.

Shuddering, she buried her face in the afghan, drawing up her knees until she was curled in the rocker like a child.

Listen. Listen to my heart.

She could almost hear the Father speak to her.

Be still. Listen.

⁊

Seneca woke up disoriented and started to turn over, but the pain in his backside quickly reminded him he couldn't.

For two days now he'd been lying on his stomach on a straw-stuffed bed in Martha McCabe's kitchen storeroom. He'd begged them not to put him in the bunkhouse with the other men, where he would be subject to constant ridicule or, worse, pity.

A feather pillow scrunched under his stomach made him fairly comfortable, but he was heartily sick of staring at the grain of the wood floor below the cot. He was sick of the knots in the wall when he turned his head to the left. The fact that Martha hadn't bothered to sweep up a little pile of dried beans, which had fallen out of the sack he saw when he looked to the right, made him want to climb the walls.

But he couldn't get out of bed for at least a week, Doc said. Seneca had no compunction about disobeying, except that it still hurt to move. He knew it would be a few weeks before he could comfortably ride again. What good was a rider who couldn't ride?

He had no idea what time it was, and it really didn't matter. He had no place to go, no one to talk to. You'd think they would treat him like a hero, since he was the one who'd brought Cane home safe and whole.

But everybody seemed to think it was his fault the boy got in trouble in the first place. The only people who came to see him were Martha, bringing his meals, and sometimes Evangeline, who wandered in to read to him after supper.

Annie was at school, of course, through most of the long days. Last night, though, she'd come into the storeroom for a jar of molasses. There was a mixture of sympathy and caution in her expression when she'd asked how he felt.

"Fine," he'd said, pretending to go back to his study of the wall.

"Do you need anything?" she'd asked gently.

You. "No, thanks."

She'd backed out of the room, cradling the heavy, golden umber jar against her stomach, her gray eyes troubled. "All right. Call if you get hungry."

Why should he feel so ashamed? Did she know he'd been drunk when he went after Cane? That otherwise he'd have easily made it over that fence?

Seneca turned his face to the wall, scooted painfully to the edge of the cot, and looked down. His Pony Express Bible lay there, still as new-looking as the day Lloyd McCabe had given it to him when Seneca took the Pony Express pledge. He reached down and brushed his finger along the glossy leather where his name was embossed in gold.

He remembered the pledge clearly: *I, Seneca Jones, do hereby swear, before the great and living God, that during my engagement, and while I am an employee of Russell, Majors, and Waddell, I will, under no circumstances, use profane language; that I will drink no intoxicating liquors; that I will not quarrel or fight with any other employee of the firm; and that in every respect I will conduct myself honestly, be faithful to my duties, and so direct all my acts as to win the confidence of my employer. So help me God.*

Except for that last—about being faithful to duties—he, Seneca Jones, had broken just about every promise in the pledge. Didn't used to bother him. But suddenly he wanted to go back and do it all over again.

"God, would you give me one more chance?" he whispered. "Not for Annie this time. Just between me and you."

He flattened his hand against the cover of the little Bible. It was cold from lying on the floor, but his skin warmed it.

At peace, he fell asleep.

❧

Annie sneezed and, because her hands were deep in flour and lard, bent her head to rub her nose against her rolled-up sleeve. Though she loved the smell of ginger, nutmeg, and cinnamon, large doses always tickled her nose.

She and Evangeline were making gingerbread people to decorate the Christmas tree. Martha wasn't feeling well and had gone to lie down. Martha seemed to be tired and ill a lot lately. Annie hoped her friend wasn't coming down with something serious.

"Evvie, what are we going to do with our holiday?" she asked her miniature assistant.

Beaming, Evangeline bounced like a jack-in-the-box on a chair pulled up to the worktable. She was covered in flour from the top of her golden head to the hem of the voluminous red apron swathed around her like a royal robe. "Can we make paper dolls?"

"Oh, I love paper dolls!" Annie turned the dough out onto the table and brandished the heavy rolling pin. "My grandma used to—"

A crash that sounded like glass shattering against the storeroom wall jerked her head around. The door had been closed all morning—a relief that she didn't have to dart by, avoiding Seneca's eyes, every time she crossed the room.

She looked at Evvie, whose eyes were round as China blue saucers. She marched to the door, holding her fisted floury hands away from her sides. "Seneca, what are you doing?"

Silence.

"Evvie and I are making gingerbread." A warning that little ears were nearby. "Do you need something?"

It was only the second time she'd spoken to him since his accident—which wasn't really an accident because he'd brought it on himself. Martha had been caring for him, saying it wasn't proper for Annie, an unmarried woman, to enter his room. The night she'd gone in for molasses didn't count, in her mind.

"Go away." His voice was surly, muffled. Was it slurred? She couldn't tell.

"Seneca, let me come in." Until he'd said to go away, she hadn't wanted to go in there. Her obstinate streak came out in bold rainbow colors. He didn't answer. "Are you decent?"

"No," he growled.

Somehow she knew he was, so she tried the door. It opened easily.

She peeked in, and there was a long, scary rush of emotion when she saw him lying on his stomach with his head in his arms. A blanket covered him to the waist, and he wore a red flannel shirt, even though the room was fairly warm. In the early days of the McCabes' marriage, the storeroom had been a bedroom. A small woodstove still squatted in the corner.

Evvie stuck her flour-powdered head between Annie's skirt and the door frame. "Pee-ewww!" she caroled. "What's that smell?"

Annie noticed it then. A yeasty medicinal odor, like the cough tonic her mother used to give her when she was a child. Buckets of it. Whatever it was, was splashed all over the wall. Then she noticed the pool of umber liquid on the floor, spreading through shards and big chunks of brown bottle.

Seneca lifted his head and propped his chin on both fists. "I told you not to come in."

CHAPTER 6

SENECA watched expressions chase each other across Annie's face, ranging from shock to disgust to compassion.

She knelt in front of Evvie. "Sweetheart, would you go wash your hands and then put your dolly down for a nap? Here, let me take your apron before you go." As if there were no hurry in the world, Annie turned the little girl, unwrapped her from the apron, and kissed her on the cheek. Smiling, she gave Evvie a playful swat on the bottom as she skipped giggling from the room.

Annie's smile faded as she turned to look at the mess on the floor and wall, then guardedly at Seneca. Wiping her hands on the red apron, she hesitated just inside the door, leaving it open for propriety.

"Come here," he said.

She drifted toward him, her eyes dark as smoke now. "Are you all right?" she murmured.

"I've been better," he said lightly. He reached for a milk stool that Evangeline had brought in, pushed it away from the bed for her to sit on.

Instead, she arranged the apron on the floor and dropped onto it, arms folded on the bed so she could rest her chin on them. Her face was mere inches from his. He almost forgot to breathe.

"I've been praying for a chance to talk to you," she said.

161

"So have I."

They stared at one another, all defenses suddenly down. He wasn't sure how it had happened.

After a moment he said, "You've got the whole man now, Annie." He watched her beautiful auburn brows draw together as she puzzled at his meaning. Then a smile slowly dawned. Her eyes brightened to silver.

She glanced over her shoulder at the mess beside the door. "Then what . . . ?"

Her hand rested so close to his, it was a natural thing to curl his rough fingers around hers. Awestruck at their slim elegance, even with bits of ginger-colored dough stuck beneath her nails, he smiled. She smelled like a cookie.

He let out a breath and answered obliquely. "I've been lying here with nothing to do but think. Late last night I talked to Billy. I can't explain it, except that it was like a light suddenly came on and I could understand what he'd been saying to me. What everybody's been saying." He looked directly into her eyes. Transparency was painful but freeing. "You were right. I wanted to be king of the world, and I was afraid somebody would look too close and find out how out of control I am."

He looked at the sweet lips he'd kissed without asking. They were now parted as if she wanted to respond but didn't know how.

He shook his head. "So I just gave it up." He released her hand in demonstration. "I surrendered my life to Christ and asked to be born again."

"Oh, Seneca."

The way she said his name, so softly, made him swallow—hard. "I've known for a long time what to do. It just took some buckshot in the seat of the pants to make me do it." When he laughed, she did too.

"I prayed for you so hard," she said.

He wiped a smear of tears off her cheek with his thumb and

looked at the wetness. Here came the hardest part of all. "Annie, you said—"

"Yes."

He blinked. "Yes, what?"

She blushed. "Yes, I will."

Even in his dismay, a tight thrill shot through him. "I wish it was that simple. I know I asked you to marry me—before, but—" He paused and considered how to undo his own monumental presumption. "It's going to be a long time before I'm the kind of man who's good enough for you." She shook her head, as if he were teasing her, but he took her hand again and jiggled it. "Annie, I've got a bad temper and a habit of cussing, and—I can't read."

"What?"

He shouldn't be so embarrassed—there were men roaming all over the West who'd never picked up a book in their lives. But Annie was a schoolteacher. "I said," he enunciated clearly, "I can't even read the Bible. I tried all morning to figure it out. I got so mad I had to throw something, and that bottle of whiskey somebody left here was the closest thing handy." He turned his face away. "How can I learn how to get control of my temper if I can't even read God's Word?"

"I'll teach you."

"What if I'm too stupid? What if it's too late?"

Annie let out a peal of laughter. "One thing you're not, Seneca Jones, is stupid." She pulled his face around. "You know what one of my favorite verses is? It's Philippians 4:13: 'I can do all things through Christ which strengtheneth me.'"

He stared glumly at her sweet, happy face. "See, that's how ignorant I am. I didn't even know that."

"Seneca," she sighed, "you have to start somewhere. But as brilliant as you are, you'll catch up and pass me in no time."

"Brilliant, huh?" He cracked a smile, then closed his eyes when her finger traced his cheek. "Oh, Annie, you'd better get out of here."

"I . . . think you're right," she said in a suffocated little voice. "But how am I going to teach you to read if I can't—"

"Bring Evvie with you next time. No more school 'til after Christmas, right?"

"Yes, that's a good idea."

He felt the bed give as she pushed herself to her feet, then a butterfly-soft brush of her lips against his cheek. "I'll be back later."

"All right." But he wouldn't look until he heard the door close again.

"Thank you, God," he whispered. "I don't deserve her, but thank you."

❧

For the next few days Annie was deliriously happy. Seneca was indeed a quick study. She got the feeling he'd have learned to read a long time ago if he'd ever sat still long enough to think about it.

Since he was young and strong, his wounds healed quickly. Before long he was able to sit by the fire in the great room, a thick pillow cushioning the seat of the big rocker. Unable to sit in his lap, Evangeline pulled up a tall stool and leaned over his shoulder, helping him struggle through her first-grade reader. She delighted in correcting him, and Annie noticed he often made deliberate mistakes just to hear the child's peals of laughter.

"No, Seneca," she would giggle, "that's *big pig*, not *pig's wig*."

"Oh," he'd say meekly and go on reading.

Seneca soon wanted to graduate to the Bible as his primer. Annie took Evvie's place on the stool beside him. She had to make a conscious effort not to put a hand on his shoulder or rest against his arm while her eyes followed his finger across the page. He, too, seemed to be suddenly aware of proprieties, red staining the tips of his ears every time he accidentally brushed her clothing.

In honor of the approaching Christmas season, he wanted to begin reading in Luke, so Annie helped him through the archaic language, explaining and pronouncing as they went. He seemed astonished to realize that God's most amazing gift had come, not through wealthy and educated people but through a carpenter and an unwed pregnant teenager. And the glorious good news of Christ's birth had come first not to kings and wise men but to rough and uneducated shepherds.

"Mutton punchers, Annie," he said, wonder in that resonant voice she loved to hear. "All those angels out in a field with a bunch of sheepherders no smarter than me."

He kept reading, while Annie, throat tight, lost track of the words in studying the streaks of white blond in his hair, the dimple coming and going in his cheek. If she'd loved him before, it was now almost a painful thing. The changes in him since his conversion made his physical beauty that much greater.

In a real sense, it had increased her own faith to watch Seneca appropriate verses he learned, face habits ingrained over years, and come out the victor. Oh, it was slow, and he slipped occasionally. Just yesterday, when Seneca walked over to the stable to watch Cane exercise Becky, Peewee Malone had taunted him into trying to ride—much too soon. He was paying for it today, wincing every time he moved.

On another level, though, Annie began to be afraid. How could she possibly hold him? Seneca was used to attention, especially that of women. Right now he was enamored only of the Lord, which was as it should be. But everybody had weaknesses. What if Seneca couldn't withstand temptation?

I'd be smashed into a million pieces, Lord. Just like that bottle of whiskey he threw at the wall.

She sat there studying her hands and suddenly realized Seneca had stopped reading. When she looked at him, his tender blue eyes were on her, not the Bible. "What is it, Annie?" he said. "You look so sad."

"You scare me," she blurted. It was not in her to withhold her feelings, though she'd tried to be patient. *He hasn't asked me to marry him yet. What if he's changed his mind?*

He stared at her. When she got uncomfortable enough to nervously get up off the stool, he took her wrist. "Wait, hold on," he said.

She reluctantly sat down again, helplessly enjoying the warmth of his hand on her skin.

"I think I know what you mean," Seneca said slowly. "You're afraid I'll fall." He paused, but she didn't answer. How could she admit such a thing? "Well, there's always that chance, but I just read something interesting here. If I understand it right, these people in the Bible—Simeon, Mary, and Joseph—they had the Holy Ghost inside to tell them things. Right?"

"Yes," Annie said.

"Well, if they did, then it seems to me you and I have that, too. Besides the Bible itself, Billy says we have the Holy Spirit to teach and help us. We shouldn't be afraid."

She thought about that. He was absolutely right. How could she have ignored the power of the Holy Spirit? She had been obedient, waiting for God to reach Seneca, learning to trust that God's way was best. Why couldn't she trust him now in her happiness?

Because I'm a woman, and I want to be held and kissed and told I'm beautiful by the man I love.

"Annie." His thumb found the center of her palm, and she melted. "You'll have to give me a little time to grow in the Lord. And—there's something else. I don't know exactly how to tell you, but we need to pray about it together."

Her heart squeezed. Fear again. "What is it?"

"In less than a year I won't have a job. Soon as the telegraph is complete between here and Salt Lake. I knew that, but there's more immediate trouble. Mr. McCabe told me yesterday that the Pony is in deep financial distress. I heard rumors when I made that trip to Summit back in November. Mr. McCabe says he hasn't been reimbursed for expenses in months. He thinks there's corruption somewhere in the chain of authority, and he's gonna go broke if somebody doesn't do something about it. He thinks—he hopes—that's what your brother's assignment is."

He sighed, his lips tightening, and continued. "Annie, I've been impulsive and wild all my life, but it's time to put away childish things. I haven't spoken—can't ask you to marry me, if I don't have a way to support you. I love you, but I need you to be patient until this thing is settled. OK?"

I love you. The words sang in her heart, even while she whispered, "But what are you going to do when the Pony shuts down?" *What are we going to do?* she corrected silently.

"You're such a good worrier." He kissed her hand, smiling. "We need to trust God, sweetheart. He'll provide something."

Delight, confusion, anxiety—Annie was filled with all three as they bowed their heads to pray together.

But in the midst of it all rose hope.

><

"Evvie, you've already got four gingerbread people on that one branch. There's no room for another one," Annie admonished as she supervised the trimming of the McCabes' Christmas tree. An exhausted Martha, who had been up since before dawn baking and dressing a turkey, watched from the rocking chair, her feet propped on a needlepoint ottoman.

"But it's a family," Evangeline explained. "The sister needs another sister. She's tired of her brother."

Annie laughed. She could sympathize.

Christmas at a Pony Express home station was like nothing Annie had ever experienced. Loud male laughter in and out all day long. Big boots thunking, tracking mud and snow on clean floors. Constant teasing, starved men, perpetual motion.

Her memories of Christmas at home when she and Micah were children, before Cane was born, were of quiet, worshipful family times. Nothing like this noisy melee of masculinity.

Sad to think this was the last time it would happen just like this. The Pony Express wouldn't be in operation next Christmas. Perhaps, though, the McCabes could stay in business with the boardinghouse, if they managed to keep it afloat.

Martha laughed too. "If you're really good," she said, "by next Christmas there might be a sister."

Evvie squealed and ran to jump in her mother's lap.

Annie looked at her friend in delight. "Truly, Martha? A baby coming?"

As Martha nodded, beaming, hugging Evangeline close, Annie turned to drape a strand of popcorn in and around Evvie's gingerbread "families." Maybe one day God would bless her and Seneca with a baby. A thrill zinged through her as she imagined snuggling a little strawberry blonde infant with Seneca's blue eyes.

Then she sighed. If he ever decided the time was right to get married. Though Seneca still wasn't riding yet, Lloyd McCabe had kept him busy caring for the horses and learning some of the clerical side of the business. Martha said Seneca was smart enough to run his own business if he wanted to.

When Annie had asked him about it, he'd shrugged. "Once the telegraph is through, who knows what will happen to the mail system? And every day it's looking more and more like war between the states. We can't count on anything right now."

Don't count on anything. But love "believeth all things, hopeth all things." How can that be? she prayed. *It's so hard to wait on you. Help me to trust you, Lord.*

She picked up a box of crocheted snowflakes and held one up to let the light filter through. Fragile, lacy, but made to last indefinitely. She nestled it onto a fragrant evergreen bough, the delicate threads clinging to the upcurving needles. *Shine through me, Lord. I know you won't let me or Seneca go.*

Suddenly the door burst open, and Cane stood panting in the open doorway. Behind him snow fell, blowing in thick gusts that almost looked like milk against the leaden sky. "Annie! Where's Seneca?"

"Down at the stable. Why?"

"They need every rider available." Cane leaned over to put his hands on his knees while he caught his breath. "Pony Bob just rode in from Solitaire—said there's been some kind of gunfight out there, and they think Micah was in it!"

"Micah? Our Micah?" Fear for her older brother shook Annie.

Cane nodded, backing out the door. "And there was a stage-coach headed this way, with Senator Gwin and Major Peele's wife in it—gone missing, too." He started to pull the door shut. "I gotta go!"

"But Cane—" The door slammed, leaving a cold draft and the wetness of melted snow on the floor. Annie looked at Martha, whose hazel eyes were wide with concern. "Seneca isn't supposed to ride yet. What if something happens to him in that storm? I can't lose both him and Micah."

***

But of course he did ride, along with every other available Pony Express rider and cavalry officer stationed at the fort over Christmas.

Annie didn't even get to say good-bye; she stood at the window, watching the men ride toward the western gates. Gates that opened onto a wilderness where wolves could tear a man to shreds without warning. Where bison lumbered in herds that, if startled into stampede, were likely to trample even the most skilled horse-men. And where a raging winter storm now cast blinding sheets of snow across the flat prairie, piling up to obliterate whatever trails had been etched into the landscape.

As they waited through the long hours of that Christmas Eve, Annie and Martha banked their fears by cooking, sewing, and trying to keep Evangeline and the boys entertained. After supper, the eight of them—including Cane and Josiah, who had begged to ride but were convinced to stay home to protect the women—re-enacted the nativity story. Evvie, naturally, chose the part of Mary, with Cane as Joseph, and her favorite rag doll as the infant Jesus.

As Annie draped a linen towel over the little girl's distinctly un-Jewish blond curls, she was informed that her part would be that of the "lonely little donkey."

Startled into laughter, Annie glanced at Josiah, who snorted and rolled his eyes. "She does this every year," Josiah said. "Whoever plays the donkey has to cart her around for the rest of the day."

"Well, Mary didn't *walk* to Bethlehem." Evvie fisted her hands on her hips. "She *rode*."

"You're absolutely right," Annie agreed, hiding a grin. Evvie did not like to be laughed at. "I'll be the lonely little donkey. Hop on."

The play proceeded without another hitch until the Madonna fell asleep in her "stable" constructed of a blanket swagged across a couple of chairs. Martha picked her up, the doll still squeezed tightly in her arms, and tucked her in her little bed. The boys, relieved of thespian duty, went off to the bunkhouse to play checkers.

Annie sat quietly alone by the fire, Seneca's Bible in her lap. She had nothing else to do, because she had long since finished her handmade gifts and had placed them, wrapped in colored paper, under the tree. Would she even have the chance to give Seneca his gift? She prayed it would be so.

She opened the Bible to the verse in Philippians she had quoted to him and found it heavily underlined. In the margin, in a bold, black motion-filled hand, she read "Annie."

Her name. Nothing else, but it told her he thought about her, prayed for her, and loved her. If the Lord chose not to bring him back to her, she would at least have that.

Holding the Bible to her heart much like Evvie had held her doll, she laid her head back against the rocker and toed it into motion. She sighed. If she had learned one thing over the last two months, it was that most things were out of Annie Fitzgerald's control. *Undoubtedly a good thing*, she thought with a slight smile.

But, Father, it just keeps getting harder and harder. I know that you won't give me more than I can bear. But I ask you to keep Seneca and the other men safe, to bring Micah home, and to strengthen my faith.

Oh, please hold me, Lord.

❧

When Annie, Martha, and the children gathered the next day around the Christmas dinner table, they were an unnaturally quiet group. Even Evvie seemed to understand that the storm howling outside the boardinghouse meant that her papa was in deadly danger.

As they bowed their heads to ask God's blessing on the food, Evvie wanted to pray first.

Ten-year-old Daniel scowled at his talkative little sister. "Don't take so long; the food gets cold."

"I won't." Evvie pressed her chubby hands together, resting her chin on the tips of her fingers. "Dear God," she said, as if addressing a letter, "it's me, Evangeline. You know, the one that wanted a sister real bad. Thank you for my nice Christmas present. Ow! Quit it, Daniel!"

When Martha restored order after several kicks had been exchanged under the table, Evvie closed her eyes again. "I told you they was mean to me," she sighed. "Anyway, I just wanted to thank you for the good food we get to eat. And thank you that you're gonna bring Papa and Seneca home safe. Tell Annie not to cry no more 'cause you're taking real good care of him." She looked up directly into Annie's tear-filled eyes and beamed. "Amen!"

"God don't always answer prayers," Cane said matter-of-factly. He picked up a bowl of mashed sweet potatoes and spooned a glob onto his plate.

"Yes, he does." Evvie's tone was equally sure. "Papa says so."

"Well, I prayed for my ma and pa not to die, and they died anyway."

Martha rubbed her forehead, her compassionate gaze first on Cane, then on Annie. "Benjamin, would you pass the bread, please?" she said, breaking the tight, thick silence that had settled around the table.

Annie took the bread basket, her appetite gone. Which truth should she hold on to? Evvie's childlike faith or Cane's bald statement of reality? She knew that God's will was sometimes impossible to understand. But she also knew that he loved his children and desired their fellowship more than anything.

Please, Lord, she prayed, *let Cane see you work in a way that will help him to trust you.* She put her arm around her brother's shoulder and gave it a sympathetic squeeze. It was a measure of his pain that he didn't shrug away.

❧

If anyone had asked Seneca two weeks ago how he wanted to die, he would have opted for a hero's death. Swift and violent, overtaking him while delivering the *mochila* but accomplished in such a way that the world would discover his fearlessness and unparalleled horsemanship.

He could never have imagined the stark terror of this utter blindness, numbness, helplessness.

Aloneness.

Snow fell on a landscape already so thickly blanketed that it was impossible to tell which direction he was headed. He was so cold that he could not feel the horse between his legs, much less his fingers and toes. Frostbite was almost a certainty. Becky lurched, staggering, striving to inch forward. He was afraid she wasn't going to make it either. Awkwardly he leaned forward to pat her neck and nearly fell off.

He'd thought he was with the rest of the group heading back to the fort. Micah had cautioned them all against falling asleep.

But none of them had slept since night before last. And the snow was mesmerizing. Endlessly white, endlessly blowing, endlessly serene. He had closed his eyes to dream of Annie. And had awakened to find the others nowhere in sight.

Were they lost, or was he?

He'd been riding, maybe in circles, for what seemed like hours, but it might have been only minutes.

No way to die, God. Like an idiot. Went to sleep. How could I go to sleep? Did you save me for this? What's going to happen to Annie? She'll die of grief.

She would. He knew it.

Suddenly, his obstinate refusal to marry her when he didn't have a job seemed like pure lunacy. Pride, plain and simple. Besides, just this morning Micah had all but assured him of a job as scout for the marshall's office. What had he been so worried about?

Please, Lord, forgive me, he prayed. *If it's not too late, help me trust you more. I've always been a man who likes to see and hear and smell things before I believe them. Pretty funny that there's nothing out here now but me and you, and I sure can't see or feel anything but cold. But I know you're here, Lord.*

And I know that Annie's praying for me. I know you won't let her down.

With a lightness of spirit that he was perfectly aware came from outside himself, Seneca strained to see through the blowing snow. It came as no surprise to finally see the stockade walls of Fort Kearny vaguely outlined against the blurry white horizon.

"Well, glory," he whispered, leaning into Becky. "You see that? The gates are open. Guess we aren't going to heaven just yet."

An eternity passed, though, before they passed beneath the unguarded stockade. Reeling in the saddle and all but frozen, Seneca reached the front of the schoolhouse, where he'd held Annie in his arms. Where he'd made up his mind that she would be his, even before God had graciously given him the desire of his heart. Home. Soon he would be home with Annie.

Suddenly Becky gave a gasping heave and pitched sideways. Seneca found himself pinned underneath the horse.

Lord, I'm so weak, he thought, struggling with clumsy hands to push, pull, anything to get free of Becky's warm, life-stealing weight. He thought he could just see the top of the post on which the schoolyard bell hung.

Ring, Christmas bells, he thought lazily. *Ding, dong, merrily on high. We nearly made it.*

CHAPTER 7

ANNIE couldn't have said what made her get up and move to the window. There wasn't anything to hear except the children arguing over the drumsticks and the wind soughing outside.

She rubbed at the freezing windowpane, trying to clear a space to look out into the gloomy street. Snow blew in dense gusts, and she could barely see across the street to the church building.

Then she thought she glimpsed a blob of some blacker darkness in the backdrop of the snow. "Cane! Josiah! Come with me!" Suddenly compelled by anxiety, she began to fling on cloak and mittens.

"What is it?" Both boys hurried to obey.

"I don't know—I think—I hope it's the men coming back." She grunted, tugging on her heavy boots.

"Annie, let the boys go." Martha was standing at the window, trying to see out. "You don't know how dangerous this weather is—"

"I've got to go too," Annie said simply. She all but hopped with impatience, her hand on the door latch as she waited for the boys to finish dressing.

"But—"

"I know they're out there. I've got to go," she repeated.

Martha hugged her hard. "All right. We'll be praying."

The three of them linked arms as they stepped into the driving snow, sinking to their knees, struggling to put one foot in front of the other. The stinging wetness took Annie's breath away, frosted her eyelashes, blurred her vision.

"Which way?" shouted Cane above the moan of the wind.

"West," Annie replied. "This way."

She hoped they were headed in the right direction, but it was hard even to tell up from down. Josiah, of the three the most familiar with the layout of the town, took the lead, staying as close to the shelter of the buildings as possible. Nobody else was crazy enough to be out in such weather.

Josiah suddenly shouted, "There! I see something!"

Blindly Annie followed the tugging of his arm through hers, praying desperately they wouldn't all die, disoriented and frozen, right in the center of town.

"Cane!" she screamed. Her brother had released her arm and gone plunging ahead, staggering through the drifts like some crazed jackrabbit. "Oh, God, help us!" She managed to keep him in sight while she and Josiah followed as best they could, zigzagging toward what seemed to be the middle of the street.

They nearly ran over Cane where he knelt, scrabbling with his hands, digging snow away from something half buried in a huge drift. Annie felt another scream build inside her throat when she realized he was uncovering the brown-and-white splotched haunches of a horse.

Becky! Where was Seneca?

She fell to her knees, as did Josiah, and the three of them dug and dug as the snow continued to fall with thick, suffocating softness. They found the horse's head; it was obvious that she was dead. Sobbing, Annie flung her arms around Becky's neck.

Her gloved hand connected with something underneath.

Galvanized, she tugged frantically at the heavy corpse, until Cane and Josiah realized what she was doing and began to help. They

176

managed to push Becky's stiff, slippery body aside, and there he was. Seneca, lying faceup and unconscious, his black hat and heavy coat still providing a measure of warmth, but he was shivering in great racking spasms that all but lifted his body from the ground.

The two boys got him up between them and looked to Annie for direction. "Where to?" Cane asked.

She thought she recognized the schoolyard bell sticking up out of the snow just a few feet away. "This way," she decided, leading off. She wished with all her heart they'd thought to bring a shovel. The best they could do was stumble along a few inches at a time, dragging Seneca like a sack of grain.

It seemed to Annie an eternity before they reached the front steps of the schoolhouse. Slipping and sliding, they got the door open and fell in a heap of quaking bodies just inside the room. Annie pushed the door shut with her foot. "Thank God," she whispered. "Oh . . . thank you God!"

Now what to do? Praise heaven, she had had the boys restock the woodpile before dismissing school for the holiday. Her own teeth chattering, she instructed Cane and Josiah to start the biggest roaring fire they could build, while she turned Seneca onto his back to assess his condition. His normally ruddy, tanned skin was like icy wax. His nostrils flared with the exertion of breathing. He was going to die if they didn't get him warm.

"Boys, help me move him close to the stove," she said. When they had done so, she began to unbutton her cloak. Without another word, both youngsters followed her example. Seneca's coat and leggings, which were of oiled buckskin, were still fairly dry, so they left them on him and simply covered him from neck to toe with the three extra garments.

"Cane," Annie said hoarsely, "you lie on one side of Seneca, Josiah on the other. We've got to get him warm."

Then she took a deep breath and knelt beside Seneca, curling across his chest. Burying her face in his neck, absorbing the shivers that racked his body, she prayed for God to minister to the man she loved, to spare the precious "jar of clay" that housed his lively mind, his beloved spirit, his God-breathed being.

Snugged together in love and friendship, the three of them shared their warmth with Seneca.

༄

Annie jumped when Seneca sneezed across the top of her head.

"Pardon me, Miss Fitzgerald, but I believe I could breathe easier if I weren't smothered by the three of you.'" His voice was weak but clear.

Cane and Josiah sprang to their feet, whooping like maniacs, and Annie put her hands on the floor, pushing upward to look Seneca in the face.

"You're alive!" she exclaimed joyfully.

"If I'm not, the beds in heaven are mighty uncomfortable. And my left ear is near burned off," he complained. "Can we move away from the stove just a bit?"

Annie scrambled to her knees and helped him sit up. She took her cloak from him and put it back on, then handed the two boys their coats. She couldn't take her eyes off Seneca.

"Can you feel your fingers and toes?" she asked, taking one of his hands and rubbing it briskly between hers.

He nodded, closing his eyes as if in pain. Then, "Becky," he gasped.

Annie was horrified to see Seneca's face crumple as he bent toward his knees. Great wrenching sobs shook his body. Aware of Cane and Josiah awkwardly turning away so as not to see their hero's grief, Annie threw her arms around Seneca, holding him close. He pressed his face into her neck, and she rocked, wordlessly comforting him.

"We're gonna be OK," she whispered. "God spared your life."

She paused, needing to ask but afraid of the answer. "Where—what happened to the others?"

"If they can all stay together, I'm sure they'll make it back." His blue eyes were red-rimmed and watery, his voice rusty, but he seemed unembarrassed by his tears. "We found Micah holed up in a cave down by Bethlehem Creek—with a couple of Pony riders and the stagecoach passengers." He closed his eyes tiredly, tightening his arms around Annie's waist. "We were on the way back, when I fell asleep and got lost—"

"Thank God we found you." She clutched him hard. "Cane said there was a gunfight. Was Micah hurt?"

"No, it turned out to be one of the other Pony riders who walked in on something he shouldn't have. Micah finally found him and got the whole mess straightened out." Seneca sat up, keeping an arm about Annie. He looked around at Cane and Josiah, who huddled on the opposite side of the stove, trying to keep warm and avidly listening to Annie and Seneca's exchange.

"I'd never have found you without them," Annie said.

"I know." Seneca turned her and drew her back against his chest, wrapping his arms tightly around her. "I have felt the direct power of God today. I'll always remember this day and know that he loves me and cares for me." He looked over his shoulder again. "Cover your eyes, boys," Seneca advised them. "I'm gonna kiss the teacher."

Both youngsters groaned in disgust and obeyed him quite literally, sending Annie into a fit of giggles. They looked like a couple of see-no-evil monkeys.

"Hurry up," muttered Cane. "I'm ready for leftover Christmas dinner."

"I've got dibs on the drumstick," Josiah declared.

⊱

The drumstick was gone, but Seneca and both hungry boys seemed perfectly satisfied with bowls of Martha's thick homemade stew and half a dozen gingerbread cookies each. Annie delighted in the way Seneca's eyes sought her again and again while he ate, leaving her feeling kissed though he never touched her.

An hour later, Lloyd McCabe arrived, to be all but strangled by bear hugs from his wife and children. He brought the good news that the other men were all safely ensconsed in their own homes.

Annie watched the happy scene, smiling. Her anxious gaze went to the door. Where was Micah?

Suddenly, as though she'd prayed him into the room, there he was, entering right behind Lloyd. He was a mountain of a man, with curly sandy hair, a thick brown mustache, and light, piercing gray eyes just like her father's. His buckskin clothing was damp with snow. Micah! With a glad cry, Annie ran straight into his arms to be lifted off the floor in a strong hug.

"Little Annie," he said over and over, as she cried into his shoulder, hardly able to get her arms around him he was so big.

At last Micah set her on her feet and released her but kept hold of her hands. They both laughed with pent-up relief and joy. He looked at her with wonder. "You are a young woman," Micah observed, shaking his head. "I told him I didn't think you were old enough to get married."

Annie's head helplessly turned toward Seneca, who looked as if he would like to crawl under the table.

"I haven't asked her yet," he said in an agonized growl, his face ten shades of red.

"Oh." Micah removed his hat and ran his hand through his damp hair. Uneasily, he looked around at the seven slack jaws of the McCabe family, who watched the unfolding drama with rapt attention.

Evvie marched up to Micah and yanked on the fringe of his sleeve. "When is Annie gettin' married? Did you know I'm gonna get a baby sister?"

The tension broke as the adults laughed, but Annie avoided

Seneca's eyes. *Was* Annie getting married? There were too many people in the room now to pursue the matter.

"Where's Cane?" Micah asked, scanning the row of multifarious young boys lined up around the table, and Annie was distracted for the next hour by the happy task of introducing her younger brother to the elder.

Except for Cane's brown eyes, they looked much alike, and it was obvious Cane would soon match Micah in height and breadth. Annie found herself more than once wishing her parents could see the man Micah had become, as well as the potential in Cane. Micah marveled repeatedly at his young brother's heroic part in Seneca's rescue. Annie watched Cane's ego swell to monumental proportions under Micah's admiration. The boy was going to be hard to live with for quite some time, she thought, amused.

Martha, still rejoicing in the safe return of her husband, allowed the children to stay up late. She offered Micah a room for the night, but he claimed business at the garrison, now that he had seen his family well cared for. He kissed Annie on the cheek, shook hands with Cane, and left by the front door in a blast of cold air.

By the time everyone had finally retired, it was nearly midnight. Seneca, exhausted from his ordeal, had been asleep in Martha's rocker for almost two hours. Annie stood beside him, a hand on the back of the chair near his shoulder. Before heading for her own room, Martha had told Annie to wake him, that she would give them ten unchaperoned minutes before sending Lloyd to play papa.

Smiling, Annie looked down at Seneca's relaxed, beloved face. He was wrapped in Martha's rose-garden-patterned afghan, his frostbitten feet wrapped in several layers of socks and propped on the needlepoint ottoman. He didn't look comfortable at all. He was going to have a crick in his neck.

And ten minutes wasn't long.

She slid her hand down to his shoulder and squeezed it gently. "Seneca."

His eyes slowly opened, and he smiled. "I was dreaming about you." He caught her hand and tugged. "Come here."

"I can't—"

He looked around. "There's nobody else here."

"I know, but—"

They stared at one another. It was obvious he was trying to figure out how to work past Micah's premature mention of marriage.

"I'm sorry—," they began simultaneously.

Annie returned Seneca's startled glance and blurted, "For what?" just before he did.

He grinned. "This is getting us nowhere. Come here so we can talk without waking everybody up." He hooked an arm around her waist and toppled her into his lap. Giggling, she put her arms around his neck, looked into his eyes, and fell silent again at the passion that suddenly flared there. He swooped his face toward hers, but she met him halfway, and they kissed hard and deep with the knowledge of what they'd nearly lost.

"Annie," he said against her mouth, "oh, Annie . . ."

"I'm here."

"Thank God. I thought I was going to have to wait 'til heaven to see you again."

"I know. I'm sorry I pressed you about—"

He groaned and stopped her words with his lips. "No, I'm an idiot. That's *i-d-i-o-t*. I love you, and I don't want to wait one more day to belong to you, and you to me. We have Micah's permission, and the preacher's right across the street." He pulled back enough to look anxiously into her eyes. "I mean if you still want to. Annie, will you be my wife?"

Joy pushed tears into Annie's eyes as she tried to speak. In the end, she could only nod and enthusiastically return his kiss. Eventually, she whispered, "I love you, Seneca Jones."

"Under God I love you," he whispered back. "I've been reading how a husband is to love his wife—like Christ loved the church." He closed his eyes as Annie traced the crease in his cheek with her finger. "I think that's what made me hesitate to ask you. That's a big responsibility."

"It is," she agreed. "But remember the Holy Spirit is here to help us both." She straightened abruptly. "That reminds me—I forgot to give you your present."

"Sweetheart, you just gave me the best present I'll ever get in my life, next to my salvation." He kissed her again, then drew back. "But what is it?" His expression was sheepish. "Nobody ever gave me a Christmas present before."

"Wait here." Annie scooted off his lap, hurried to root beneath the debris under the tree, and came back with a square package wrapped in red paper and tied with colored ribbons. She put it in Seneca's hands and watched as he delightedly handled it, obviously enjoying the pleasure of anticipation. She waited anxiously while he carefully opened it. He seemed reluctant to disturb the paper or the ribbons.

"I made it," she said, unsure of his expression as he fingered the embroidery on the plain blue fabric covering his Pony Express Bible. "I know it's not much—"

Seneca kissed her, halting her embarrassment. "You made it. It's beautiful." He proudly read the verse she'd embroidered on the outside: "'I can do all things through Christ which strengtheneth me.' You taught me that, Annie."

"And you've taught me that God answers prayer," she said, holding his face in her hands. "Not always in the way I want him to, but always in a way that's best for me. Oh, Seneca, I love you."

He was about to reply when Lloyd McCabe's stern face appeared in the doorway that led to the family bedrooms. "You two better bank the fire and skedaddle before Martha has a hissy," he said. They heard him mumbling to himself as he turned and stomped back down the hall. "Crazy woman. Told her we should leave them alone. Wasn't doing nothing but reading the Bible. . . ."

Annie stifled her laughter in Seneca's shoulder. He squeezed her tight, the Bible pressed between them. "We'd better get up before we have Evangeline in here wanting a story," Seneca said. But he tipped her face up again. "Kiss me one more time, Annie."

She did.

RECIPE

THIS RECIPE reminds me of Christmases when my children were small. We would dig through a drawer to find the "gingerbread people" cookie cutters, roll out the dough, and get flour from one end of the kitchen to the other. Both kids loved to stand beside me on chairs and "help" cut and decorate—and of course eat a lot of dough! I'm hoping these delicious cookies bring you lots of great Christmas memories too!

—Beth White

Gingerbread Cookies

3 cups all-purpose flour
¾ cup firmly packed dark brown sugar
1 tbsp. ground cinnamon
1 tbsp. ground ginger
½ tsp. ground cloves
½ tsp. salt
¾ tsp. baking soda
¾ cup (1½ sticks) unsalted butter, slightly softened,
   cut into 12 pieces
¾ cup unsulphured molasses
2 tbsp. milk

In a large bowl, combine the first 7 ingredients. Scatter butter over dry mixture; combine with pastry blender until mixture resembles fine meal. Gradually stir in molasses and milk until dough is evenly moist and forms a soft mass.

Divide dough into quarters. Working with one portion at a time, roll dough ⅛ inch thick between two large sheets of parchment paper. Leaving dough sandwiched between the parchment layers, stack on cookie sheet and freeze 15–20 minutes.

Adjust oven racks to upper- and lower-middle positions; heat oven to 325°. Line two cookie sheets with parchment paper.

Transfer one dough sheet from freezer to work surface. Peel off top parchment sheet and gently lay it back in place. Flip dough over; peel off and discard second parchment sheet. Use cookie cutters to cut out gingerbread people, transferring shapes to parchment-lined cookie sheets with wide metal spatula, spacing them 1 inch apart. Set scraps aside. Repeat with remaining dough until cookie sheets are full. Bake cookies until slightly darkened and firm in center, 15–20 minutes. For even baking, rotate cookie sheets front to back and switch positions top to bottom in oven halfway through baking time.

Cool cookies on sheets for two minutes, then remove with spatula to wire rack and cool. If you wish to thread cookies for decorations, punch holes in them with a drinking straw when they're just out of the oven and still soft.

Gather dough scraps; continue rolling between parchment paper, freezing, and cutting out shapes until all dough is used.

Store cookies in an airtight container. In dry climates, cookies should keep about a month.

A NOTE FROM THE AUTHOR

DEAR READER,

Having lived most of my life in Mississippi and Alabama, I've never experienced a winter on the Great Plains. If I did, I'm sure I'd be, like Annie Fitzgerald, "one frosty Magnolia"!

Isn't it great how our God-given imagination can take us to places we might never otherwise get to visit? If you live in a northern climate, try to picture a Christmas dinner where everybody dresses in shorts and sandals (like my family often does). Or maybe you're like me and can only experience the smell and sensation of a snowdrift in your mind.

Sometimes I try to imagine what heaven will be like. Now there's a place I want to go! The Bible assures me that I'll get to see it one day. Not because of any "reforming" I've done in my own life, like Seneca tried to do. Not because I'm any better than anyone else, as he imagined Annie was. But I'll be in heaven because I've put my faith and trust in Jesus, the one who gave his life to rescue me.

I don't have a good enough imagination to picture streets of gold and mansions on every corner. I can't comprehend a place where no one ever gets lost or cold or lonely. But because of the peace and joy Christ has placed in my life even now, I know that there is such a place. And the way to get there is through Christ! Won't you give your life to him today?

Blessings,
Beth White

ABOUT THE AUTHOR

ELIZABETH WHITE grew up in Southaven, Mississippi. A "real-life" music teacher, she always dreamed of following in the footsteps of Louisa May Alcott, her all-time favorite writer. She kept very busy studying classical voice, flute, and piano, singing in contemporary Christian bands, playing in Mississippi State University's Famous Maroon Band, and participating in church missions trips. Nevertheless, Beth could usually be found with her nose firmly planted in a book.

After a five-year stint in Fort Worth as a bank teller, she moved to the beautiful Gulf Coast of Mobile, Alabama, with her minister husband. After the birth of their two children, Beth decided to beef up her music education degree with some English courses. One fiction-writing course was all it took to get her hooked.

A love of romance, combined with a strong desire to tell stories illustrating Christ's incomparable love for his children, draws Beth to writing inspirational romance. Her first novella, "Miracle on Beale Street," appears in the HeartQuest anthology *Dream Vacation*. Watch for her upcoming novella, "The Trouble with Tommy," in the anthology *Sweet Delights*.

Beth somehow finds time to write amidst her busy schedule of teaching a second-grade Sunday school class, teaching piano lessons, directing a middle school band program, and keeping her own two middle-schoolers out of trouble—besides the responsibilities of being a pastor's wife! Her main goal in life, however, is to remain in an intimate relationship with Jesus Christ.

Beth welcomes letters written to her in care of Tyndale House Author Relations, P.O. Box 80, Wheaton, IL 60189-0080, or you can E-mail her at bethsquill@aol.com.

WISHFUL THINKING

Peggy Stoks

To Jane

CHAPTER 1

"HOWDY-DO . . . Miss Wilcox?"

"Afternoon," Elizabeth Wilcox replied after a pause, looking over the smiling, nattily dressed gentleman who had walked up the drive along the south side of her modest house.

The fellow's appearance was neat to a fault. Even in the wilting August morning, his suit and shirt were well pressed, and a fine serge hat sat at a jaunty angle upon his head. Though the wind stirred up a fine dust from the road, it appeared as though none had dared settle upon his dapper clothing. As he drew close to the porch, she noticed he held his left hand behind his body.

This spruce man must be the widower who had made the 150-mile move from Minneapolis, slightly north and a good ways east of Marshall, Minnesota. Hattie Crabtree had heard from Jane Pruitt, who had heard it first from Emma Graham, who had it on good authority from Irvetta Auerbach, that a Mr. Determan of the Twin Cities had purchased the house and twenty acres next to Betsy's property. The news had set a full two-thirds of the Marshall Ladies' Sewing Circle buzzing like so many bees.

"Elmore Determan's the name," the bewhiskered gentleman announced, extending the nosegay of orange coneflowers he had hidden behind his back. "Seeing as how we're going to be neighbors, ma'am, I brought these daisies for you. And might I say, while it's true the Lord's earthly garden holds such a variety of radiant flowers, all pale in comparison to your delicate beauty."

Struck dumb by his flattering words, Betsy's hand stilled on the handle of the barrel churn she had been steadily turning. For a few moments the liquid inside continued sloshing, then it too fell silent, overtaken by the sibilant sounds of innumerable insects and conjoined twitters of robin, meadowlark, and bobolink.

Radiant flowers? Delicate beauty?

What nonsense.

"Rudbeckia," she responded, throwing out the first thing that came to her mind. "Rudbeckia is the proper name for those flowers, Mr. Determan. You picked them down near my ditch, didn't you?"

His smile grew only wider, creasing his face in a most pleasant way. "Yes, ma'am, I did."

She noticed that his eyes were every bit as blue as the summer sky behind him. How did a man full grown manage to have about him the air of a carefree, impenitent little boy? she wondered. Extending the bouquet toward her, he lifted his eyebrows. A green inchworm and two black spiders adorned his offering, each crawling its own direction across the profusion of petals. Lord only knew what other insects his posy contained.

"Will you take them? Please?"

Gesturing toward the stairs, she sputtered, "You can set them there. I have to get this butter churned."

"I'd be happy to give you a hand." A second later, his jacket lay next to the flowers on the wooden steps, and he rolled up his sleeves. His arms were strong for a city man, she noticed, and sunbrowned. His shoulders, too, appeared to be the sort that had managed their fair share of work over the years.

He chuckled. "Surely you don't eat all this butter yourself, Miss Wilcox. Why, you'd be fat as a little tusker if you did. Move on over now, ma'am, and let me have a go at this."

Under his capable hand, the crank turned smoothly and the rhythmic, sloshing sound resumed. If Betsy was flabbergasted to have had to slide quickly down the bench as her new neighbor made himself at home, she was even more shocked when his voice lifted in song.

"Shall we gather at the river,
Where bright angel feet have trod,
With its crystal tide forever
Flowing by the throne of God?
Yes, we'll gather at the riv—"

"I most certainly do not eat all this butter myself, Mr. Determan," she said, finally finding her tongue and interrupting the spiraling chorus. "I keep a small amount for myself and sell the rest," she replied, shooting her new neighbor her most disapproving expression.

"Is it good?"

"Why, most certainly!"

"I might buy some if it's good." His twinkling gaze lit upon her, disarming the tart response on the tip of her tongue. For heaven's sake, Mr. Elmore Determan had a *dimple* right in the middle of his cheek.

What manner of man brought flowers to an utter stranger of the opposite sex, took over her chores, and had the indecorous manners to sing one of those newfangled gospel songs at the top of his lungs? The fatuous type who frequented camp meetings and tent revivals, no doubt. Why, the old fool had to be seventy years if he was a day.

You're no spring chicken yourself, Elizabeth Wilcox.

Glancing down at her own knuckles that had grown more knotty with each passing year, she realized she had passed her sixty-eighth birthday in May. With her only sister and both parents having passed into the hereafter, there was no longer anyone to make an occasion of the Ides of May, as her father had always referred to the day of her birth.

For over thirty years she had taught school. Teaching had been a good vocation, and her savings had enabled her to purchase this modest homestead and acreage where she had spent the past ten years of her life. There had been a time when she had grieved over the realization that marriage and motherhood had indeed passed her by, but all in all, she considered herself richly blessed by the many pupils she'd had the occasion to teach. Some of her former students wrote to her still.

And even though she had retired from the schoolroom, every Sunday morning she led twenty-three students, ages seven to twelve, in ninety minutes' instruction of Bible teachings, Christian living, and, for good measure, a sprinkling of the virtues of convention and etiquette. Today's youth were simply not being raised with the same values that had been instilled a generation earlier.

She glanced askance at her new neighbor, whose white beard waggled as he whistled the remainder of his tune. With what kind of manners had he been raised? she wondered. Did he suffer from a lack of instruction, or had he cast aside a proper upbringing in favor of living so impetuously? What had his wife been like?

Gracious, why did she care?

"What do *you* think heaven will be like, Miss Wilcox?" Mr. Determan inquired in a cheery tone. "Do you expect we'll gather at the beautiful, silver river with all the saints?"

"I'm sure I don't know."

"But you believe Christ died for your sins, don't you? That the Son of God came to give hope and peace to fallen mankind?"

"Yes, good sir, I am well aware of my catechism."

"Well, praise the Lord for that! Hallelujah!"

Even as she wondered at the intrusive and highly personal nature of his subject matter, he continued speaking.

"Yessiree, I used to think all the Jesus-dying-for-my-sins busi-ness was all a bunch of fiddledy-hoo, until I met the man."

Betsy felt her face draw into a prunish expression. "You've met Jesus Christ?"

Elmore Determan's blue eyes twinkled, and a merry smile creased the tanned, wrinkled face. "Oh yes, I have. I met him at a revival back in '75, and he's been at my side ever since."

Betsy cleared her throat and lifted her brows. "You have no way of knowing I taught school for thirty-four years, Mr. Determan, nor that my greatest vexation with students was caused by care-less, imprecise speech. Now, there's only you and me on this bench. I do not see the Lord. Perhaps what you meant to say was that you experienced some sort of religious fancy, or that after years of dissolute living you repented of your wicked ways and de-cided to follow the path of righteousness?"

"No, I meant what I said." His hand stilled on the churn while his expression waxed gleeful . . . and if she wasn't mistaken, just a bit mischievous. "I take it maybe you haven't met him up close, then. Perhaps one day I can introduce the two of you."

She was right: he *was* one of those religious extremists. How otherwise perfectly sensible people could get caught up in such mania was beyond her. Church was church, and religion was reli-gion. It was only seemly to follow the customs and heritage set forth by the noble men and women who had gone before them. Talking about the Lord as if he were sitting right on this bench? That was . . . what was the word he had used? *Fiddledy-hoo.* She al-lowed herself the pleasure of a slight, disdainful sniff at his outra-geous comments.

"I make it a habit of introducing him around, on the off chance a person might not be acquainted with the great Jehovah. I won't be on this green earth forever, but I aim to spread the Good News as far and wide as I can before I go. Yessiree, this old ticker of mine could give out any minute," the white-haired gentleman went on, winking broadly as he patted his chest. "And then, as I always say, it'll be 'no more Elmore.' "

His laughter was booming, genuine and infectious, causing her pursed lips to loosen a little. *No more Elmore.* How much mileage had he gotten out of that particular witticism over the years? she wondered, watching him in his merriment. His features were pleasantly arranged, she decided, noticing his chin, his nose, the shape of his brow. And as hale and spry as he appeared, she would not be surprised if his heart should beat another full score of years.

"This may be wishful thinking on my part, Miss Wilcox," he said, raising snow-white brows and gazing into her face with those lively blue eyes. "But as we're going to be neighbors, it seems only right that we should become better acquainted. I was wondering if I might bring over a few ears of sweet corn around suppertime? If you were to supply the butter and salt, we could have ourselves a feast of grain. See, that way, too, I could gauge whether your butter's any good—"

"I'll have you know my butter is excellent, Mr. Determan. You will find none better in these parts." As she fired off her retort, she realized she had just provided tacit consent for the wily old man to enjoy his sweet corn at her dinner table. Oh, why had she taken his bait? It was a well-known fact that single men and widowers were ever in pursuit of a woman's good cooking.

Her neighbor stood and stretched his long legs. "Well, then. I look forward to sampling your fresh, good butter, Miss Wilcox. You have a big pot of water boiling, and I'll shuck the corn before I come. See you about five?"

Betsy could think of nothing to say as he paused at the bottom of the stairs, favoring her with another of his winning smiles. Nor was she able to formulate a suitable response as he tipped his hat and strolled past the hollyhocks. Only when he reached the dirt drive and lifted his arm in a confident wave did she shake her head in disbelief at what had transpired.

For all her elocutionary skills, she'd just been rendered speech-less.

Returning to her original position on the bench, she set her hand on the metal handle of the churn and stared after her new neighbor. She may have been outmaneuvered this time, but as sure as the dawn, she would not allow such a thing to happen again. She would be well prepared when Elmore Determan returned with his ebullient faith, his jovial manner, and however many ears of husked sweet corn.

Yes, Elizabeth. You'd best be prepared.

Giving the crank a halfhearted turn, she experienced a strange, winded feeling as she recalled her neighbor's blue gaze. Heaven above, was it possible for a person to be thrown completely askew by a pair of eyes? a dimple? a sprightly grin? Or had she simply become muzzy-headed from the heat?

Turning hard on the crank, she was surprised to find herself humming the very tune to which she had, a short while ago, taken exception.

CHAPTER 2

ELMORE whistled as the pile of cornhusks at his feet grew larger. It was too hot to be indoors or even sit on the front porch, so he'd moved his cane rocker from beneath the eaves out to the yard, where he rocked contentedly in the welcoming shade of an elm tree.

For all the years he'd spent living in the city, he had not forgotten the uniqueness of a late August afternoon on the prairie. Wide open and windy, yet sultry, rich, and heavy. Something about this month was peculiar from all others, he mused, perhaps due to the gentle yet persistent welling up from the earth and its growing things, a ripening into maturity that stippled the air and piqued the memory.

He closed his eyes and recalled Augusts gone by—Augusts he had spent living on the plains rather than in the noisiness of the city. Some of the prairie years he had spent coopering; others he had farmed. He couldn't complain about his years of city work or city living, but he preferred the sight of the spreading land, the tall waving grasses, the freedom of the wind.

He could no longer deny he was slowing down. In a few weeks' time, he would celebrate his seventieth birthday. His mouth formed the word: *seventy*. How could that be? he wondered, a faraway smile forming on his lips. Where had the years flown? Inside, he didn't feel any older than he did as a young man of nineteen, but his aging, more-often-than-not-aching body insisted upon the truth in that seemingly unbelievable concept: he would soon begin his eighth decade of life.

Was it in the Lord's plan that he would live until ninety? a hundred? He chuckled. Ah, such things were not for him to know. With the wind in his ears and the weight of a succulent ear of corn between his hands, he raised his face and gave silent thanks to the Creator for giving him life and for allowing him to return to the prairie he had always loved. *This* was where he wanted to live out the remainder of his earthly years, however many there may be.

Opening his eyes, he glanced at the modest property he had purchased. A house with three rooms. Pasture on either side of the small barn out back. An empty chicken coop. He didn't need more. As the previous owner, an aging widow, had done, he would rent most of his twenty acres to the farmer living north of him. Upon making the real estate transaction, he had learned that James Pennington, the farmer, also rented farmland from other neighbors . . . among them, Miss Elizabeth Wilcox.

A pleased expression settled upon his face as he thought of the intriguing, exacting woman he had met today. He didn't know what had possessed him to stop and gather a bouquet of daisies— *rudbeckia*—he amended, recalling the crisp yet lilting sound of her voice, nor what had inspired him to use such embellished speech upon making her acquaintance. He only knew that with each response she gave, he found himself enjoying her company all the more. And to tell the truth, he had rather enjoyed making mischief with the very proper Miss Wilcox. He imagined she had endured enough naughty schoolboys over the years for his rascality to be of too much consequence.

Setting down the husked ear of corn, he reached for another and paused to examine the tuft of silk protruding from the end. It had dried to a crispy brown, indicating its readiness. Margaret, his wife, had been in her prime when he'd lost her to childbed twenty-four years ago, along with his only son and namesake. His smile faded. Meg had been thirteen years younger than he, filled with life—and plenty of sparks and fire to go along with all her vivacity.

The pain of losing her had faded over the years, yet sometimes . . . he sighed.

Sometimes, when he really stopped and thought, he was aware of his loneliness. Most times, it did not trouble him. After Meg's passing there had been plenty to keep him occupied. Raising his daughter, Clarice, keeping food on the table, and, of course, spreading news of the Savior wherever he could. A gentleman at his church back in Minneapolis had exclaimed some years ago, "Determan, it seems as though your objective is to distress the comfortable and comfort the distressed!"

He had never forgotten those words, nor had he quite known in what manner the fellow had rendered them. But if that was what his plain talk about Jesus had accomplished over the years, then perhaps his outspokenness wasn't an entirely bad thing.

He thought of Clarice and sighed again. Clarice and her husband lived in New Ulm, a thriving town situated approximately halfway between Marshall and Minneapolis. No doubt, as soon as her schedule permitted, she would be traveling westward on the Number Eighty-One to inspect her father's domicile and cluck her tongue.

Allowing his thoughts to amble, he found himself wondering how Clarice and Miss Wilcox would get on. One eyebrow went up as he decided most likely, not well at all. Thankfully, there would be no occasion for them to meet. Humming an even livelier rendition of the gospel he had sung for his gingery neighbor this morning, he began shucking the ear of corn in his hands. Yessiree, taking his supper next door tonight would be just the thing. In fact, he rather hoped their conversation would continue on the same note on which it had left off.

"Rudbeckia," he said aloud when he had closed the chorus, trying to mimic the exact precision of speech and depth of reproach she had uttered in that single word. Ribbons of green cornhusk and whitish yellow silk fell to the ground while he sought just the right diction. "Rud*beck*ia. Rud*beck*-ia." There. That was it— "Rud*beck*-ia."

"Rud*beck*-ia," he repeated in falsetto, delighted that he had captured the essence of her articulation. Genuine laughter bubbled up from inside him, and he again realized how very much he was looking forward to spending more time in the company of Miss Elizabeth Wilcox.

⤳

Many times Betsy had appreciated the amount of trouble to which the settler of this humble prairie homestead had gone by culling dozens of cottonwood saplings from the edges of nearby Lake Marshall and transplanting them onto the property. Now well established, several of the trees topped fifty feet in height. Today the ever-present prairie wind rustled pleasantly through countless green, triangular-shaped leaves, and in the relative shelter of the grove of cottonwoods on the west side of her home, Betsy set up her outdoor table with great care . . . and determination.

Mr. Elmore Determan might have inveigled himself to dinner, but she would not play hostess to any sort of impropriety: they would take their meal outdoors.

A crisp white cloth went down first. Armed with a miniature hammer and several brads, she tacked the fabric into place beneath the rough tabletop. For this open-air meal she had decided in favor of her everyday plates rather than the few pieces of fine china she owned. These she lifted from the seat of her chair and set on the spread with a decisive thump. The artful old gentleman would have to be content with what he got. What nerve he possessed . . . first challenging the quality of her butter, then inviting himself over to try some.

To be truthful, his departure this morning had left her in a curious frame of mind. Foremost, of course, she retained a degree of irritation caused by his presumptuous manner and outlandish claims. And adding insult to injury was that catchy, unbefitting song he had burst out singing while churning her butter. No matter how many times she had tried ridding her mind of its first verse and refrain, one or the other would steal back like a thief in the night, causing her no little consternation.

But as she laid a knife and a cup by each plate, she realized that something like a challenge also stirred within her. She was actually looking *forward* to seeing her new neighbor again. How could that be? Especially since he irritated her so?

Perhaps she was merely experiencing a feeling similar to the one she used to have when faced with a particularly vexing student. She was proud to recollect that in all her years of teaching, she had never been bested by a pupil. It may have taken some time to establish the rules and boundaries, but she had found that stern discipline tempered by fairness and small amounts of clemency had served her in an excellent fashion. But before she could think of how she might apply a similar strategy to her new neighbor, his voice gave her a start.

"Are you nailing down the plates so they won't blow away, or are you worried I might abscond with your dishes?"

Whirling about, she was confounded to see the very gentleman about whom she had been preoccupied for hours. How had he sneaked up on her? She'd been glancing toward the lane every few minutes to spot his arrival. With a sack—presumably filled with corn—he gestured toward the hammer and nails lying near one of the plates. His blue eyes sparkled while he waited for her reply.

Caught off guard yet again, Betsy could not seem to manage a clever retort, or for that matter, any sort of retort at all. Of their own accord, her hands flew to her apron and smoothed away its creases. *Why did you do that?* she immediately chided herself. *He's going to think you're overly concerned with your appearance—or even preening, of all things. Irvetta Auerbach might still be trying to catch herself a man, but she hasn't got the sense to know she's too old for such foolishness.*

"I'm not ready for you yet," she finally sputtered, gathering up the hammer and brads and sliding them into her roomy apron pocket. Feeling hot and snappish and slightly winded, she was dismayed to find herself once again taking notice of her neighbor's smart appearance and arresting features. He was as neat and crisp as he had been earlier in the day, while she felt as wilted as an uprooted weed.

His lips twitched, and it struck her that along with his burlap sack, he carried with him an air of suppressed amusement. Fifty years ago she might have cared to engage in happy-go-lucky banter with a member of the opposite sex, but such departures from conventional conversation were simply not seemly for persons of their age and maturity. Surely he must realize that . . . *if* he possessed any of the latter.

Reaching deep into her inner well of fortitude and experience, she found the composure to acknowledge his ridiculous greeting. This morning he may not have realized that she did not care to be trifled with, but she must set forth that line of demarcation without any further delay. "For your information, Mr. Determan," she began in a no-nonsense tone, "I have no intention of nailing down my plates—which would no doubt shatter if I were to attempt such a thing, nor do I host any real suspicion that you wish to flee with my dishes. If your curiosity must be satisfied, I used these implements to fasten the tablecloth to the underside of the table."

"Yes, ma'am." He nodded, waiting as though he sensed she had more to say. She might even have believed he was earnestly considering her words if not for the glint of mischief she detected in his gaze.

Lifting her chin in a way that had never failed to let her pupils know she meant business, she went on. "I would also appreciate, sir, if you would cease and desist addressing me in such a colloquial manner. I am not the sort of woman who cares to be trifled with."

Her neighbor puckered his lips and let forth a low, admiring whistle while shifting the bag of corn from one hand to the other. "I'll bet you turned out some right fine students over the years, Miss Wilcox. Some real big talkers."

Irritation with her new neighbor pricked her even more strongly than before. "Did you hear what I said, Mr. Determan? I do not wish to be spoken to in a playful manner, handled idly, indulged, mocked, ridiculed, or anything else of that ilk. Nor do I care for flirtation or coy remarks. Certainly I make myself clear."

Up went the snowy brows. "Certainly! I heard you loud and clear, Miss Wilcox. We both did." His face creased into an outright grin. "Me and you-know-who. Now where would you like me to put the corn?"

Betsy couldn't help the frustrated *ooh* that escaped her as she gestured abruptly toward the porch. With an obliging nod, he turned and started for the house, leaving her staring at his back and hotly aware that he had once again tied her tongue in knots. Half of her wanted to call out that he could just march himself straight back home, while the other half wanted him to stay long enough so she could give him a proper dressing-down.

As if he'd read her mind, he looked over his shoulder and grinned. *What an exasperating man*, she thought, trying to formulate what she might next say to him. Moments later he reached the foot of the porch steps. "Why don't I have myself a seat on this perch you have up here," he called, turning a second time, "and wait out-of-doors till you ring the dinner bell. You but say the word, Miss Wilcox, and I'll carry our meal to your winsome little table." She thought he may have even winked, but with the way the late-afternoon sun struck his face, it was impossible to say. She'd known him only half a day, but she wouldn't put it past him.

"It would also be my pleasure to help you with the dishes after our alfresco repast." He sounded out of breath after he'd climbed the three stairs and settled his frame onto the bench. He set the corn at his feet. "You're very kind . . . go to such trouble . . . least I can do." His playful manner had vanished, and his last words had been spoken in a gentle, gracious manner.

"It's . . . no trouble," she found herself replying, helplessly studying the bewhiskered gentleman who had doffed his hat, closed his eyes, and leaned his head back against the side of her house. How could it be that a few minutes ago she was ready to give him a swift rebuke but now felt her anger dissipating in the face of his disarming appearance?

"I'll just take this and go inside," she muttered, bending to retrieve the corn. Not waiting for a reply, she hurried into the kitchen. The water she'd set on the stove was boiling at a good clip, creating what she supposed must be a tropical climate inside the already sweltering room.

Fresh perspiration moistened her neck and back, but she knew it wasn't just the temperature of the kitchen that unsettled her so. What *was* it about Elmore Determan that kept her as ruffled and rattled as . . . as she didn't know what? she asked herself, setting the bag of corn on the table. There was simply no word to describe how she felt.

In the short course of a single day, this solitary man had unbalanced her to a degree that thirty-four years' worth of schoolroom students, school boards, and superintendents had never managed. Withdrawing the hammer and nails from her apron, she shook her head at all of Mr. Determan's silly repartee. But when she thought of him, what appeared in her mind were not his merry blue eyes or his impish smile but the unguarded, almost defenseless expression upon his face as he'd closed his eyes and reclined in her porch seat. Something about that picture twisted her heart in an uncomfortable, unfamiliar way.

She put the corn on, then opened the icebox and removed the butter crock. What was she doing having supper with such a . . . such an unusual man? she wondered with no small amount of anxiety. Her movements were choppy and hurried, not calm and deliberate as they usually were.

What did she have in common with Elmore Determan except for shared residence in Lyon County? What would they talk about over their meal? Another thought struck her. What if he had fallen asleep on her front porch? How would she wake him? *Should* she even awaken him?

Nothing in her life had prepared her for such a predicament, and she almost wished he had never come over. Yet, if she was honest with herself, there was a part of her that was the tiniest bit glad for a change in the sameness of her days.

CHAPTER 3

"YOU DON'T say, Betsy! He fell asleep right on your porch?" Hattie Crabtree's mouth formed a perfect O and her swiftly basting hands came to a complete halt as she looked around at the assembled members of the Marshall Ladies' Sewing Circle. Even the *clackety-clack* of Jane Pruitt's sewing machine treadle had fallen silent.

Aware of all eyes upon her, Betsy regretted saying anything about her new neighbor having come to supper. But as Irvetta Auerbach had progressed from broad hints to outright nosiness about the Twin Cities widower who had moved next door to Betsy, Elizabeth had ended up giving a brief synopsis of Mr. Determan's visitation earlier in the week.

This week the Marshall Ladies' Sewing Circle was meeting in the Pruitts' handsome sitting room in downtown Marshall, while the group continued their goodwilled efforts making warm winter clothing for the less fortunate souls of Lyon County. Fourteen of the group's twenty-one members were present this warm and muggy afternoon—eleven busy with various implements of stitchery, the other three knitting caps and mittens.

"Oh my, whatever did you do?" Emma Graham exclaimed, dashing Betsy's fervent hope of someone introducing another topic.

"Well, I woke him up, of course," she answered more sharply than she intended, but seeing the deliciously intrigued expression on Irvetta's face irked her.

Miss Irvetta Auerbach was far too fanciful and impulsive for a woman of her fifty-some years, Betsy had decided a good while ago. Though her appearance was in no way unpleasant—plain features tending a bit toward pudginess, clear hazel eyes, and dark hair, which in the past several years had taken on an admirable shade of gray—she had never married. Perhaps that was why the woman was an enthusiastic and incurable romantic, working tirelessly at promoting the matrimonial state in whatever way she could.

"Did you *still* take your meal together?" Irvetta persisted. "Did he like your butter?"

"He seemed to," Betsy answered evasively, distinctly recalling that in tandem with the basket of bread she'd set alongside the corn, Mr. Determan had all but emptied her butter crock. What she didn't reveal was that he had heaped lavish amounts of praise upon her throughout the meal—for her bread, her buttermaking, her hospitality—and once he'd even commented on the rare color of her eyes . . . as if brown eyes were unusual. What nonsense. A lesser woman might easily have been swept away by such flattery.

"I heard he *lived* in these parts for a time, back in the seventies," Irvetta was saying.

"He did? I do not recall ever making his acquaintance," Jane commented, puzzled. An elegant woman in her midfifties, she was considered one of the pillars of the rapidly growing town of Marshall.

"I didn't know him in the early days, but he turned up at church last Sunday," Mabel Dunn contributed, nodding her approval. The eldest member of the circle at eighty-one years of age, Mabel looked like a tiny, fragile, snow-white bird. She raised her right hand for emphasis, thimbles glittering on her third and fourth fingers. Her voice possessed that precarious tremor peculiar to persons of her maturity. "He sang louder than the choir and congregation combined."

"He was quite inappropriate." Anna Dilley's already flushed cheeks became the color of cherries. "The way he shouted 'hallelujah' and 'amen' throughout Reverend's sermon—why, my children scarcely behaved themselves for wanting to snicker all during the service. And what's more," she grumbled, clearly outraged, "he wasn't the least bit embarrassed. He seemed to be enjoying himself!"

Elmore Determan singing at the top of his lungs in church? Betsy wasn't at all surprised by Anna's remarks about her new neighbor. What amazed her, however, was the number of circle members who responded to Anna's commentary with amusement. Did none of them have proper respect for Sunday worship?

"I believe I'll come to your church next week!" Emma declared to a fresh round of laughter, her eyes crinkling with merriment. "If the Second Coming were to occur right in the middle of our service, I have often wondered how many would be awake to notice."

"Has Mr. Determan joined your congregation, Anna, or will he be visiting around?"

"If he's making the rounds, it sounds as if we need to prepare for him!"

Questions and comments flew riotously about the room until Mrs. Dilley spoke over the assemblage. "I sincerely hope this man has made his first and last visit to our evangelical association," the red-cheeked matron concluded, stabbing the needle back through her cloth. "And I don't find any of this amusing, ladies. Elizabeth, what do you have to say?"

Finding herself once again at the center of attention, Betsy hesitated. With everything inside her she agreed with the younger matron's assessment of Mr. Determan's lacking social graces, yet she was shocked to find herself experiencing a flicker of loyalty toward the dapper gentleman who had sat at her table and asked her about herself.

"I wonder if he's looking for a new *wife?*" Irvetta postulated, drawing the gazes of thirteen sets of eyes. "I heard that his wife died years and years ago, but you know a man's never too old to be looking. And for that matter, we aren't either."

"Well, I'm not looking at any man," Hattie announced with vinegar in her tone, silencing the titters that had begun at Irvetta's last remark. "But widowers? If you ask me, they're all looking. Since John died, you would not believe the number of old gallants who've come out of the woodwork, thinking I'd be overjoyed to say 'I do' and begin starching their shirts."

"Not *all* widowers are like that," Irvetta objected, gesturing toward Betsy. "Why, I'm sure Mr. *Determan* is nothing of the sort, *is* he?"

"How could I say? I hardly know him."

Irvetta, having yielded herself to the rapture of her fertile fancy, did not heed the stern look Elizabeth directed her way. "Well, you can *never* tell what will happen," she trilled. "Think of it, Betsy! Maybe Mr. Determan's falling asleep on your porch was his way of choosing you! Like Ruth slept before Boaz, only in reverse. Remember three years ago when Stanley Foley proposed to Grace Emery? Now who would have ever thought those two would make a pair? But look at them today, happy as larks. And then there's Mr. Forbes and Ada Kinmore, and do you remember Florence Johns—"

"We remember, 'Vetta," Emma interrupted patiently. "But I think you're a bit premature in linking Mr. Determan's name with our Elizabeth's. They have only shared a single, neighborly, get-acquainted meal. That hardly puts them in the same alliance as some of these other couples."

Couples? Betsy quelled a most unladylike urge to snort. Who said anything about her and Mr. Determan being a couple?

Gazing directly at Betsy, Minnie Bernhard spoke up from the far corner of the room, her knitting needles having resumed their blurring speed. "I met your Mr. Determan the other day in town. Came around a corner and there he was. My, Elizabeth, did you notice his eyes? I thought them arresting. Or maybe it was the way his face lit when he smiled—"

"Pardon me for interrupting, but did any of you hear that a Mr. Haney of Minneapolis is going to buy out Wakeman's Drugstore?" Emma flashed a sympathetic glance toward Betsy as if to say she was sorry this applesauce about Elmore Determan had gone on as long as it had. "I hear he wants to put in a soda fountain, and he's also planning to—"

"Mr. Haney! Oh, how could I have forgotten? I *did* hear about him!" Irvetta interjected, looking as though she might explode. "And listen to this: he's *never* been married. Just think, next month we will have yet *another* eligible bachelor in town."

Thankfully, the conversation turned completely to the new-comer, a graduate of the University of Minnesota's pharmacy department. Betsy tried listening with interest as Irvetta relayed each piece of information she had learned, but as she worked at setting the sleeve into the girl's nightgown in her lap, she couldn't keep her thoughts from her unusual new neighbor, the man with the bright blue eyes and ready smile who trumpeted his praises of the Son of God for all to hear.

The man who had thought to bring her a spray of rudbeckia.

≯

"Do you ever find yourself at all lonely, Miss Wilcox?"

"Lonely?" Betsy reflected on Mr. Determan's question, slightly less wary of him than she had been upon first making his acquaintance. However, he possessed a mysterious quality that continued leaving her off-kilter more often than not. They had now shared three meals in less than two weeks, and this evening they sat side by side on her porch seat—with as much space between them as she could manage—sipping lemonade.

"Are you asking if I am lonely, as in *desolate* and *forlorn?* I should say not." She sniffed. "With my friends, the various works in progress in the Marshall Ladies' Sewing Circle, and the large number of pupils in my Sunday school class, I am really quite preserved from loneliness."

"Yes, of course," he replied thoughtfully. After taking a sip of his beverage, he sighed with contentment and gestured toward the western sky, where the setting sun illuminated a bank of fleecy clouds. "Would you take a look at that? Who could ever dream up such furious, glorious beauty? In fact, such a sight makes me want to fall to my knees and—"

"Yes, yes," she interjected, quite afraid he might do just that . . . and ask her to join him. "What made you ask if I was lonely?" She couldn't stop herself from inquiring, a defensive feeling having risen in her breast while replying to his initial question. Gripping her glass more tightly, she forced herself to take an unhurried sip before asking, "Do I *appear* to you to be lonely?"

His blue gaze fastened upon her with an expression she couldn't quite fathom, while a half smile played about his lips. In all her days she had never met such a person as Elmore Determan. That first day she had wanted to dismiss him without so much as a fare-thee-well, but during their meal beneath the cottonwoods she had become aware of a secret sense of enjoyment while in his company. Certainly Irvetta Auerbach must *never* be privy to such information.

"Yes indeedy, you appear to have your life in quite efficient order, Miss Wilcox," he replied, nodding.

"I 'appear' to . . . what do you . . . well! I hear you are visiting churches all over Marshall. Are *you* lonely, Mr. Determan?" she sputtered, wishing at once she hadn't recklessly turned tables and asked such a personal question of this unsettling gentleman. Only the Almighty knew how he might answer. But before she could moderate her reply, he chuckled and slapped his hand on his thigh.

"Am I lonely? I don't think I can count the number of women who have tried chasing me down over the years, believing they were doing their Christian duty to preserve me from loneliness."

Chasing him down? What arrogance! Oh, heavens, surely he didn't think she was.

Betsy didn't allow herself to finish the ludicrous thought. Despite the evening's coolness, she felt her face heat. In all her born years, she had never made a fool of herself by pursuing any man. That wasn't to say that in her prime she hadn't had a few fellows come courting. Things had just never . . . worked out. And after so many years, there was nothing romantic left inside her—and certainly not inside Mr. Determan, either.

"After Meg passed . . ." He surprised her by sighing and growing reflective. "After she was gone, I didn't feel called to take another wife, even though it might have been easier on Clarice to be raised with a woman's gentle touch in the home."

"Clarice?" she exclaimed, setting aside her discomfiture at the information he had divulged. "You have a daughter?"

"Oh yes, I have a daughter," he replied in an enigmatic tone.

A silence settled between them, and they each sipped their lemonade. It shouldn't surprise her that he had a daughter, she told herself sensibly; it was just that she had not thought of him as a father. Where *was* this daughter? she mused. On the other side of the country? Abroad? Didn't she care that her father was alone in a southwest Minnesota prairie community amongst strangers? And what of Meg? she wondered not for the first time. When had she died? Of what? Were there other children?

"I figure you're probably burning with curiosity down at the southern hemisphere of this bench there but are far too polite to ask, so you're hoping and praying I'll tell you more."

"Really, Mr. Determan!" she objected with a *tsk*ing sound. How could a person stir such a tender emotion inside her one second and exasperation in the next? "You needn't feel obligated on my account."

"Not in the least," he replied with a grin. "I can tell how badly you want to know."

"*Hardly*," she replied with a sniff. "If you were to walk off into the sunset without saying another word, I should not care one whit."

His booming laughter rang out, scattering a cluster of grackles that had settled in the yard below. "But, Miss Wilcox, what if my old ticker should give out while I am in the process of disappearing into that magnificent, resplendent sunset?" Winking, he patted his chest. "You would never know what you wish to know about me, and then, as I always say, it'll be no more—"

"Oh, you and your japery! The only thing the matter with your ticker, as you call it, Mr. Determan, is that it is filled with wisecracks and tomfoolery. I declare, you ought to call yourself '*go-more* Elmore,' for you appear more robust than all of my church elders combined."

"Why, Miss Wilcox, I had no idea you felt that way about me . . . or your church elders."

Betsy's face took on fresh color. "For pity's sake, Mr. Determan, you have never grown up."

" 'Whosoever shall not receive the kingdom of God as a little child, he shall not enter therein!' "

By now she felt two full beats behind her vexatious neighbor, and what was more, she knew he was enjoying himself to a colossal degree. While she strove for a fitting comeback to his revival preacher-style execution of that particular verse of Mark's Gospel, he unsettled her yet again by continuing in the contemplative tone he had used just a short while earlier.

"I was grown once, Miss Elizabeth Wilcox, but when I met up

with the Lord Jesus Christ, I decided to enter my second child-hood." He sighed and stroked his beard. "You see, I didn't know how to laugh about anything back in those old days, and I sure as shootin' didn't know the first thing about finding joy."

"After your wife died?"

"Yes, after Meg died, and every year before that, numbering back to '29. That's the year I came into this world, but I like to think I *really* began living in '75."

"After you attended that revival," Betsy couldn't help adding dryly, her opinion of such events much on the same level with ring fights and that offensive Buffalo Bill Wild West Show that would soon be coming to town. She had never understood how even good people seemed to lose every bit of common sense at such as-semblies, giving into excessive sentimentality, emotion, and even histrionics.

"That's not the half of it. Would you like to hear about how Jesus—"

"Perhaps another time, Mr. Determan," she said, though not unkindly. She didn't care to hear about such zealous goings-on but hoped she hadn't hurt his feelings by cutting him off.

A short silence passed while the evening wind soughed through the cottonwoods. Betsy took another sip of lemonade, nearly choking at his next words.

"Miss Wilcox, do you think you might find yourself able to call me Elmore? I hear around town you're known as Betsy." His face lit with an appealing smile, and he continued speaking, not allow-ing her an opportunity to reply. "And while you're thinking about that, I'll give you something else to chew on. This might just be wishful thinking, Miss Betsy Wilcox, but I'd like you to be my companion next Tuesday to the Wild West Show."

Time seemed to stop in its tracks. Was he merely seeking a *com-panion* . . . or something more? Had Irvetta Auerbach actually seen smoke where there was fire? Of all things—the Wild West Show? Oh, good heavens, now what?

"Why me?" was all she could seem to articulate.

"Why you? That's a good question, indeed." His whole face lit with pleasure as he took in her perplexed expression. "Because you are a virtuous woman, and I can see that you have a fear of the Lord."

"But—"

"No *buts* until you hear me out." He held up his hand, his joviality mellowing into an expression that was somehow tender and penetrating all at once. "Let me say that I appreciate your company more than I've appreciated any woman's in a long, long time. You possess a particularly fine mind, and for some reason, that inspires me to ruffle your feathers. Yes indeedy, in the short time I've known you, you've given me great enjoyment."

She gave him *enjoyment?* When had she ever been told something like that?

"You could choose any eligible woman in Lyon County, Mr. Determan. You need not choose me," she argued. Really, she was feeling a very odd throbbing deep within her chest as well as the inability to draw a full breath. Was *her* heart acting up?

"The Lord placed me next door to you, Miss Wilcox. I figure he must have done so for a reason."

"We hardly know one another!"

"We become better acquainted each time we see each other."

"But I'm too . . . *old* for such foolishness."

"Fiddledy-hoo."

"Fiddledy-hoo back!" she scoffed, seeing his features crease with delight.

"Will you take in the Wild West Show with me next Tuesday, Betsy Wilcox?" he proposed, eyebrows raised.

"I most certainly will not! I cannot abide such raucous, dusty, disorderly—"

"Hold up!" He raised his hand. His grin softened, and he inclined his head toward her. "I have one more thing to say."

"And what might that be?" Her retort was thorny, yet the tender expression on his face caused her to hold back the remainder of her opinions. She watched him sigh, and he turned back to face the setting sun.

"Betsy," he finally spoke, "I believe I am a little bit lonely."

CHAPTER 4

O
NLY fifty cents' admission to see the greatest exhibition in
the entire world! Twelve hundred men and horses in action! A veritable institution of heroes! For the very first
time, see Roosevelt's Rough Riders in the Battle of San Juan Hill
in the absolutely, positively most realistic reproduction of this famous battle you will ever see!"

As Elmore guided his buggy horse through the throng, Betsy
cringed at the derangement into which the pleasant town of Marshall had fallen. Barkers were seemingly everywhere, blaring the
marvels of Buffalo Bill and his traveling show. Already uncounted
numbers of spectators had descended upon the city for this one-of-
a-kind event, and they continued pouring in by all means possible.
The noise and dust were indescribable.

"Have you ever seen such a marvel in all your days, Betsy? There
have to be more than ten thousand here already, and it isn't even
noon yet!" Seated to her left on the narrow surrey bench, Elmore
radiated pure delight. Nearly shouting to make himself heard, he
added, "The Northwestern and Great Northern have been running special trains all morning."

"I've no doubt the saloons are overjoyed for that," she responded under her breath, still not over her displeasure about
Marshall becoming wet again after a two-year dry spell.

Why had she given her consent to come to such a frightful affair? In the past several days there had been countless moments during which she had nearly gathered her skirts and marched to the house next door to tell her neighbor that he could go on and see the western wildman and his production without her. But each time she resolved to do that, she remembered the expression on Elmore's face, the sound of his sigh, and his revelation after he'd asked her to accompany him to this extravagant show.

"Betsy, I believe I am a little bit lonely."

It made no sense that a single sentence could strike her so deeply. Yet in the space of those nine words, this man had taken the liberty of using a diminutive of her given name and had plucked uncomfortably at her heart as well. Was it because he had allowed her a glimpse of the humanness that lay beneath his cheerful, confident exterior, or was it because his admission, like a tuning fork, had caused a faint hum inside her?

Was she lonely?

"Isn't this a grand affair, Betsy? Look at the crowds! Smell that popcorn! Are you hungry? thirsty? What would you like to do first?" he offered gallantly, finding a spot to park in the hitching area. "Besides going back home," he added with a waggish grin as he set the brake and dismounted from the buggy. "If I know you at all, I'd guess that's what you're thinking right about now."

Lifting her eyebrows, she favored him with a reproachful expression while he assisted her to the ground. Unfazed, he chuckled and boldly tucked her arm inside his.

Taken unawares, Betsy gasped and pulled her arm free. "Mr. Determan! You can't do that!"

"I can't? I just did. And furthermore, you felt rather nice snugged up next to me."

If Betsy's heart had pounded oddly the evening he had declared his interest in her, it jigged to a breakneck tempo at this moment. His touch had lit through her like the electric lights the townspeople switched on at dusk—fast and bright. Kingdom come, what was happening to her? Swallowing hard, she glanced around to see who was in the vicinity.

With a wink, he inclined his head toward her. "Don't worry; I don't think anyone noticed."

"Oh . . . you!" she sputtered. "I never should have come!"

Still near her ear, his voice resonated with feeling. "Maybe not, but I'm awful glad you did. You're one dandy woman, Betsy. Now, if you're not hungry or thirsty, what do you say we investigate that row of vendors we just passed? I know your walls must be begging for a souvenir of this great day."

Elmore didn't try taking her arm again, but she was aware of his hand at her elbow several times as they perused what seemed like a limitless amount of merchandise. Accustomed to living the majority of her years alone, the closeness and touch of another human being—not to mention that of this dapper new neighbor—was far beyond disconcerting.

The mood of the crowd was one of suppressed excitement and festivity, but she scarcely noticed. Never had she imagined a man so attentive, and she found herself so distracted that she could barely think. At nearly every booth and stand, he tried interesting her in a trinket or two or ten. Finally, to appease his generous nature, she allowed him to purchase her three postcards of the Wild West Show.

"Now I have my souvenirs, Mr. Determan, and I thank you for them," she said, tucking them into the small bag she carried.

"You're most welcome." His smile was warm as he regarded her with those brilliant blue eyes. "You could have more than that, Betsy. All you have to do is—"

"Yoo-hoo, Elizabeth! Is that you, dear? I can't *believe* you're here!"

Turning her head, Betsy was dismayed to see Irvetta Auerbach bearing down upon them, her plump face aglow with pleasure.

The uneasy, conspicuous feeling she'd had upon setting out with Elmore Determan returned instantly, making her wonder just when it had left her.

"Good afternoon!" Irvetta cooed upon reaching them. "You *must* be Mr. Determan. I've heard *so* much about you."

Lifting his hat, Elmore bowed formally. "And I sincerely hope I live up to each of the fine tales you've heard, madam. May I ask what you are called?"

Remembering her manners, Betsy made the introductions, hoping her giggling, clearly enchanted acquaintance would promptly be on her way. Fortune, however, did not smile upon them so.

"Did the two of you make the trip to town *together*?" Irvetta inquired, making no move to walk on as she glanced between the two of them. Her eyebrows lifted expectantly, as if she were about to hear the most interesting news in the world.

A beaming Elmore did not disappoint. "We did indeed make the trip together, Miss Auerbach. What's more, when I asked Betsy to accompany me to this dazzling display of horsemanship, she accepted at once."

Accepted at once? Betsy nearly stamped on his foot. "I did no such thing! In fact, I very nearly did not accompany you at all."

A knowing smile developed on Irvetta's pink mouth, and not for the first time, Betsy thought that if the woman had a window in the center of her forehead at moments such as this, one could watch the wheels of her mind clacking round and round with ever-increasing velocity.

"Why, E-*lizabeth*," she gushed, "at our last sewing circle, I remember you sharing your opinion of the Wild West Show." Tilting her head toward Elmore, she added, "It must have been the *company* that changed her mind."

"You must be right, Miss Auerbach. I know I have greatly enjoyed Betsy's companionship since we shared our first meal together. That would be the first of three, in case anyone might be keeping count." His smile broadening, he gave a conspiratorial wink. "The way I see it, time's a-wasting. This old ticker of mine could give out any day now, and then, as I always say, it'll be . . ."

Betsy grimaced as he delivered his quip and basked in Irvetta's delighted giggles. Things were moving too quickly, and in absolutely the wrong direction. Her mischievous, fantastical neighbor had no idea of what he was getting himself in for with a newsmonger such as Irvetta Auerbach.

And what was worse, he was involving *her* as well.

"Betsy, you have an absolutely *charming* suitor! This is the most exciting thing to happen in Lyon County since . . . since I don't know when!" Irvetta exclaimed, still flushed from her laughter. "I need to run along now, but I look forward to hearing *all* about your day at our next circle!"

Elmore chuckled as their visitor melted into the crowd. "She's a busy one, isn't she?"

"And you aren't?" Betsy snapped, raising her chin. "I don't suppose you know what you've just done."

"I have a pretty fair idea. And might I add that your loveliness is magnified with such color in your cheeks?"

Loveliness? Her outrage increased at his brazen compliment, while the word *suitor* burned in her mind. Why had Irvetta gone and said such a thing? And she would continue spreading her prattle to everyone with whom she came in contact. *Did you know I just saw Betsy Wilcox with that new man, Elmore Determan?*

Suitor, suitor, suitor.

Betsy drew in a breath and released it, feeling both helpless and out of control. At the age of sixty-eight she had no business entertaining a gentleman caller; she was far too old to be wooed and serenaded. Besides, she'd heard enough talk about widowers over the years to know the only thing they wanted was a woman to cook for them, clean up after them, and nurse them when they ailed. And really, what did she know of Elmore Determan . . . except that in all respects he resembled an overgrown, wizened, ten-year-old boy?

"Shall we find our seats? According to my other ticker, it's half past one."

"I think, instead, Mr. Determan, we should find your buggy."

"Really!" His eyes twinkled, merry and warm. "That's quite a walk if all you want is a little smooch. Why, I'd be pleased to save us both the trouble and give you a peck on the cheek right this minute."

Elizabeth felt as if she were outside of her body, watching in disbelief, as Elmore bent toward her. Light as a butterfly's touch, his lips grazed her cheekbone. Straightening, he wore an enormously satisfied expression. "There, now. If your Miss Auerbach is still watching, she'll have no doubt as to my intentions."

"Your intentions?" Betsy's disembodiment ended abruptly in a cascade of hot and cold shivers. Her eyes sought his, finding what she feared would be revealed there.

"Don't you know? I'm courting you, Betsy," he affirmed, his gaze both ardent and eager. "I had a long talk with the Lord about this, and he thinks my taking up with you is a splendid idea."

"W-well . . . ," she stammered, the crowd of several thousand, the dust, the noise all fading to the background of her awareness. "What if *I* don't?"

"Maybe you ought to discuss matters with him before you make any rash decisions."

"Who are you calling rash? I'm not the one going about kissing *you* in public!"

"You could, you know, if you really wanted to."

"I have not been acquainted with you even one full month." Not deigning to respond to his repartee, she reasoned from another angle. "Besides what you have told me about yourself, I do not know the first thing about you. Perhaps 'Elmore Determan' is merely an alias for a man of unscrupulous character who moves from town to town, bilking unsuspecting women of their assets. You could be dangerous—even wanted!"

Elmore threw back his head and guffawed. "Dangerous?" he was finally able to utter, still chortling. "I can assure you I am not the least bit dangerous, but a fellow likes to fancy he is wanted . . . at least a little."

"Stop your . . . your *fiddledy-hoo*. I'm serious."

Raising his hands in a palms-up gesture, he shrugged. "I am, too."

"What have you ever been serious about?"

"Well, now that you've asked, for the first time in a quarter century, I find myself having serious thoughts of a certain woman. That would be you," he added with a wink.

"But why me? Why now?"

Where was the measured calm in her tone, the reliable voice that had carried her through more than three decades in the schoolroom? Her last words had sounded every bit as strident as something Irvetta might utter.

"Why you?" he mused, guiding her out of the increasing stream of foot traffic to an empty space between vending carts. With a buffer of canvas on each side of them, the rising din of the crowd was slightly muffled. His hand moved from her elbow, seeking her hand. This time, however, she did not pull away but allowed her fingers to lie limply between his. Perhaps she was in the midst of a dream; none of this was really happening.

Or was it?

"I believe I like you, Betsy, because of your honesty. Half the time, I think you'd just as soon tell me to jump in Lake Marshall as you would pour me another glass of your delicious lemonade. But I also think, the other half of the time you like me coming over and rattling your cage."

Before she could form a reply, he went on. "I haven't pressed this, but I also think you're a beautiful woman. And it's not just your pretty little face that enchants me; it's what lies behind it."

To her mortification, tears sprang to the corners of her eyes. Jaws trembling, she swallowed. He had called her *beautiful*. Glancing at the wrinkled hands that covered hers, she wondered at the sense of a man saying such a thing during her waning years. Why not years ago—before the bloom of her youth had withered to dust?

He sighed, gazing wistfully into her eyes. "As for your other question, 'why now?', I don't have as clear an answer for you. It was like the Lord tapped me on the shoulder after all these years and said, 'She's the one, Elmore. I've been saving her for you.'"

"Impossible!" Betsy contended, swallowing past the thickness in her throat. "And for as long as you continue insisting that the Lord walks around all day with you, taps you on the shoulder, and whispers such flights of fancy in your ear, I cannot give you any more of my time. We have nothing in common."

"Balderdash. We have more in common than you realize. Now, this might just be wishful thinking, but I was hoping you would allow me to escort you to church this coming Sunday."

"I . . . no!"

"Why not? Aren't you going?"

With the memory of the sewing circle conversation burning afresh in her brain, she searched frantically for a reply. At the same time, she suddenly recalled that her hand was still sandwiched between his, and she snatched her fingers free. "I do not even know why I am here with you today."

He tipped his hat and made a slight bow. "Because today is my seventieth birthday, and I wanted the pleasure of your company as I celebrate."

Today was his birthday? Why hadn't he made mention of that before? And why had he sought *her* company during such a landmark day in his life? Once again, she was at a loss for words.

"Will you let me take you to church Sunday, Betsy? I'll behave . . . I promise."

"Why don't I believe you?" she disputed, alert to the growing flickers of ambivalence inside her.

"You could look at it this way, my sweet. If a man were granted the privilege of praising the Lord in the company of such a fine woman as yourself, wouldn't it follow that he would want to be on his very best behavior? And if he were denied such a privilege, mightn't he go on by himself and perhaps take it upon himself to act up a bit?"

"As in singing and shouting at the top of his lungs in a respectable house of worship?" She eyed him squarely. "Mr. Determan, that's blackmail!"

His eyes danced with mischief. "What time shall I come by for you?"

Just then, a cacophony of bugles sounded, heralding the start of the show.

"Tell me later!" he shouted with a grin, taking back her hands with the excitement of a small boy. "Come on, Betsy-fretsy, our adventure is about to begin!"

CHAPTER 5

E LMORE couldn't remember when he'd passed a more glorious afternoon. The sights and sounds of the incredible show in progress far exceeded the descriptions that had been carried in the *Lyon County Reporter*.

The Wild West arena was enormous, and now, before their eyes, the charge up San Juan Hill was being reenacted—complete with a reproduction of the hill itself, a blockhouse, trenches, and barbed-wire fencing. To add to the drama, those on the imitation battlefield were not actors but valiant soldiers who had participated in the engagement in southern Cuba. Roosevelt's Rough Riders were represented, as were ex-regulars and volunteers of the United States Army, and even Cuban revolutionaries.

Finally the hill was taken, and the crowd erupted with wild emotion. Next to him, Betsy continued observing the goings-on quietly, without adding to the whooping and cheering from spectators on all sides of them. Even so, he would bet her sharp gaze hadn't missed a thing. A spreading feeling of contentment coursed through him as he continued stealing glances at the petite, dignified woman beside him.

Elizabeth Wilcox was really something.

At his age, he'd certainly not expected having his head turned and heart stirred in such a way. He'd been alone for so long, com-

233

fortably so, but now . . . something was drastically different. A long-extinguished spark had ignited upon making her acquaintance, and since then, thoughts of this pretty, prickly woman had filled his mind.

Though Margaret, his wife, had been much different, he had been deeply in love with her. Thirteen years his junior, Meg had been vivacious and sweet. She'd been an attentive and loving mother to Clarice, whom they had conceived during their first Christmas together, soon after their marriage.

Meg's barrenness for the next eleven years had been a great source of grief for her, and he remembered well their joy when she became certain she was carrying again. The months of confinement had gone well, with only the usual discomforts women suffered while with child. Even as she entered her labor, there was no forewarning of the hemorrhage that had come upon her, swift and deadly as a silent sword to her vitals.

He'd been forty-six when Meg had died; Clarice, twelve. Meg and the baby had been gone two months when he'd noticed a handbill for a traveling gospel event, promising abundant hope and new life to all who attended. From the depths of his despair he'd latched onto those assurances and gone to the assembly with his despondent, unwilling daughter in tow.

Once there, it hadn't taken even two hours for his spiritual conversion to occur. Even now, nearly a quarter-century later, tears sprang to his eyes when he recalled that moment of understanding: Jesus Christ had died so sinners such as he, Elmore Determan, could go to heaven. No sacrifice, ever, was comparable to the Son of God's death on the cross. How could he have walked around for so many years, oblivious to the Father's plan of salvation for mankind? Meg had known, he'd concluded in retrospect, but he'd been blind, deaf, and dumb to the truth.

How deeply he regretted his many years of unbelief—more than half his lifetime. While it was true he'd never been anything but hardworking and law-abiding, he had not honored the greatest commandment: to love God with all his heart and mind and strength. It wasn't until that night that the eternal significance of those words became manifest.

Who knew how things might have turned out if only he'd known the Savior before that?

But even after all these years of being a Christian, he still wondered if it had been a mistake to take Clarice to the revival that day. Not because she'd been too young to hear the gospel and decide for Jesus, but because it had overwhelmed her . . . and ultimately divided them.

As far as he knew, his daughter's heart continued to be locked up as tight as it had been the day they'd laid her mother to rest. Over the years he'd tried everything he could think of to reach her, but it was as if the more deeply he loved Jesus Christ, the further she'd retreated from him and the Lord.

Nonetheless, in gratitude for the gift he'd received, he resolved to spread the love and joy of the Lord wherever he went, until he no longer had breath to do so. Lately, there had been moments during which catching his wind was more difficult than it had ever been, making him wonder if that day might not be too far around the corner. At times, it seemed he could feel and hear his blood rushing through his veins. Though he had no fear of his own passing, he continued harboring worry for the loss of his daughter's soul.

"Have you fallen asleep again, Mr. Determan?" Betsy's distinctive voice tickled his ear, and his lips twitched at the unmistakable disapproval in her tone. She was as different from Meg as day was from night, but he knew there was a woman of great substance and intelligence beneath her prim and proper exterior. Mentally shaking off his weighty thoughts, he opened his eyes and took in his companion's appearance.

It wasn't difficult to see past the network of fine lines on her face to the maiden she once was. Clear brown eyes sat over a straight, pert nose. Her cheekbones were set high, creating a most lovely plane extending downward to her jawline. Perched above the oval of her face and upswept silver hair was an understated black silk hat, finishing her appearance with grace and dignity.

"I can't thank you enough for accompanying me today," he declared in the waning roar of the crowd. "What a fine birthday this has been!"

"I should think your Buffalo Bill has more to do with it than I."

"You might be surprised, Betsy dear."

Eyes widening at his endearment, she made no comment. Her fingers twisted the cords on the bag she carried while the battle scene was cleared of its mock casualties and sharpshooter Annie Oakley was announced.

"Pardon me for a short while," he said, as nature called.

She waved him on, and he made his way to the row of backhouses behind the stadium, hoping he might be back in time to watch some of Annie Oakley. But on his return to the stands, a bit winded from his exertion, he stopped at a flower cart to catch his breath. While there, he selected an arrangement of chrysanthemums, cattails, and bittersweet to surprise Betsy.

Thinking he might save steps as well as disrupt fewer people on the way back to his seat, he decided to reenter the stands one entrance down from the one he exited. The report of a rifle rang out, followed by the cheers of thousands. He wished he could see more of the shooting exhibition, but at the same time, his steps seemed to be costing him much energy. Slowly climbing the wooden ramp up to the seating, he caught sight of a familiar face out of the corner of his eye, and for a long moment, his gaze locked with that of his daughter's.

Clarice Determan Wilson appeared as startled to spy her father as he did her, but then, pasting a spurious smile on her face, she lifted her arm in a nonchalant greeting, making no effort to rise. She was perhaps ten feet up in the stands, only twenty feet over and a row or two up from where he and Betsy had been taking in the show. She sat amidst a group of finely dressed women, and he surmised that she and her important friends had come here on one of the special trains this morning to watch the show.

Clarice now was older than Meg had been when she'd died, but her resemblance to her mother continued to be remarkable. But whereas Margaret had been petite and soft-spoken, Clarice had grown to an ample size and was often corrosive. With a sad, slight nod toward her, he continued back to his seat, his enjoyment of the day extinguished.

Had Clarice intended to make contact with him while she was in town, or would she have slipped back to New Ulm as quietly as she had come? he wondered, suspecting the truth was his latter supposition. He'd written her twice since he'd moved and had given her more than sufficient notice of his plans to move before that.

Did she even remember it was his birthday?

His heart ached with both heaviness and pain as he slipped back into his seat beside Betsy. Why was he so weary? Right this minute, he wanted nothing more than to go home. Taking several deep breaths, he tried gaining control over the shroud of sadness that had settled upon him.

"Are those flowers for me, Mr. Determan, or did you intend to hold them the remainder of the afternoon?"

Shaking his head, he handed the festive-looking spray to Betsy. With questioning eyes, she accepted the gift and offered her thanks. On the field below, Annie Oakley and Buffalo Bill began shooting down balloons that had been released to great heights. He watched, detached.

"Those two did the most senseless, dangerous things," Betsy offered when their display of skill had come to a close. "Can you imagine holding a silver dollar and allowing someone to shoot it from between your fingers? What if one of them should miss?"

"If they still have all their fingers, I would reckon they don't miss."

"Yes, but . . ." She trailed off, turning to look at him. "Are you well? You don't sound like yourself." Her gaze swept over his face. "Or look like yourself. Have you become ill?"

"I'm a little tired," he allowed, forcing a smile.

"You should be home." Her concern was clear. "It would be a sacrifice for me to miss the remainder of the show, but I would do that for you."

Despite his gloom, a brief, genuine smile replaced his artificial expression. "Miss Wilcox, I believe you just made a joke."

"I may have," she continued in what he assumed was her finest, take-charge schoolmarm voice, "but I truly do not think you look well. Your color has changed, and it appears to me that you're breathing harder."

"Well, then, Betsy-fretsy, will you take me home?" he asked, longing for the rest and comfort of his bed.

"I most certainly will." Gracefully managing the bouquet and her bag, she rose and extended her hand.

❧

Even though Betsy insisted she was perfectly capable of driving the four miles home, Elmore took the reins when they were seated in his buggy. Gone were his optimism and jaunty manner; he drove out of town in a silence utterly uncharacteristic to everything she knew about him.

But what did she really know of Elmore Determan except that he was a widower who today celebrated his seventieth birthday? With another sidelong glance in his direction, she was even more troubled by the change that had fallen over him during such a short space of time. All day he'd been as exhilarated as a third-grade boy to see the Wild West Show, yet in the space of a quarter hour, he'd been ready to walk out without a backward glance. Had he become feverish? He stared straight ahead, his hat fixed low over his brow, his jaw set.

"Is there anything I can bring you?" she asked as they neared her drive. "I have a new bottle of Kodol's Dyspepsia at home."

Briefly his blue gaze lit upon her. "There's nothing the matter with me that a little tincture of time won't cure."

"You're certain?" Even his eyes were different, she noted, as if the brightness behind them had been doused.

She felt even more helpless when he dropped her off, thanked her for her company, and turned the horse and buggy around for home. Bent over the reins, he looked as though he was heading into a blustery storm rather than setting off in the pleasant September afternoon.

As she entered her kitchen, an idea sparked. She had saved a little chicken in its juices from the previous day, and she was well stocked with vegetables. Perhaps he would find a bowl of hot soup restorative. If she put some water on to boil right now, she could have it ready within the hour.

She removed her hat, pulled an apron over her head, and began bustling about the kitchen. Once a fire was going in the stove, she set out the ingredients she would use. The carrots, especially, would have to be finely diced so they cooked quickly, she thought, but then they would also have the added benefit of being more easily digestible.

Once again she found herself thinking of her blue-eyed neighbor, wondering at the cause of his indisposition. He had never mentioned any health problems to her, save his wordplay about his heart. That aside, the sudden disappearance of his normally ebullient spirit caused her no small amount of worry.

When the vegetables were diced, she slid them into the steaming water. To save time, she boned the leftover chicken and chopped the meat into tiny pieces, rather than boiling the meat from the bones as she normally did. Adding a little hot water to

239

the roasting pan that had held the chicken, she loosened the rich brown juices and carefully poured the concentrate into the soup pot. Salt, pepper, and dried parsley followed.

Someday she would have to make Elmore a proper soup, but this would have to do for now. Surveying her simmering creation, she still carried the sense that something was undone.

Or was it sympathy because no one had made a fuss over his seventieth birthday?

He might not feel like eating cake today, but she could just as easily bring one over with his soup as not. The stove was hot, and perhaps it would do his heart good to have some bites of raisin-spice cake . . . to know she was thinking of him.

Just what are you thinking of him, Betsy?

A jolt went through her as she realized she had slid into thinking of him in more than a neighborly sense. That wouldn't do at all. He may have clearly stated his intentions toward her, but that didn't mean persons of their age had any business engaging in courtship. Why, they would be a laughingstock! The talk of the town!

Thanks to Irvetta, no doubt you already are the talk of the town.

With a frustrated sigh, Betsy took a large saucepan out of the cupboard and began gathering the items she needed to make the cake. What was Elmore thinking? Where did he think his courtship of her would end? In marriage?

As if at sixty-eight years of age she would don a fine dress and stand before a clergyman with Elmore Determan. What bunkum. She poured a cup of water in the pan, sloshing a little over the edge, then added raisins, sugar, butter, cinnamon, and ground cloves. Once that had boiled five minutes, she would cool the fragrant mixture to lukewarm before adding flour and baking powder.

But even while she took a cake tin from the shelf and greased its inner surfaces, her mind spun at the whimsical thought of marriage to Elmore Determan. If such an impossible, improbable thing were to happen, didn't he realize they dwelt in the twilight years of their life span? One or the other of them could very well be meeting their maker any one of these years now.

Setting down the pan with a clatter, she realized she had to put an end to such outlandish thoughts at once. She was Elmore Determan's neighbor, and nothing more. Because she had always striven to be a good neighbor, she would bring Mr. Determan his soup and a fresh spice cake to acknowledge his birthday, but sick or not, he had to be set straight about the nature of their relationship. In her mind, she uttered a brief prayer that almighty God would help her neighbor come to his senses as far as realizing his age, as well as quash his desire to court her.

Dusk had fallen. After lighting the lamps and completing her food preparations, she read distractedly from a book of poetry until the cake had finished baking. The soup, too, was done, and smelling delicious. Carefully pouring half into a canning jar, she screwed on the top and nestled the hot container in a commodious basket amidst several tea towels and the entire cake still in its pan.

With renewed determination, she donned her cloak and lit the outdoor lamp, which hung on a peg near the door. Managing the lamp and the basket would be toilsome, but the sooner she made her delivery—as well as making things clear to Mr. Determan— the sooner she would be back home, enjoying her soup, and have this most disconcerting day behind her.

Full darkness had enveloped the countryside. In the east, a half-moon had risen above a backdrop of low clouds. The air had turned chill, a mild foretaste of Minnesota's coming winter. After clearing her drive, she walked down the road to her neighbor's and was nearly to his house before she noticed an unfamiliar conveyance parked outside.

Who would be visiting? Or had he fallen gravely ill? One of the horses nickered as she passed by; she approached the porch with quick steps, her anxiety stirred more greatly than her curiosity.

Setting the lantern at her feet, she knocked at the door, shifting the weighty basket from her right arm to her left.

She felt, rather than heard, the approach of heavy, determined footfalls, and then the door was wrested open to a distance of no more than nine inches.

"Yes? What is it?"

The face staring outward at her belonged to a female in her middle years. At one time she might have been described as beautiful, but the twin tolls of time and excess weight, combined with the open hostility in her gaze, rendered her hard-featured.

Who was this woman? Why was she here?

Where was Elmore?

"What's your business?" the woman demanded, gesturing toward the basket.

"Mr. Determan was feeling poorly earlier, so I brought him some—"

"Wait—I remember who you are," the woman proclaimed with a censorious tone. Her pale eyes narrowed as she peered more closely at Betsy's face. "You're that woman who was with my father today at the show."

CHAPTER 6

WALKING home in a state closely akin to shock, Betsy tried recalling whether she'd ever been spoken to or treated in such a manner in all her born days. Elmore's daughter's words—*"you're that woman"*—echoed round and round in her head, for she had spat them forth with the abhorrence one might reserve for snakes or other hideous creatures. After that, she'd snatched the basket from Betsy's hands and briskly closed the door in her face.

Appetite forgotten, Betsy entered her good-smelling home with a heavy heart. How *was* Elmore? She'd never gotten to ask. Perhaps he was sleeping, and the daughter—had he once mentioned her name was Clarice? —was merely being protective of his respite.

The animosity on the woman's face, however, had told another story. Recalling the conversation she and Elmore had shared over lemonade last week, she realized he had never told her any more about his family and his life.

Oh yes, I have a daughter.

He'd been so full of mischief that evening that she'd almost forgotten that cryptic remark. In the silence that had fallen afterward, the expression on his face should have told her the subject was a doleful one for him. But he had started up with his tomfoolery again soon afterward, and between that, his invitation to the

Wild West Show, and his unexpected disclosure about his lone-someness, she'd all but lost her wits.

Yet again.

Keeping up with Elmore Determan was like attempting to watch every exploding kernel in a basket of popcorn. Never had she imagined such a person as he. Energetic, impetuous, mischievous, outrageous . . .

She recalled the cast of his features during the drive home. He had not been well. Had his daughter come to care for him? she wondered, rejecting that theory as she reasoned he had been perfectly fine until midafternoon.

What on earth was the matter with that woman? And what kind of care would Clarice give her father, anyway? Betsy was aghast to think of her kind neighbor being tended with so much bitterness. With such a person as his daughter about, his sunny nature would never be restored.

Though Betsy never said her prayers until she had put on her nightgown and brushed her hair, she made an exception in her routine and bowed her head. *Almighty God,* she began, searching for how she might best ask for help, *please grant Elmore your healing. If he needs to be tended, I suppose there's no reason I can't help him until he's better. Just send that dreadful daughter on her way. Amen.*

Sighing, she picked up the three postcards he had purchased for her that afternoon. Bold claims and busy, detailed illustrations covered the face of one. Another advertised the cities in which the Wild West Show had played. Buffalo Bill himself adorned the third—a tall, dignified man with a white goatee.

After looking more closely at each of the cards, she set them aside, her glance lighting on the spray of autumn flowers Elmore had brought her. The vivid chrysanthemum heads were full and flawless, set off by the striking scarlet blaze of bittersweet. With a sad smile, her finger stroked the velvety texture of the cattail.

She realized she had enjoyed their outing today after all.

〜

"Mr. Determan?" Betsy called after knocking. Opening his door a crack, she repeated his name.

"Come in, come in!" he invited, his voice sounding far off and sleepy. "Are you finished with church already?"

"I am. I asked the Gardners to drop me here so I could see if you needed anything." Letting herself in, she hung her cloak on the row of hooks inside the doorway and assessed her neighbor's modest home. He must be in his bed, for there was no sign of him in either the front room or what she could see of the kitchen.

She'd spent most of Wednesday alternately worrying about him and stewing about Clarice and her rudeness. Though she had not seen any further signs of the unfamiliar carriage, she told herself another driver could have left his daughter to stay with him.

But what if that was not the case? What if Elmore was ill . . . and alone?

By Thursday morning she was over her constraint. Besides wanting to lay eyes on her friend and ascertain his wellness, she was thoroughly incensed about his plump, dark-haired daughter snatching the basket from her hands—and she was determined to have it back. Bright and early she'd marched next door with a half dozen warm muffins, only to learn that Clarice had departed Tuesday evening.

Elmore, weak, wan, and apologetic, had answered the door. After visiting briefly, she'd gone home and made a proper soup, simmering beef, vegetables, and barley together to make a rich, nourishing noontime concoction. Each midday since, she'd called upon him, finding him a pale replica of the brash man who, only a month ago, had strolled up her drive with a bouquet of flowers he'd picked from her ditch. He continued insisting he was fine, merely a bit under the weather, but she was not satisfied in the least with his assurances.

"How are you feeling today?" she inquired, concerned that he had been abed this late in the day. His bedchamber was situated off the kitchen, so he appeared in the kitchen at the same time she did.

"I got the paper read and didn't find myself in the obituaries, so I reckon I can't complain." A grin creased his features, and to her relief, she noted his color was better today. Hair combed, cheeks fresh shaven, he wore a dark wool sweater, instead of his usual suit coat, over his shirt. "I was just having myself a little snooze."

"What do you suppose was ailing you?" Doing her best to ignore the flip-flops her heart made at his appearance and roguish smile, she couldn't help but think of his expression as the sun coming out from the clouds after a long spell of bleakness. "You didn't say much this week when I was over."

He shrugged. "I figure maybe the Wild West Show was too wild for this old man."

"I hardly think so," she commented dryly. "It has been my observation that you possess more energy than a sackful of Mexican jumping beans."

"Some days, Betsy dear. Just some days." In his blue eyes were tenderness and warmth. "Can I get you anything? A cup of tea?"

A pang went through her at his endearment, and she realized if she were to curtail his familiarity with her, she needed to do it now, before he grew secure in thinking her feelings mirrored his.

"No tea, thank you," she began, clearing her throat, "but there is something we must discuss before I leave."

"Might her name be Clarice Determan Wilson?" His smile faded. "I notice you haven't commented on making my daughter's acquaintance. After suffering the remarks she made to me, I have no doubt she treated you in an equally unpleasant manner."

"It isn't my place to say anything," Betsy replied, feeling her blood rise at the memory of their meeting. *Even though she insulted me, snatched my basket right out of my hands, and slammed your door in my face.*

"I never did finish telling you about Clarice, did I?" He sighed and sat down at the table, allowing his weight to rest heavily against the back of the chair. "I recall beginning, but I don't believe I ever finished."

"That's correct, but you do not owe me an explanation." As she spoke, Betsy found her emotions in wild disorder. The curious part of her wanted him to elaborate, but her circumspect side knew if she sat down and listened, she would have even more trouble extracting herself from the tangled mess she was in.

"She and her husband live over in New Ulm. To my everlasting regret there have been no children, but they have themselves quite a little money," he continued, raising an eyebrow and gesturing toward the other chair. "A fellow might call them big fish in a small pond. . . ."

Against her better judgment, Betsy took the seat opposite her neighbor, telling herself she would redirect the conversation as soon as it was polite to do so. To her consternation, a full quarter hour had passed before she glanced up at the clock again. His account of his relationship with Clarice had been riveting, though sad.

"But you're her father," she protested, unable to believe a difference in faith could cause such division of close family members. "Doesn't she know how much you love her? It's quite apparent, even to me."

"I tell her, but she stopped listening to me years ago." Another sigh issued from him, followed by a slight cough. "Meg's dying was the beginning of the wedge between us. I think Clarice still blames me for her death . . . because of the baby, you understand. My acceptance of Jesus Christ only drove the wedge deeper. Besides that, she had it in her head that I ought to have remarried to provide a 'proper' home for her. When that didn't come to pass—"

"Why didn't you marry again?" Elizabeth blurted before thinking the better of holding her tongue. A man as handsome and outgoing as Elmore Determan should have had no difficulty finding a mate.

"Why? I never before felt called to take another bride."

Uncomfortable with his reflective tone, Betsy quickly remarked on the first thing she could think of. "You might have become a preacher, then. With your newfound faith and zeal, you would have been perfect for the job."

"Well, I can't say I didn't give that some thought, but again, I never received the call. You see, Betsy, a man's got to be clear about the Lord's leading before he makes such momentous decisions." His gaze was gentle and penetrating all at once. "I've been wondering . . . are you acquainted with the sound of his voice?"

For as long as she'd lived, Betsy had bristled at the notion of God speaking privately to individual persons. What inanity. Were such revelations preceded by a clap of thunder so one could be certain of the Almighty's identity?

Of course not.

The Creator spoke through his written Word and through various prophets of history. Over the years, it had been her observation that someone who said, "The Lord told me this, that, or the other thing," usually stood to gain the most by his or her supposed sign from heaven.

"Mr. Determan," she said with a sniff, "God rules the heavens and the earth, but he certainly does not *speak* to ordinary people."

"Are *you* certain, Betsy Lou? Have you never felt a particular stirring in your heart—"

"Aha! You admit, then, you do not *hear* a thundering, majestic voice coming down from on high?" Ignoring the license he had taken with her name, she was intent on making her point clear.

"No, I can't say as the Almighty has ever thundered at me, but he speaks to me all the same. His voice comes as the softest breath of breeze over a hushed stillness."

"You're saying God whispers to you, then?" Frustrated by his fanciful rhetoric, she couldn't help the edge that crept into her tone.

"You might say that," he replied earnestly, not appearing to have taken offense at her discourtesy. To the contrary, he seemed intent on explaining his experience to her in great detail.

"In fact, Betsy dear, I'd go so far as to say the Holy Ghost whispers right into my heart." Though fatigue lingered in his features, his eyes sparkled brilliant blue as he leaned forward. "Would you like to know what he told me about you?"

Acute nervousness eclipsed her inflammation, making her heart beat like the wings of a wren taking flight. Goodness, had her hands begun trembling as well? She shook her head, telling herself that now was the time to set him straight about the nature of their relationship. But her tongue remained tied in a row of knots as he continued speaking.

"He thinks we should marry . . . and I'm inclined to agree." Appearing quite satisfied with himself, he sat back in his chair and waited for her to speak.

Apprehension gave way to full-fledged panic. Springing to her feet, she scurried to the sink, putting as much distance between them in the small kitchen as she could.

If she was not mistaken, she had just received a proposal of marriage. "Mr. Determan," she began weakly, finding her voice. Why was it so difficult to draw a breath? "Do you think me lacking wits and common sense alike? I have lived on this earth in an unmarried state for sixty-eight years. I cannot suddenly up and wed a man whom I have known scarcely one month. What would people say?"

"Fiddledy-hoo! They'll talk less if we marry than if we keep courting."

"But why, after living twenty-four years as a widower, would you choose to marry *me*?"

The affection in his expression caused her racing heart to skip a beat. "Because, Miss Elizabeth Wilcox, you are a jewel among women, a rare treasure, a blossoming rose. You possess an abundance of both wits and common sense, and your mind is keen. You are not given to frivolity—"

"But—," she tried, feeling her cheeks grow as pink as wild columbine.

"And because neither of us is getting any younger," he continued sweetly. "I moved back to the prairie to live out my remaining years, but I never expected to find such a fitting companion to share them with. Betsy, I love you. In placing me next to you, the Lord has blessed me in my old age beyond my wildest dreams. To me, it feels like Christmas—and I'm getting the best gift of all—you."

With effort, he rose from the chair, then knelt. "This may be wishful thinking, Betsy Wilcox, but will you do me the honor of becoming my wife?"

CHAPTER 7

I DECLARE, Elizabeth, I don't believe I have *ever* seen you looking so down in the mouth. You've scarcely said a word today. Are you and your suitor no longer an item?"

With studied nonchalance, Irvetta pressed the bottom hem of the apron she had sewn. Her eyes sparkled, however, and the atmosphere in Betsy's home became electrified in the ensuing silence.

Elizabeth had avoided the September circle for this very reason, but as she was scheduled to host the October meeting, she couldn't very well not attend. Today, sixteen of the group's twenty-one members were present, packed into her small house like pickles in a jar.

"Why, last month at Emma's I told everyone you looked so happy together at the Wild West Show," Irvetta prattled on, "as if you were *made* for one another. I remember saying to myself, now *there's* a match if I've ever seen one." Addressing the group, she added, "Some of you may not know Mr. Determan has been coming to our Sunday services for the past three weeks, but he's been sitting four rows back from Betsy. And afterward? I notice she still rides home with the Gardners. Wouldn't it make more sense for Mr. Determan to bring her home? After all, they *are* right next door."

Tiny, elderly Mabel Dunn spoke up. "So he's turned up at your church now? I rather miss him. Does he still sing with as much gusto?"

Irvetta appeared nonplused. "Why no, come to think of it. I hear him, but not in the way Anna described. The way she told it, you'd have thought he was hooting and hollering while turning handsprings down the aisle."

"That's because he *was* all but doing those things," Anna Dilley pronounced, launching into a harangue about the silver-haired man's indiscretions during worship.

Betsy knew that somehow she had to make it through the sewing circle without saying much at all. Elmore had indeed begun attending her church the week following his illness, but despite his earlier gleeful assurance of misbehavior should she not accompany him, the gravest indecorum he had so far committed was being more animated than the majority of the congregants.

She had been right to refuse his offer of marriage . . . hadn't she? Why, it was sheer madness to rush into matrimony with a man she hardly knew. And at their ages! Practically speaking, how would they ever go about merging two so very different lives?

As they often did, her thoughts turned to that September Sunday afternoon back in his kitchen. She remembered the dignity with which he had arisen from his knees, the sad smile and nod he had bestowed upon her. Oh, why was there such a strange, squeezing pressure in her heart whenever she thought on that moment?

Anyone watching her afterward would have shaken her head at the sight of a woman in her Sunday best, scurrying home as if the hounds of hell were nipping at her heels. The tears had spilled down her cheeks once she'd reached the safety of her dwelling, and she cried as though she hadn't cried in decades . . . possibly ever.

Was it out of self-pity that she had wept so? she wondered, feeling her throat grow thick even now. Or was it from a sense of loss at the realization she would pass from this world without ever being wed? She thought she had accepted her spinsterhood, but perhaps deep down she hadn't.

Stop it, Betsy, she reprimanded herself, pushing her needle and thread through the cloth she held. *Your life has been good. What a privilege it is to have been charged with the teaching and formation of so many young minds. That is the Lord's will for your life, not dashing off to the altar willy-nilly now because you know you'll never have another chance.*

In defiance of the stern talking-to she'd given herself, her mind promptly served up a vignette of poignant recollections: Elmore strolling up her drive in his dapper hat, a spray of rudbeckia hidden behind his back; his sprightly grin, a pair of twinkling blue eyes, an incorrigible sense of humor. Not to be forgotten was his hearty laugh—and his equally uninhibited faith.

Of all the things about him, it was his religion that unsettled her the most. The way Elmore talked about Jesus Christ was pure exaggeration. Utter hyperbole. But still, the things he'd said wafted through her mind at odd times, causing her both unrest and confusion.

Ever since she was a little girl, she had gone to church each Sunday, accepting Jesus as her Savior when she was nine. But over the years that special relationship had faded, overcome, she supposed, by the realities of life. Each night she said her prayers without fail. Yet not once in all her years could she say she'd ever experienced anything similar to her neighbor's fanciful spiritual adventures.

"Yessiree, I used to think all the Jesus-dying-for-my-sins business was all a bunch of fiddledy-hoo, until I met the man. . . . Are you acquainted with the sound of his voice? . . . He thinks we should marry."

Enough! She knew she had to stop thinking on Elmore Determan before her heart became seriously involved. Though they were different as cat and dog, something about him had stirred her. Softened her.

Frightened her.

Why would he possibly want to marry her? she asked herself, unable to get him out of her mind. There was no way she could change her life so drastically now; she was too settled in. Too set in her ways. *"I can't,"* she'd blurted out to him, watching the hopeful light in his eyes grow dim. Since that day she had avoided him as much as possible, not understanding why memories of the times they'd shared should keep coming to mind. Nor did she understand the degree of grievance she felt about the dark-haired woman he called daughter.

At long last, the sewing circle ended, and she was left in quiet . . . but not peace.

October passed into November while Minnesota readied itself for winter. Each morning frost gilded the fields and grasslands, while day and night a cold, cutting wind wailed over Lyon County. Long gone were the sweet-singing summer birds, leaving behind their hardier cousins to forage during the inhospitable months until spring.

A thick glaze of ice covered the horse's stock tank this morning, requiring a few blows to break through. After seeing to his outdoor chores, Elmore trudged back toward the house, observing the low-hanging clouds to the northwest. What he saw was only a confirmation of what his bones had already told him: a change of weather was on its way. His upper back ached something fierce.

As he did every time he was out, he gazed at Betsy's house and uttered a prayer for her well-being. Pausing to catch his breath, he studied her neat home and the curl of smoke rising from her chimney. Did she ever think of him? he wondered. He saw her bundled form outdoors from time to time, but she didn't spare a glance in his direction. How he missed her company, her companionship, their budding friendship.

After this many years, Father, why would you have me fall in love with a woman who wants nothing to do with me? You told me to court her; I know you did. But now I don't understand. I thought your plans for Betsy and me were to . . .

Entering the house, he hung up his hat, bringing his mental dialogue to a close. The Lord had heard it before. And as his respect for Elizabeth Wilcox demanded, Elmore would not press his suit. Perhaps he was wrong, but at times, he could have sworn she was secretly amenable to his courtship. The way she had fled his kitchen after his proposal spoke to the contrary, however, as did the many days and weeks of silence since then. After shucking out of his coat, he rubbed his arms, noticing that they felt heavy and achy, in addition to his back pain. A granddaddy of a snowstorm must be on its way. He had planned to attend the big football game this afternoon between the Marshall Eleven and their rivals from the sister town of Tracy, but he didn't fancy making his way home in a blizzard. He would have to keep an eye on the skies.

The pot of coffee he'd started before his chores was done, filling the air with its rich aroma. Lately, coffee hadn't seemed to agree with him. Nor had many other foods. Even though he hadn't eaten yet this morning, he already noticed a twinge of the indigestion that had plagued him for the past several weeks. He hadn't felt right for a long while, and he couldn't help but wonder if his troubles with Betsy and Clarice had simply made him heartsick.

Though the situation with Clarice was nothing new, each time they associated he felt fresh pain about their estrangement. She had been particularly vitriolic the evening after the Wild West Show, doing her best to heap shame on him for having escorted Betsy to the event. He suspected, deep down, she felt guilty that he'd spotted her in town. Hence her unannounced visit later that day.

It was an encounter he could have done without, especially since he'd been feeling punk. If Clarice had noticed his affliction, she hadn't commented. He remembered being so weary, so tired, that he'd actually fallen asleep while she was talking. Once he'd awakened, she'd had more choice words for him, but then she had departed in a rush.

A dispirited smile touched his lips as he remembered finding the basket of food in the kitchen. At once he'd known it was from Betsy, and his heart swelled with gratitude.

How he missed her.

With a long sigh, he put a pan of water on to boil, deciding a bowl of mush was probably the best thing for him. Taking a seat at the table, he opened his Bible to Proverbs, seeking the Lord's counsel on all the matters of his heart.

The past week had passed especially dolefully for Betsy, and she retired early Saturday evening. Even the prospect of seeing the eager faces of her Sunday school students failed to buoy her spirits because she knew, chances were, Elmore would attend the service afterward.

Oh, how her nerves stood on end each Sunday morning with the knowledge that he was seated behind her. Furthermore, the sound of his voice lifted in song never failed to elicit memories of the humid August day he'd walked up the drive and introduced himself. In the space of five minutes he had flirted with her, flattered her, helped with her churning, sung to her, questioned her faith, and invited himself to dinner.

There could be no man on earth like Elmore Determan.

Though she purposed not to think of him, she couldn't help it. And when she said her prayers at night, she couldn't seem to conclude without asking God Almighty to keep her neighbor safe.

"*I've been wondering . . . are you acquainted with the sound of his voice?*" What a strange question he had asked. Acquainted with the sound of God's voice? Did Elmore truly hear the voice of the Lord—and what's more, so often that he was *familiar* with it?

Though she didn't really believe so, his question plagued her . . . made her wonder. From the still darkness of her bedroom each night she spoke toward the heavens, yet in her lifetime she had never heard a reply.

No thunderings, no whisperings.

Completing her preparations for bed, she put out the lamp and climbed between the smooth, chilly sheets. For some reason as she began her prayers, the Old Testament story of Samuel came to mind. Three times the boy was called in the night, and thinking it was Eli the priest who summoned him, he went to the older man each time, saying, "Here am I." Finally Eli discerned it was the Lord calling Samuel, and instructed him to say, "Speak, Lord; for thy servant heareth," if the child should hear the voice again.

"Speak, Lord; for thy servant heareth," Betsy whispered into the night, feeling as foolish and embarrassed as one of her students who had misspoken in class. There was a big difference between her and Samuel: God had already been calling Samuel. Quickly, she commenced with her usual prayers, brought them to conclusion, and closed her eyes.

It seemed she had been asleep only a few minutes when she was awakened by a persistent knocking. "Miss Wilcox," came an urgent male voice. "Are you there, Miss Wilcox?"

Alarmed and confused, Betsy sat up, reaching for her wrapper. "Who is it?" she called, her feet shrinking at the coldness of the floor.

"It's Pennington, your neighbor. There's been some trouble."

"What kind of trouble?" she called, her confusion waning as she hastened through the kitchen. The glow of her neighbor's lantern shone into the room once she'd unlocked and opened the door. His kind but angular features were grim.

"I hate to be the one to tell you this, Miss Betsy, but Elmore . . . well, he collapsed. Dr. Taft's got him, and Elmore was asking for you."

CHAPTER 8

NEVER had the trip to town taken so long as it did tonight, Elizabeth thought frantically, scanning the dark for the first signs of Marshall's lights in the distance. Jim Pennington had filled her in on what he knew of Elmore's affliction—which was precious little—and now they rode in the buggy in silence, each wrapped in their own thoughts.

Apparently the men had met up at the Athletic Park to watch the high school football game. During the second half, Elmore had cried out and slumped forward. Fortunately, Pennington explained, Dr. Taft had also been attending the game in case any of the athletes should become injured. In no time at all, the physician had removed the stricken man to his office and residence.

"Yessiree, this old ticker of mine could give out any minute. . . ."

Along with the memory of her neighbor's playful words came the stabbing realization that perhaps he *did* suffer from some type of heart disease. He certainly hadn't *acted* like a man with a weak heart, but with him, who could know?

". . . and then, as I always say, it'll be no more Elmore."

What if he died—or was already dead? Betsy suppressed a rush of tears at the thought of her exuberant neighbor lying still and cold. No more Elmore? Life would be dreadfully empty without him. At the same time she wondered how this one man, met so late, could have managed to make such an impact on her life.

The night pressed down upon them without benefit of moon or stars. Though no snow had fallen, the sky remained as choked with clouds as it had throughout the day. At long last she spied a glimmer of light ahead; minutes later they arrived downtown and parked in front of the physician's office.

An electric light burned at the entryway, emitting a strange, artificial glow. While she and Pennington approached the modest brick structure, she couldn't help but think that nothing about this night seemed real. Pennington knocked, and the door was soon answered by the town's newest and youngest physician.

"Come in, come in. You must be Miss Wilcox. I am Dr. Taft."

"How is he?" Pennington asked, dispensing with social niceties.

In reply, the younger man put his index finger to his lips before motioning them farther into his combination office and home. He had kind eyes, Betsy noticed before he turned, though he scarcely seemed of an age to shave, much less to have acquired any sort of competence in medical matters.

"Mr. Determan is resting," he announced after leading them into his personal office. Gesturing to the pair of chairs before his desk, he invited them to be seated.

"Have you settled in on what the matter is?" Pennington asked, still standing. "Can we see him?"

"In answer to your first question," the physician began, "I believe our patient has suffered a paroxysm of cardiac disease."

Betsy felt her heart sink. Cardiac disease. Tears welled in her eyes when she recalled her annoyance at Elmore's witticisms about his old ticker.

"You may see him *briefly*," Dr. Taft continued, "but I must caution you. In the treatment of such a condition, it is of paramount importance to keep the patient free from apprehension and anxiety. What you say and how you act before him could be of the greatest benefit or the most dire consequence. I must ask: are either of you aware of who his next of kin may be?"

"His daughter . . . Clarice Wilson," Betsy murmured, remembering the embittered woman who had answered her father's door. "She lives in New Ulm."

"Very good." The young physician nodded. "I'll notify her first thing in the morning. Now I can treat Mr. Determan here for a day or two, but my facilities are a far cry from a proper hospital. If he doesn't . . ." He paused, clearing his throat before beginning again. "Rather, should he become well enough to be moved, she may want to take him—"

"Just what are his chances?" Pennington interrupted, his brow furrowing. "You don't sound very optimistic."

"I'm doing what I can for him," Dr. Taft said simply. "We'll just have to wait and see how his body responds now to rest and medicine."

Icy fingers of fear squeezed Betsy's heart while the physician led them to the treatment room where Elmore lay. A wall sconce cast muted light from the side of the room opposite the bed, causing her ailing friend to be swathed in shadows.

Or was he already beyond his ailing?

He didn't appear to be breathing, and he lay so still. She was afraid to go nearer, not ready to learn what she didn't want to know.

"Mr. Determan," the physician said gently, taking his patient's wrist. After a few moments, he gave a satisfied nod. "Mr. Determan, your Betsy is here to see you."

Slowly, Elmore's eyes opened. Spying her, his lips traced upward in the faintest of smiles before he yielded to his body's demands for rest. As his eyelids fluttered closed, she couldn't help but wonder if that was the last of his smiles she would ever receive.

"Dr. Taft, may I stay here?" she blurted out, not able to bear the idea of her neighbor being alone, without loved ones near during such a time.

"Why, of course," replied the physician graciously, though his expression registered obvious surprise. "It isn't much to look at, but I have an extra room down the hall."

Tears sprang to her eyes as she bid Pennington good night and was led to a clean but starkly furnished room. "I'll call you if anything changes, Miss Wilcox," the younger man promised. "Mr. Determan's heart was feeble when he arrived, but perhaps his laying eyes upon you will strengthen its function as much as the medication I've given him." With a musing smile, he tipped his head and added, "He was most insistent about wanting you brought to town. He cares a great deal for you, I believe."

With a soft click, the door closed. Sinking onto the narrow bed, Betsy ruminated on the fact that Elmore's feelings for her had never been in question. It was her emotions toward him that were riotous and jumbled, painful and confusing.

With so many thoughts and worries swimming in her head, she thought she would never be able to sleep. But sometime during her prayers she must have nodded off, for she awakened to Dr. Taft's footsteps outside her room.

Startled, she gasped. "Is he . . . ?"

"Shh," he said, moving inside the room to cover her with a blanket. "I've just given him more medication, and I came to check on you too. He's the same. Go back to sleep."

Closing her eyes, she tried to do that. Several times she dozed, only to jerk back to wakefulness with the feeling that she was falling, falling from the sky. Strange dreams and disturbing thoughts visited her in the remaining hours until dawn. Each time she awoke, she did so with the sense that there was some knowledge a slight bit beyond her grasp, which, if she could have stayed asleep, she would have been able to discover.

When murky gray light began filtering into the room, she arose and lifted the window covering. It was snowing, thin and depressing flakes carried in swirling sheets on the northwesterly wind. What would today bring? she wondered, hearing footsteps in the hall. Had Elmore already departed this earth to be gathered at the beautiful, silver river of which he had once sung?

Oh, Elmore, her heart cried. *You tried to love me, and I wouldn't let you.*

"I have some warm water for you, Miss Wilcox," came the doctor's voice through the door. "Breakfast will be ready soon."

"Thank you, Dr. Taft," she called, overcome with relief at the news he hadn't borne. Opening her door, she found a pitcher of steaming water, a towel, and a washcloth waiting for her. The warm water felt heavenly on her face, cleansing away several layers of the physical and mental exhaustion that clung to her. She couldn't imagine how the poor doctor must feel this morning. Between serving her and tending Elmore, he probably hadn't gotten a wink of sleep.

A fresh spasm of worry gripped her as she thought about her good-hearted neighbor. Had he passed the night comfortably, or had he suffered? She wanted to do something—anything—to help him, but she felt so helpless, so out of control. If he died, she didn't think she could bear it, but in the back of her mind was also the fear that if he survived, Clarice would take him to New Ulm and then she would never see him again. With shaking hands, she removed the pins from her hair and did the best she could with a finger-combing before sweeping it back up into its usual style.

A short time later, in the kitchen, she bowed her head while Dr. Taft asked a blessing over their eggs and toast. Afterward, she learned that though Elmore had spent a fairly comfortable night, he was by no means out of danger.

"Mr. Determan is not a young man." The physician chose his words carefully, speaking with great tact. The skin beneath his eyes was swathed with shadows, testimony to his lack of sleep. "And I suspect the natural process of aging has advanced the organic changes within his circulatory system. He tells me he has not suffered any disease of the heart, but the symptoms he has described to me and has experienced over the past few months relate another story. I also observed significant dropsy in his lower limbs."

With a sigh, he set down his fork and pushed his plate forward. "The good news is that there are some excellent medications available that can be tried."

"And the bad?" Betsy asked in a choked whisper.

His compassionate eyes met hers. "They may not be effective. I promise you, Miss Wilcox, I will do what I can. However, despite our best efforts, this may very well be his time."

No! she cried out from deep inside her soul while scalding tears traced down her cheeks. Why did the thought of losing this man hurt so much? *If you are willing, God*, she beseeched, *please spare him.*

"Ma'am?" The doctor's concerned voice penetrated through her grief. Glancing up, she saw he had extended his handkerchief toward her. "When you feel ready, I'll take you in to see him."

Nodding, she wiped her eyes. When she was finally able to speak, she thanked the physician for his many kindnesses. Now, with her emotions under some semblance of control, she was ready to look in on Elmore.

What she wasn't ready to do, however, was bid him farewell.

⤶

For a moment, Elmore had experienced the most dreadful fear. *I'm dying,* he remembered thinking, feeling as though a lumber wagon had suddenly parked itself across his chest. He had been aware of his body pitching forward in the football stands, but he had been powerless to stop himself, unable to breathe, unable to move.

Then, nothing.

He gathered he hadn't died when he'd awakened in this room, a young man making an assiduous examination of his form. The fellow had introduced himself as Dr. Taft, informing him that he'd had a bit of trouble with his heart. Over the physician's shoulder he'd caught sight of Pennington's face, and he knew the situation was much more grave than the doctor was letting on.

Is this it, Lord? he'd asked wonderingly. *This really isn't so bad after all. If you're taking me, though, I'd like to see Betsy one last time before I go.*

Dr. Taft had nodded to his whispered request, and Pennington had gone to fetch Elizabeth straightaway. To say good-bye, he surmised. Despite his hopes and wishful thinking, he realized she wasn't going to become his wife. She would have been a corker. Beneath her prim schoolmarm facade, he'd found her an utterly fascinating mixture of contradictions. Straightlaced and proper, yet not a bit bashful about speaking up and calling a spade a spade.

She was a strong woman and an intelligent one. He had also come to believe that the tenets of her faith in Jesus Christ were solid . . . if perhaps a bit *too* solid. Since making her acquaintance, he'd prayed for her to strike up a joyous, vibrant relationship with her maker. It was his opinion that she didn't possess so much a bitter heart as one encased in a bit of crust.

How he'd longed to be the sandpaper that smoothed that brittleness away.

He read the fear in her eyes when she'd come in to see him, and he'd wanted to soothe her, reassure her he wasn't afraid to die, but he didn't have the energy. The medications Dr. Taft had coaxed down his throat throughout the night had eased his pain, made it a little easier to breathe . . . and made him so tired. He'd also found that if he lay perfectly still, the dreadful air-hunger did not come upon him. Only now did he remember that his father had died the same way. How could he have forgotten the elder Determan's cries for air—*Atemnot*—in his native German?

He slept again, and when he roused, Betsy was seated at his bedside. Intent upon her reading, she didn't notice his wakefulness immediately, so he took the opportunity to study her appearance. What a fine and lovely woman she was. Though their courtship had not progressed far, he was deeply grateful for the few months they'd had together.

"Oh!" she said with a start, glancing up at him. "You're awake. Are you in pain? Shall I get the doctor?"

He shook his head slightly. With no small amount of effort, he freed his hand from the covers and extended his fingers. A strangled sound escaped her, and she took his hand between her own. Twin tears fell from her eyes as she gazed at him, and then, an instant later, she lowered her face to their entwined fingers.

"Oh, Elmore," she wept, her voice muffled, "I am so sorry—"

"Shh," he managed, squeezing her fingers with what little strength he had. Her slender back shook as she labored to restrain her tears.

"I . . . love you. Remember . . . love never . . . fails." His words came slowly, in a whisper.

"But *I* failed." Her words were raw with regret. "How can I ever—"

He stilled her words by pulling his hand from between hers, his fingers seeking the softness of her hair. One pin, then another, hampered his efforts. How he wished he might have made her his bride and seen her glorious silver hair down about her shoulders, unfettered.

She turned her head toward him, a question in her tear-dampened eyes. A long moment passed, and then, with shaking fingers, she reached up and began removing the pins from her hair. Elmore closed his eyes as the warm strands fell from her twist, caressing his knuckles, his arm.

Thank you, Father, for the gift of this woman.

While he prayed, he was aware of her taking his hand in hers again, bringing it to her cheek. Suffused with a perfect peace, sleep overpowered him, and he remembered no more.

CHAPTER 9

FOR BETSY, the next days passed with excruciating slowness. Dr. Taft continued treating Elmore with a combination of medications he hoped would increase the elasticity of his heart, remedy the dropsy, and relieve his pain. At times she was hopeful that the physician's medical regimen was working, but then she would sit at her friend's bedside, taking in his pallid complexion and frequent episodes of short-windedness, and her hopes would plummet.

Word about Elmore spread quickly. By Sunday afternoon, she'd had half a dozen invitations to dinner and offers to spend however many nights in town she wished, yet she could not bring herself to leave the doctor's residence. She wanted to stay—no, she *needed* to stay—as near to Elmore as possible. After the way she'd treated him, it was the least she could do.

What a fool she'd been to throw his affections back in his face. Not only a fool but a coward as well. He had offered her his very heart, and she'd run from his presence like a frightened pup. He'd scared her . . . her feelings had scared her. Though she hadn't been sure before, at this juncture in time she was certain: she loved Elmore Determan.

And now he might die.

Emma Graham and Irvetta Auerbach had called midweek,

bringing a delicious assortment of foods. The day before, Emma had driven out to Betsy's and packed a bag of clean clothing and personal items, a gesture Betsy deeply appreciated. Jim Pennington had stopped to say he was seeing to both her place and Elmore's, and that he would be pleased to do so for as long as necessary. In addition, several women from church and from the sewing circle had also visited; consequently, Dr. Taft's kitchen was overflowing with good food and drink.

The young physician continued being a kind and generous host, but Betsy knew that having his home and medical practice turned upside down was taking a toll upon him. He had wired Clarice as he'd promised, and yet again, but no reply had come. On one hand Betsy felt relief, wondering if things might not be better for Elmore this way. She knew how their estrangement grieved him. But on the other hand, she worried about what would become of him. He couldn't stay at Dr. Taft's indefinitely, yet the physician did not believe he could tolerate a journey of any distance . . . even back to his home.

On Friday, a solution to the problem presented itself when Jane Pruitt paid call. She and her husband were perhaps the most well-to-do couple in the area, owning a large home three blocks from Dr. Taft's.

"Why don't we have Mr. Determan moved to our home?" she offered after listening to Betsy's concerns. "It's just a short distance away, and that way, Dr. Taft will be nearby. You'll come, too, Betsy. We have plenty of room."

In the end, that was exactly what happened. Dr. Taft gave his consent for Elmore to be moved to the Pruitt home and personally supervised the process. Once his patient was installed in a stately bedchamber of burgundy and yellow, he produced a written list of instructions. On it were times and dosages of medications to be given, a recommended diet, and a regimen of exercises for his limbs.

"Now, I'm sure this looks intimidating, but it really isn't," he said to Betsy and Jane over tea in the Pruitt's lovely parlor. "Miss Wilcox has watched me enough to have more than a general idea of what I've been doing for Mr. Determan."

"But what if he should—," Elizabeth began weakly, realizing she wouldn't have the doctor's presence to fall back on.

"Whatever it is, ring me on the telephone, and I'll be right over. I've already promised to stop by every day. Furthermore," he replied, leveling his gaze at Betsy, "I have the utmost confidence in your care."

"Perhaps we could hire a nurse," Jane suggested.

"Perhaps," Dr. Taft agreed, "but I have a feeling Mr. Determan will soon declare himself one way or the other."

A lump grew in Betsy's throat as she thought of her life without Elmore. *Oh, Lord,* she questioned, *why did you bring such a man into my life only to take him so soon?*

"As you know, Doctor, prayer can move mountains," Jane was saying, "and there are people all over Lyon County praying. If the Almighty is willing, Mr. Determan will be restored to health."

"I sincerely hope so," he responded, setting his cup in its saucer. After checking his watch, he stood. "Thank you for your hospitality, Mrs. Pruitt, but I must beg your leave. I have two more appointments scheduled this afternoon. And, Miss Wilcox," he said, turning toward her with a nod, "Mr. Determan is fortunate, indeed, to have such a devoted . . . friend."

Elizabeth felt herself color, but not because of the brief, awkward pause while the physician searched for a word to describe her relationship to Elmore. It was because his compliment was so far from the truth. If he only knew how she had run out on his patient weeks earlier, opposing the love Elmore had tried so patiently to bestow, he would have an entirely different opinion of her character.

At Jane's coaxing, she took a bath after Dr. Taft's departure. Elmore was asleep, and Jane promised to sit with him until Betsy bathed and refreshed herself. "Take a nap if you need to," she urged. "You must be exhausted. I have nothing pressing this afternoon; I'll stay with him as long as necessary."

Truly, Betsy hadn't intended doing more than washing up and getting back to Elmore, but the Pruitts' bathroom was a marvel of modern luxury. Running water—both hot and cold! The bathtub was like no other she'd seen, and once she filled it and slipped into its enveloping warmth, she could hardly think of moving again.

Oh, Lord, she thought, *here I sit in comfort while Elmore's life hangs in the balance. I've tried to show him I care for him, but what more can I do?*

As she closed her eyes and laid her head against the back of the tub, time seemed suspended. Could any of this really be happening? Here she was, Elizabeth Wilcox, bathing in a rich woman's home, grieving over a man who had just a short while ago declared himself her suitor. Her life, lived innocuously for sixty-eight years, had suddenly undergone a great upheaval. What more could happen?

Do you want him?

Yes! her soul resounded before she had even comprehended that a question had been asked. Opening her eyes, she found herself staring at the busy hearts-and-flowers wallpaper pattern. Though she knew no one had come into the room, she turned her head and glanced around. Nothing was different; not a thing was out of place. A round clock ticked steadily on a shelf. Her towel remained folded and undisturbed on its rack near the sink.

Had she heard a voice, or was her mind playing tricks on her? She sighed, the sound of her breath loud in her ears. She had heard that persons lacking sleep sometimes suffered hallucinations. After days of worry and interrupted slumber, could such a thing be happening to her? Though she didn't feel delusional, perhaps she was.

Do you want him? Do you want Elmore?

Again came the whispering question, somehow a part of her yet not a part of her at all. All at once, her heart began pounding like the hooves of a horse in full gallop. The story of Samuel leapt back into her mind, as did the self-conscious words she'd uttered into the night: *Speak Lord; for thy servant heareth.*

She wiped her face with a washcloth, aware her hands were trembling. Did almighty God deign to speak with her? Surely she hadn't heard his voice . . . or was this indeed the voice of which Elmore had spoken?

Gone was her exhaustion, her languor. She felt as though she could leap out of the tub and run a hundred miles. Did she want Elmore? With all her heart she did. But what did the question mean? she wondered, her contemplation cut short by an urgent rapping at the bathroom door.

"Betsy," cried Jane, "hurry! Come quickly!"

To Betsy's anxious query, there was no reply. Only a minute or two passed until she was out of the tub and back into her clothing, but it seemed like hours. *Oh, Elmore.* Had he taken a turn for the worse? Had Dr. Taft been summoned?

Heedless of the disarray she left behind, she opened the door and hurried through the Pruitts' princely bedchamber. As she entered the hallway, she heard not only Jane's voice but an unfamiliar female voice raised in anger.

"I don't know what you people expect of me. The doctor already told me he can't be moved."

Jane's reply was too soft to make out, but all at once Betsy knew to whom her friend was speaking.

"Well, does he need me right this minute?" Clarice fumed. "Don't you understand how exhausted I am? We returned from Chicago yesterday, and I had to climb right back on another train today. As if I didn't have enough trouble finding the doctor's," she went on, "I had to *walk* all the way over here besides."

Taking a deep breath, Betsy rounded the corner. To her dismay, the two women stood right outside Elmore's door. How could he have helped but hear every word? she thought, feeling sick. No-

271

ticing Betsy's presence, Jane turned a grateful and pleading look her way, while Clarice's eyes narrowed.

"What is *she* doing here?" The question was blunt and rude.

"I've been helping to care for your father," Betsy replied firmly, stepping forward. With each step, her trepidation fell away, until she was standing before the pair of women. She might have been intimidated by Elmore's daughter before, but it wasn't going to happen again. Nor would she allow Clarice to upset her father.

"Dr. Taft wasn't equipped to keep him any longer, nor did he think a trip of any distance would be beneficial to his health. This good woman, Mrs. Pruitt, was gracious enough to open her home to both of us." With a nod toward their hostess, who appeared white faced and shaken, she added, "Perhaps we could have some tea prepared . . . in the parlor?"

"Yes, yes. I'll see to it at once." Only too happy to take her leave, Jane departed with swift steps.

A long moment passed while Betsy and Clarice regarded one another.

"Shall we go downstairs and wait for our tea?" Betsy forced herself to speak graciously.

"I don't want tea. As long as I've come all this way, I'm going to see my father."

With the physician's cautionary advice about not upsetting Elmore utmost in her mind, Betsy replied, "Of course, but perhaps we might have a word downstairs first."

Pushing past Betsy with a wordless glare, Clarice entered the bedchamber.

Now what, Lord? Betsy found herself praying as she stood alone in the hallway. *Elmore is already so ill, and this visit could very well be the death of him. On the other hand, this hateful woman is his only flesh and blood.*

Taking a fortifying breath, she stepped into the room. Elmore lay with his eyes closed, covers drawn up to his chin, looking helpless and pale. Clarice's progress had halted a full six feet from the bed, and Betsy noticed her shoulders shook.

"Clarice?" She spoke softly, feeling a rush of compassion for this hard woman. "Your father loves you very much. He told me so not long ago." Chancing to lay her hand upon the younger woman's arm, Betsy was surprised when it wasn't immediately shaken off.

A sound from the bed drew their attention. Elmore was awake, extending a trembling hand from beneath the covers. "Clarice," he entreated, his voice sounding as fragile as fine china.

"No!" she wailed, fleeing the room.

In the wake of his daughter's departure, Elmore's gaze locked with Betsy's. Tears brimmed in his brilliant blue eyes. A sob racked his chest, then another.

"Oh, Elmore," she cried, going to him, her heart breaking along with his. "For whatever it's worth, I love you." His fingers gripped hers fiercely as he wept. "I love you! I've been such a fool. Can you ever forgive me, my dearest? The Lord spoke to me today, and he asked me if I wanted you."

Raising her face toward the ceiling, she cried, "My answer is yes!" Tears slid down her cheeks as she realized the enormity of what had occurred this day, and she closed her eyes in awe of it all.

You really spoke to me, didn't you? All these years, and I never believed such a thing could happen. And on top of that, I'm in love. Glory, I thought this old body was dead! I never dreamed of feeling such a way! Oh, Father, what a hard-hearted, stiff-necked old woman I've been. I beg your forgiveness, as I beg you for a second chance with Elmore. Please heal his heart. I want to be his wife, and I want to live at his side until you choose to part us.

The pressure on her hand increased, and she opened her eyes, hoping to see Elmore's love for her reflected in his eyes. But to her horror, she saw his face gripped with pain, his chest flailing for breath. As she simultaneously shouted for Jane and reached for the medication on the nightstand, his grasp on her hand loosened.

Please! she implored first to the heavens, then to her beloved. *Not now! Please, not now!*

CHAPTER 10

THE TOWN of Marshall was ready for Christmas. Decorations hung from streetlamps and storefronts, and cheery greetings rang in the frosty air. A soft snow fell, blanketing the streets and sidewalks with whiteness.

Betsy arrived at the church early, wanting some time to herself before the service began. She had taken great pains with her appearance, wishing to honor Elmore in every way possible. The air in the sanctuary was cool, smelling of candle wax and faintly of pine.

A crèche had been placed near the altar, a figurine of the Christ child lying in the straw. She bowed her head at the holy scene as she approached, remembering Elmore's words: *"Love never fails."* How was it she had gone to church all these years and never really understood how deeply almighty God loved each of his people?

How deeply he loved *her*?

Christmas had never meant so much to her as it did this year. The simplicity of the gospel teachings penetrated her soul and flooded her being with understanding. God loved his people so passionately that he came to earth in a way to which mankind could relate. Jesus was born, he lived among common folk, and he felt every human emotion. Above all, he loved.

It had taken a man, a one-of-a-kind fellow with bright blue eyes

275

and a joyful, mischievous spirit to teach her the truth about God's love. Oh, how her heart had been torn asunder these past months. In all her years, she had never experienced such things as she had since making Elmore Determan's acquaintance.

In her mind's eye, she again saw him strolling up her drive, presenting her with a bouquet of flowers he'd picked from her ditch. Tears moistened her eyes, and she knelt before the altar. *Oh, Lord,* she began, not able to find any words to express what she felt. Minutes passed, and she heard the door open and close, then the sound of hushed voices.

Was it time already?

Footsteps sounded behind her. "Betsy?" came Emma's gentle voice. "We came a little early for you, dear."

Rising, Betsy wiped her tears and gratefully received her friend's embrace.

"I brought you something," Irvetta offered, an unashamed tear trickling down her cheek. "Here," she said, reaching in her bag and producing an exquisitely embroidered handkerchief. "It was my mother's."

"Thank you." Deeply touched, Betsy wasn't surprised when more wetness spilled down her cheeks.

"Heavens, look at all of us standing around weeping," Irvetta said with a sniffle. "You'd think we were about to attend a *funeral* rather than your wedding, Betsy! Now, that handkerchief has a hint of aquamarine on the edge, so you can decide if you want it to be something old, borrowed, or blue. I *do* hope you've got something new."

Just then, Reverend Fraser entered from the side door, his face wreathed with pleasure. "Good morning, ladies. I see we have in attendance one bride. Has the groom arrived?"

"Not yet, Reverend," Betsy replied, her heart leaping as the big front door opened again. Turning, she felt a flush of pleasure and nervousness at the sight of Elmore's tall figure, flanked on either side by Ronald Pruitt and Dr. Taft. A bouquet of red and white flowers was tucked in the crook of his arm. Like a butterfly, Jane hovered about them, her face breaking into a wide smile when she caught sight of Betsy.

"Truly, we are beholden of a miracle," Reverend Fraser spoke out, watching Elmore's slow progress down the aisle.

"What better time of year?" Betsy said softly, glancing first at the baby Jesus, then at her husband-to-be. The virgin's words came to her: *"Be it unto me according to thy word."* Who could ever fathom the plans and goodness of almighty God?

A short time later, the guests were assembled, and the ceremony began. Betsy's breath caught in her throat at the emotion she saw reflected in Elmore's eyes. Since the day he'd collapsed, he had made an astonishing recovery. Even Dr. Taft had said there was no earthly accounting for the turnaround in his health. True, his strength was not complete, but he had progressed to being up for short periods of time without suffering.

As Reverend Fraser directed, Elmore laid his hand over hers and made his vows. Then, impossibly, at the age of sixty-eight, Elizabeth Wilcox was wed. Elmore's kiss was lingering, making her blush, and drawing laughter from the circle of friends gathered.

"There will be a reception and luncheon at the home of the Pruitts," the pastor announced, "to which you all are welcome."

From the corner of her eye, Betsy caught sight of a solitary figure at the rear of the church. Had Elmore noticed? she wondered, squeezing his hand. He had mailed a wedding invitation, together with a long letter, to Clarice, but there had been no reply.

"Well now, look who's here," he whispered to her as they carefully negotiated the steps down from the altar. "A little wishful thinking, a little more prayer, and look at the things that can happen."

"You and your wishful thinking," Betsy murmured as they received a hail of congratulations and well-wishes. Burying her nose in the spray of hothouse roses her husband had so tenderly presented to her, she smiled and urged, "Go to her, Elmore, before she leaves. I'll be waiting for you."

"Hallelujah! After all this, you'd better be!" His face creased into a grin that she knew would never stop turning her heart end over end. "I love you, Betsy-fretsy."

And I you, Elmore, my Christmas miracle.

EPILOGUE

BETSY WILCOX and Elmore Determan were wed on Christmas Eve 1899. Instead of settling in one home or the other, they sold both properties and purchased a snug house in Marshall. Electricity was installed, and a small addition was made, complete with a bathtub and water heater.

Elmore never regained his former vigor but lived happily and thankfully for another five years before departing peacefully in his sleep. During that time, a tenuous bond between Clarice and Elmore was reestablished, which grew stronger as the years went by.

After Elmore's death, Betsy was visited regularly by her stepdaughter until Betsy's passing in 1907. It wasn't until 1915, upon suffering ill health of her own, that Clarice opened the Bible Betsy had left to her. To her great surprise, she discovered within its pages a letter addressed to her in Betsy's hand, dated six months before the older woman's death.

Upon reading the tender missive left to her by her father's wife, Clarice put her head down and wept. Afterward, with her head still bowed, she sought the Lord for the first time in decades, unable to resist the legacy of love poured out upon her by her earthly father . . . and her heavenly Father as well.

RECIPE

I'm not sure how far back this recipe goes, but I can trace it back at least as far as my mother's grandmother. When I was a little girl, I remember my Grandma Ivy telling me this was a popular cake back in the "olden days" because it did not require any eggs. It is easy to make, and your home will smell wonderful as the spices cook together with the raisins and brown sugar. Those watching their calories may want to finish the cake by sprinkling a little powdered sugar over the top. A recipe for penuche icing is included for anyone wishing to throw caution to the wind.

— Peggy Stoks

Sensational Spice Cake

1 cup packed brown sugar
⅓ cup butter
1 cup water
1 cup raisins
1 tsp. cinnamon
½ tsp. ground cloves
1 tsp. baking soda
2 cups flour
1 tsp. baking powder

In a saucepan, combine first six ingredients. Heat to boiling and simmer for five minutes. Set aside to cool.

In a small cup, dissolve baking soda in a teaspoon or two of hot water. Pour into above cooled mixture. Add flour and baking powder, stir until blended. Bake in greased 8x12 pan at 350° for approximately 25 minutes, until a toothpick inserted into the center comes out clean.

Penuche Icing

½ cup butter
1 cup packed brown sugar
¼ cup milk
1¾ to 2 cups powdered sugar

Melt butter in saucepan. Stir in brown sugar. Heat to boiling; cook and stir over low heat for two minutes.

Stir in milk. Return to a boil, stirring constantly. Cool to lukewarm.

Gradually stir in powdered sugar, until icing is of a good consistency to spread.

A NOTE FROM THE AUTHOR

DEAR READERS,

A woman from my town fell in love last year. Seemingly overnight, this very sensible, highly educated former missionary turned into the giddiest, giggliest, most exhilarated person I've ever seen. Some days I don't think her feet came within six inches of touching the ground! Her age might surprise you, for she wasn't in her teens, twenties, or thirties . . . but well into her sixties.

Even before I was privileged to watch this romance unfold, I had already submitted the proposal for "Wishful Thinking," complete with a sixty-eight-year-old heroine and a just-about-to-turn-seventy hero. I knew I was taking a chance with this far-from-typical love story, yet the scriptural theme I had chosen for the novella—*love never fails*—inspired me to press on.

All the confirmation I needed came the day my radiant friend confided her feelings for a certain gentleman. That morning, I knew beyond all doubt that the capacity in our hearts for romantic love does not diminish with age. I wondered then, and still do . . . does it perhaps become even greater?

Beyond the simple telling of a tale, I hope the elements of Betsy and Elmore's story inspired you in some way to love your dear ones even more dearly. My mother died just before I began writing this story, her body finally succumbing to the cancer against which she had fought so valiantly. I tell you this not to elicit your sympathy but to remind you that life is precious, and so are people. Our time on this earth is fleeting, and how well we love while we are here is at the heart of our Christian existence.

How do we love? First, we look to God and remind ourselves that we are created in his image and likeness. First John 4:8 gives us a very basic but oh-so-important tenet of our faith: God is love. Our calling as his children is to show forth his image and to be transformed into the likeness of his Son. This happens as we love our Creator, love our families, love our neighbors.

It is my prayer that none of us would be afraid to live—or love—fully. It may be difficult, and yes, it may even hurt, yet our heavenly Father has given us his word that such love will not fail. May his peace be with you as you do his will.

Sincerely,
Peggy Stoks

ABOUT THE AUTHOR

PEGGY STOKS lives in Minnesota with her husband and three daughters. She has been a registered nurse for nearly twenty years but recently resigned her hospital nursing position to be a stay-at-home wife and mom, and to cope with the logistical challenges of getting her daughters to their various school, church, and athletic activities. A homebody at heart, Peggy loves to cook and bake, and especially enjoys making jams and jellies. She also enjoys reading, gardening, swimming, tackling home-improvement and decorating projects, and getting outdoors to walk through the nearby woods as often as she can. She has published two novels as well as numerous magazine articles in the general market. She is the author of the HeartQuest novel *Olivia's Touch* and its sequel, *Romy's Walk* (available spring 2001). Peggy's novellas appear in the HeartQuest anthologies *Prairie Christmas*, *A Victorian Christmas Cottage*, *A Victorian Christmas Quilt*, *A Victorian Christmas Tea*, and *Reunited*.

Peggy welcomes letters written to her at P.O. Box 333, Circle Pines, MN 55014.

Current HeartQuest Releases

- *Magnolia*, Ginny Aiken
- *Lark*, Ginny Aiken
- *A Bouquet of Love*, Ginny Aiken, Ranee McCollum, Jeri Odell, and Debra White Smith
- *Dream Vacation*, Ginny Aiken, Jeri Odell, and Elizabeth White

- *Reunited*, Judy Baer, Jeri Odell, Jan Duffy, and Peggy Stoks

- *Awakening Mercy*, Angela Benson

- *Faith*, Lori Copeland
- *Hope*, Lori Copeland
- *June*, Lori Copeland
- *Glory*, Lori Copeland
- *With This Ring*, Lori Copeland, Dianna Crawford, Ginny Aiken, and Catherine Palmer

- *Freedom's Hope*, Dianna Crawford
- *Freedom's Promise*, Dianna Crawford

- *Prairie Fire*, Catherine Palmer
- *Prairie Rose*, Catherine Palmer

- *Prairie Storm*, Catherine Palmer
- *Prairie Christmas*, Catherine Palmer, Elizabeth White, and Peggy Stoks
- *Finders Keepers*, Catherine Palmer
- *A Kiss of Adventure*, Catherine Palmer (original title: *The Treasure of Timbuktu*)
- *A Whisper of Danger*, Catherine Palmer (original title: *The Treasure of Zanzibar*)
- *A Touch of Betrayal*, Catherine Palmer
- *A Victorian Christmas Cottage*, Catherine Palmer, Debra White Smith, Jeri Odell, and Peggy Stoks
- *A Victorian Christmas Quilt*, Catherine Palmer, Debra White Smith, Ginny Aiken, and Peggy Stoks
- *A Victorian Christmas Tea*, Catherine Palmer, Dianna Crawford, Peggy Stoks, and Katherine Chute

- *Olivia's Touch*, Peggy Stoks

Coming Soon (early 2001)

- *Sweet Delights*, Terri Blackstock, Ranee McCollum, and Elizabeth White

- *Freedom's Bell*, Dianna Crawford
- *Hide and Seek*, Catherine Palmer

HEART
QUEST.

Other Great Tyndale House Fiction

- *As Sure As the Dawn*, Francine Rivers
- *Ashes and Lace*, B. J. Hoff
- *The Atonement Child*, Francine Rivers
- *The Captive Voice*, B. J. Hoff
- *Cloth of Heaven*, B. J. Hoff
- *Dark River Legacy*, B. J. Hoff
- *An Echo in the Darkness*, Francine Rivers
- *The Embers of Hope*, Sally Laity & Dianna Crawford
- *The Fires of Freedom*, Sally Laity & Dianna Crawford
- *The Gathering Dawn*, Sally Laity & Dianna Crawford
- *The Last Sin Eater*, Francine Rivers

- *Leota's Garden*, Francine Rivers
- *The Scarlet Thread*, Francine Rivers
- *Storm at Daybreak*, B. J. Hoff
- *The Tangled Web*, B. J. Hoff
- *The Tempering Blaze*, Sally Laity & Dianna Crawford
- *The Torch of Triumph*, Sally Laity & Dianna Crawford
- *Unashamed*, Francine Rivers
- *Unveiled*, Francine Rivers
- *A Voice in the Wind*, Francine Rivers
- *Vow of Silence*, B. J. Hoff
- *Winter Passing*, Cindy McCormick Martinusen

Heartwarming Anthologies from HeartQuest

Dream Vacation—Sometimes the unexpected can be the best thing for your heart! Whether it's a chilly winter's evening or a sunny, warm afternoon, let authors Ginny Aiken, Jeri Odell, and Elizabeth White sweep you away to three very special vacation destinations.

A Bouquet of Love—An arrangement of four beautiful novellas about friendship and love. Stories by Ginny Aiken, Ranee McCollum, Jeri Odell, and Debra White Smith.

A Victorian Christmas Cottage—Four novellas centering around hearth and home at Christmastime. Stories by Catherine Palmer, Jeri Odell, Debra White Smith, and Peggy Stoks.

A Victorian Christmas Tea—Four novellas about life and love at Christmastime. Stories by Catherine Palmer, Dianna Crawford, Peggy Stoks, and Katherine Chute.

A Victorian Christmas Quilt—A patchwork of four novellas about love and joy at Christmastime. Stories by Catherine Palmer, Ginny Aiken, Peggy Stoks, and Debra White Smith.

Reunited—Four contemporary stories about reuniting friends, old memories, and new romance. Includes favorite recipes from the authors. Stories by Judy Baer, Jan Duffy, Jeri Odell, and Peggy Stoks.

With This Ring—A quartet of charming stories about four very special weddings. Stories by Lori Copeland, Dianna Crawford, Ginny Aiken, and Catherine Palmer.

HEART
QUEST®

HeartQuest Books by Catherine Palmer

A Town Called Hope series

Prairie Rose—Kansas holds their future, but only faith can mend their past. Hope and love blossom on the untamed prairie as a young woman, searching for a place to call home, happens upon a Kansas homestead during the 1860s.

Prairie Fire—Will a burning secret extinguish the spark of love between Jack and Caitrin? The town of Hope discovers the importance of forgiveness, overcoming prejudice, and the dangers of keeping unhealthy family secrets.

Prairie Storm—Can one tiny baby calm the brewing storm between Lily's past and Elijah's future? United in their concern for an orphaned infant, Eli and Lily are forced to set aside their differences and learn to trust God's plan to see them through the storms of life.

Prairie Christmas (anthology)—In "The Christmas Bride," by Catherine Palmer, Rolf Rustemeyer can hardly wait for the arrival of his Christmas bride, all the way from Germany. You'll love this heartwarming Christmas visit with friends old and new from A Town Called Hope. Anthology also includes novellas by Elizabeth White and Peggy Stoks.

Treasures of the Heart series

A Kiss of Adventure (original title: *The Treasure of Timbuktu*)—Abducted by a treasure hunter, Tillie becomes a pawn in a dangerous game.

A Whisper of Danger (original title: *The Treasure of Zanzibar*)—Jessica's unexpected inheritance turns out to be an ancient house filled with secrets, an unknown enemy . . . and a lost love.

A Touch of Betrayal—Stranded in a dangerous land, Alexandra must face her fear . . . and escape the man determined to ruin her life.

Finders Keepers series

Finders Keepers—Blue-eyed, fiery-tempered Elizabeth Hayes is working hard to preserve Chalmers House, the Victorian mansion next to her growing antiques business. But Zachary Chalmers, heir to the mansion, has very different plans for the site. And Elizabeth's eight-year-old son, adopted from Romania three years earlier, has plans of his own: He wants a daddy—and this tall, handsome man is the perfect candidate.

Hide and Seek (coming in early 2001)—Luke Easton wants to be left alone to nurse his broken heart, raise his daughter in peace, and complete

HEART
QUEST.

the renovation of the Chalmers Mansion. Jo Callaway prizes her privacy
too. She doesn't want her new friends to ask too many questions about
her mysterious past. But fighting for common goals begins to forge a
bond between Luke and Jo that neither expected—or welcomes.

HeartQuest Books by Peggy Stoks

Olivia's Touch—Olivia Plummer desires nothing more than to honor God by using the healing touch he has given her—a gift that has been honed and perfected under the watchful eye of her beloved grandmother.

Eastern-trained doctor Ethan Gray, disillusioned by the pampered rich of Boston, risks his medical career to set up practice in rural Colorado. There he can help people who are truly in need. Immediately upon his arrival, he clashes with the town's "healer," Miss Olivia Plummer. He knows all about her type—those who endanger lives with folk remedies and old wives' tales—and flatly forbids her to continue.

But when his hand is injured, Ethan is forced to accept Olivia's help. Watching her work, he finds himself captivated by her bravery, her beauty, and her passion for helping the sick. And Olivia is drawn to Ethan's disarming tenderness. Still, he stubbornly refuses to support her efforts to obtain a state medical license. Must Olivia choose between the promise of love and fulfilling God's call on her life? *Book 1 in the Abounding Love series.*

Romy's Walk (coming in spring 2001)—Schoolteacher Romy Muller has never questioned God's goodness. At least not until a tragic accident leaves her close to death. Granting what the doctor predicts will be Romy's dying wish, her would-be suitor, Jeremiah Landis, marries her. But Romy doesn't die; nor does she willingly accept this new chapter in her life. A battle rages inside her soul: Is God sovereign, or is he not? Join Romy and Jeremiah as they struggle to accept God's will for them, complicated by the obstacles that challenge their growing love. *Book 2 in the Abounding Love series.*

The Beauty of the Season—A determined suitor risks everything to help a vulnerable young woman overcome her wounded past. This novella by Peggy Stoks appears in the anthology *A Victorian Christmas Cottage.*

The Sound of the Water—A sports hero, intent on serving God and making things right with his first love, returns to his hometown and the girl he left behind. But will Holly's disillusionment with God forever be a barrier between them? This novella by Peggy Stoks appears in the anthology *Reunited.*

Crosses and Losses—On Christmas Eve in snowy St. Paul, Minnesota, a cherished Crosses and Losses quilt opens the door of healing and love for a grieving young couple. This novella by Peggy Stoks appears in the anthology *A Victorian Christmas Quilt.*

Tea for Marie—In rural Minnesota, love springs unexpectedly from the ashes of disaster. This novella by Peggy Stoks appears in the anthology *A Victorian Christmas Tea.*